HUSH money

Also by Jean Femling:

Backyard

Jean Femling

HUSH money

St. Martin's Press   New York

Design by Judith Stagnitto

Library of Congress Cataloging-in-Publication Data

Femling, Jean.
Hush, money.
p. cm.
ISBN 0-312-02931-4
I. Title.
PS3556.E475H87   1989   813'.54—dc19   89-30145

First Edition

10   9   8   7   6   5   4   3   2   1

To Marcel

Acknowledgments

My thanks to Bob Ray, the best writing teacher I know of, for his canny criticisms and suggestions. Betsy Rapaport early on made some valuable observations about the novel's structure. Jim Richardson shared his knowledge of the boating world. Lou Ross and Chuck Ross provided background on insurance operations, and Jane Schaffer was especially helpful. Maxine O'Callaghan and Kaye Klem, among other writers, gave me feedback and encouragement; and I value Don Stanwood's ongoing hospitality as much as his perceptive and articulate critiques. Most of all I thank the fire-bringer, Marcel Mathevet—Parisian, wherever he is.

HUSH money

A telephone ringing in an empty apartment has a nagging, hostile sound. I was halfway up my steep outside stairs, running sideways to keep from banging my toes into the concrete, when the ringing stopped.

My hand slid up the cold, wet iron railing coated with the heavy dew of an October night on the California coast, which spread a sparkling mist over the street and harbor lights. An hour before, I'd been down at Newport Harbor finishing dinner on board the *Caminante* with my old friend Rick and his new friend Judy, and the non-chemical glow lingered on.

When Rick and I split up two years before, it had been my doing, and maybe I still felt a little guilty. Rick is the kind of guy you love forever, only now he was like a brother. When he told me he was bringing this Judy person along on his cruise down from Monterey, I said "Great," and meant it, but I was worried. What if she wasn't good enough for him? Judy almost was; in fact, I liked her a lot. Calm, and funny, didn't miss a thing. When she got up to stir the chili and I saw the way Rick looked at her, it was wonderful.

They said good-bye to me on the dock with their arms around one another, and at the same moment they stepped apart as if thinking, Poor Moz, she doesn't have what we have; let's not rub it in.

Wrong number, maybe. Certainly not my boss calling this late. Investigating auto-insurance claims, which I do for a living, can generally wait till morning. Maybe it was Bobby-Lew Manahan, boy-wonder realtor, who's been yearning for us to share a peak experience at his place on the ocean front in Laguna with the glass-walled shower overlooking the surf. Bobby and I were going nowhere, which he'd probably figured out already.

By now I pretty much know which part of my life I can plan, and men aren't in it. They just happen, and a good thing, too. When I turned thirty, two months earlier, I'd waited to be hit by that horrible depression everybody dreads, the first step off the hundred-foot pole, and it never showed up. Hey: I found out I could fly.

At the top of the stairs I let myself into my nest, and slid the brass bolt that shuts out the world. It's a one-bedroom place, "Single Adult No Pet," built over a triple garage stuffed with my landlady's precious antiques. In the southwest corner by the big windows there's a round birch table where I can check out the weather and plan the day over my Granola.

My tastes run to Danish modern, oiled woods and leather when I can afford it, but my landlady, Mrs. Chaney, keeps sneaking her Orientalia up here "temporarily." Stuff that won't go into her jam-full main house, like the five-dragon folding screen, and the ceramic elephant end tables glazed in gaudy yellows and blues, with the trunks sticking out to catch your shin.

"The real goods, Moz," Mrs. Chaney always says, giving me

2

her long-eyed Tennessee backwoods look. "Now, *this* is the style that suits you."

Somehow Mrs. Chaney has snapped me into that whole Blue Willow world of pagodas, bound feet, and opium dens. I'm half-Filipino, five-three and fairly assertive. Color? Wet adobe, as Rick so nicely put it. Mrs. C. is five-nine, built like a tractor, and can tell you to the dollar what her Biedermeier is worth; but she wouldn't know a mandarin from a Bantu.

I was eating banana yogurt and waiting for Johnny Carson, single America's pacifier, when the phone rang again.

"This is Nurse Kale in the emergency room at Coast Community Hospital. Could I speak to Martha Brant, please?" She had an aggressively soothing voice, designed to flatten potential waves of hysteria, and it set off my adrenaline alarm.

"Speaking. Hospital? Why?"

"We have a patient here who's just been brought in, a Richard Tyler?"

"Rick! Yes, I know him. What's happened?"

"He's been seriously injured, and we need to get in touch with his family right away. He had your business card in his pocket, and we'd like to—"

"How bad is it?" She didn't answer right away, and a sick dread climbed into my throat.

"The doctor's with him now and I'm really not able to say. Some sort of boat accident; explosion, I believe. We have a girl here who was involved also, but there's no identification at all on her. If you could possibly—"

"Ask her if her name is Judy."

A sigh of exasperation. "I can't do that, because she's unconscious; which is why I'm talking to you." Nurse Kale, dealing with one of the world's incompetents, spoke with exaggerated patience. "Now, if you'll just answer a few questions—"

"No! I mean yes, I'm coming right down. What kind of explosion? Oh, that's right, you know nothing. Who shall I ask for—what did you say your name was?"

"Nurse Kale. That's K-A-L-E. I'll be right here all night."

Kale, Kale. I'd written it twice on the notepad I keep by the phone. Don't stop to think about anything; just go.

I jammed my feet back into my sneakers and grabbed my purse and jacket—was that Johnny Carson? since when had his hair turned white?—and remembered to lock the door and slam it so it caught. Maybe he's dying, I thought. People do. I started down the stairs hanging on to that slippery railing, weak-kneed and shivering like a wet dog.

A trip like that has its own awfulness. You have X number of miles to cover, and God himself can't get you there any quicker. The streets were mostly still and bright-glazed, it was like driving through an empty bowling alley. I ran a few red lights but not many; I've seen some gruesome accidents caused that way and I couldn't do Rick any good on a stretcher along-side him.

I should've asked more questions. An explosion? Oh, sure. What really happened to them? Maybe somebody suckered Rick with a sob story, and then robbed and beat up both of them, set it off to cover up everything. Rick always was too trusting. Two years before, Rick had pulled me out of deep quicksand and given me back myself. He was the best friend I had in this world: as long as Rick was in it, I could go on believing in the possibility of good. Just let him live. . . .

The hospital's emergency entrance is down an incline, so that you actually go into the basement of the building. I opened the door and pulled myself up tall, because people tend not to take small brown persons seriously.

It's the smell that hits you first—chemical, alien, and there must be fresh blood in it. Or maybe it's the fear that makes you breathe shallower so that you don't take in very much.

Under the flat no-shadows light of the waiting room, several messy civilians waited on benches. Two guys had brought in a friend of theirs with a bloody scraped-up face and arm; a mother in a red plaid shirt bounced her screaming baby. In contrast, the two tidy policemen talking to a nurse, and the hospital personnel all in white, added a note of order. I interrupted the conversation.

"I'm here to see Rick Tyler. Is he still alive?"

"Certainly." Nurse Kale, according to her badge, was offended by my question.

"I'm the one you just called, Martha Brant. Where is he? I need to see him right now. Don't worry, I'm perfectly calm; I just have to see for myself."

"If you'll wait a few minutes, I'll find out. . . ." She headed back into the treatment area, with me right behind her. I saw Rick beyond a white cotton curtain in a little booth on the left and went in to him. The light was dimmer here, and I thought, good; it'll be easier on his eyes.

Rick was laid out on a high rolling table with his shirt off, uncovering about a yard of smooth tanned chest, lean, his ribs visible. They'd already put an IV needle into one hand, and tied his arm to the metal bed frame. When I spoke to him he turned his head slowly, and his free hand moved a little, the fingers flaring. Blood had spread around his left ear and dried black on his cheek and neck, and I could see it was still wet in his ear. I bent over him on the other side and murmured his name.

"Rick? Can you hear me?"

He quit moving, but he was still breathing steadily. His jeans were smeared with chili, and filthy. Nobody was paying any attention to him, there were plenty of other things going on. I reached out and picked away a bit of the dried blood on his jaw.

"Stop that!" Nurse Kale snapped behind me. She looked genuinely disturbed. "We leave that alone deliberately. It's an open pathway to the brain: there's too much risk of contamination."

"I'm sorry, I didn't realize."

"He has a probable skull fracture," she told me. "They'll be taking him up to X-Ray in a few minutes. Dr. Marcus has already seen him briefly. He'll be in again later."

"But is he . . ." I couldn't even think what to ask her about Rick.

"He's already getting some medication to help keep his brain from swelling," she said. She added that Judy's chest had been crushed; they'd taken her straight into surgery, they couldn't wait.

"But how did it happen?"

"I understand that some boats blew up down at the harbor. You'll have to ask the police about that, they're here doing their report. And we need you to fill out some papers." Of course.

She went away again and I took Rick's free hand, warm enough but just dead weight, and held it. It felt familiar, the squared-out bottom thumb joint and the long, calloused fingers. I told him he was going to be fine because he was so strong, and that he was mending already. His face was still . . . the long jaw and the nose with a jog in the bridge, like Peter Ueberroth's. . . . I remembered the night Rick got his nose rearranged like that and I wanted to cry, but I knew I couldn't; not yet.

I gave him a little till-later peck on the shoulder, and went out to the admissions counter.

"It's fortunate we were able to locate you," Nurse Kale said. "We need information on the next of kin, and we have just nothing on the girl at all. To start with, what's her name?"

"Judy." I didn't remember her last name, didn't know if Rick had even told me. Her billfold must still be on the boat.

The Kale woman slid over a batch of admittance forms, but I had to leave them mostly blank. Medical insurance? I checked yes, even though I'd bet they didn't have any. I could see they were getting emergency care; but what would happen after that? And then I would have the job of calling Rick's parents, and giving them a horrible little midnight surprise. After I'd talked to the police.

Officer Parker was a fox, razor-trimmed, sharp as a recruiting ad and polite to boot. "Real crazy how it happened," he said. "Just a one-in-a-million thing.

". . . Nah, it wasn't your friends' boat that blew up at all," he said. "It was another one entirely, moored two over from them. A yacht being restored by its owner. For some reason as yet unknown, the cabin exploded, and *whong!* Drove this big hatch cover right through your guys' hull. Fiberglass, isn't it?"

Officer Parker shook his head as if suggesting, "Fiberglass—what do you expect?" but with more sense than to say it.

"Slammed into the both of them together," the other cop said.

"If you'd planned it, you never could've done that," said Parker.

"But what made the other boat blow up?"

He shrugged. "That's up to the fire marshal. He'll be the one investigating it. Don't you worry, they'll give it their best shot." He shifted, getting ready to leave. "Damn shame about your friends; really. Anyway, they're alive, which is more than you can say for the guy on board the yacht. He was burnt to a crisp."

"Totaled," said his partner. "They hadn't identified him yet, last we heard. The coroner's office retrieved him, so now it's their problem."

"When your number's up, it's up," said Officer Parker.

"I guess you're right," I said. But I wasn't going to tell Rick's parents that.

It must've happened right after I left; maybe fifteen minutes—my God, just a little earlier and I would've been in it, too, and bashed up like they were. Or at the morgue, like the other man. Why them, and not me?

Explosion; fuel, gas tank. So what had set it off, then? And who was the unlucky soul who got killed?

Nurse Kale handed over Rick's wallet, looking dubious even though she'd called me herself, and pointed me toward the pay phones. The wallet was good leather, a present from his folks, I'd guess, but about worn out, curved to the shape of his body and rimed with white where it had gotten soaked at least once. Inside was a wadded-up notice dating from last year that his auto insurance was overdue and was being canceled. I couldn't find anything about Judy, except a picture of the two of them cheek to cheek in a K-mart photo booth, grinning like monkeys.

Rick's parents lived in San Jose. When I finally got their number, his stepfather answered. "What? Who's this?"

I told him what had happened. "Oh my God," he said. "Oh my God. Where did you say you were? Hold on a sec, I'll get his mother."

The halls around Intensive Care were dark and quiet—naturally; it was the middle of the night. When Rick was clean and settled, they let me in to see him again. He was wired six ways and attached to the little green screen that showed the pattern of his heartbeat, steady and consistent; naked under his sheet and deeply unconscious now, but healthy-looking, rosy and relaxed—as if at any minute he would wake up and give me that shy, long-jawed grin, and stretch and walk away, trailing his web of wires and tubes.

Eventually Dr. Marcus appeared, a tall, tired man with a scooped-out hairline and a night-shift pallor.

"Tell me the whole story," I said. "All the possibilities."

"He has a compound fracture of the skull, this plate right here," Dr. Marcus said, massaging a spot behind his own left ear. "It's—oh, about three centimeters long. Actually there are two fractures, it makes a sort of Y."

"Oh. And how serious is that?"

"Well, there's always the possibility—in fact, I'd say the inevitability—of damage to the brain in a trauma this extensive. Now that doesn't necessarily mean you'll see gross permanent impairment. Actually, we don't even know what is involved as yet. At the moment we're administering medication to slow the swelling of the brain, to prevent as much damage, that is, further damage, as we possibly can. It's a massive bruise, if you like." He pantomimed the brain smacking against the skull case, first one side and then the other.

Then the good doctor, standing with his head tilted and two fingernails snapping together, endured my questions. What were the chief dangers?

"Internal bleeding, obviously. Clotting—he's getting some anticoagulant but we can't give him very much, you can see the problem one way or the other. Possible paralysis, which in some cases is only temporary. We just—don't—know."

"But if you had to guess, what?" I asked. "Based on your experience."

"If he makes it through the night, I'd say he's got a good chance," the doctor said.

"—Of being okay?"

"Of surviving."

I asked about Judy, but she was still in surgery, and would be for a couple more hours. I stood around for a while longer, useless, with nothing to do but picture Rick bobbing and slobbering in a wheelchair. I wanted to howl and smash something, use my teeth and claws on whoever was responsible. But I knew where I could make a little difference. I headed for the harbor.

2 Pacific Coast Highway, which runs through Newport Beach parallel to the waterfront, was almost deserted now. I parked in the darkened lot of the yacht brokerage at almost the same spot I had earlier that day, when I first came down to see Rick and Judy. Rick's 25-foot boat, the *Caminante*, was moored around front, opposite the turning basin at the inner end of the harbor.

I got out my flashlight and camera. The least I could do was provide some solid information to help Rick and Judy file damage and injury claims against the owner of the other boat.

Even before I got around to the waterfront, the ugly stink of wet, charred wood filled the wind, along with the steady throbbing of a motor, which turned out to be a generator pumping water out of the damaged yacht. Under the floodlights, the burned-out sailboat still rode the water in trim.

I remembered looking at the boat earlier, in daylight, when

Rick had pointed her out to me. She was a beautiful 40-foot wooden ketch with a sweeping hull and the deck slightly rounded so that the water would run off; she was, in fact, all curves, except for the two immense spruce masts. Now portholes and doorframes were blackened, but the masts rose up straight as ever.

From the head of the floating dock I could see the gaping hole torn in the hull of the *Caminante*. I should've been in a hurry to get on down there and find Judy's wallet, I had her people to call yet; but I dragged my feet, not wanting to go back into the boat.

Trash littered the docks and the water, and the blast had broken the big window in the yacht brokerage. The waterfront jogs in just at that point, so that the side wall of the Snug Harbor Restaurant overlooks this section of the docks. Anyone upstairs would've had a ringside seat for the event. Like a finals match at Wimbledon.

Farther along the pale strip of floating dock, out in the shadows, two men were pointing and arguing in low, sharp tones. Some sailboat's rigging had been torn loose and hung down, rattling when the night breeze moved it. Otherwise the harbor stretched undisturbed in all directions, millions of dollars' worth of power boats, sportfishermen with flying bridges and radar equipment on top, yachts with living rooms big enough to have sofas and table lamps, and stickboats—sailboats—with their swaying masts stuck up at all angles, like a burned-out forest.

I stopped to look at the damaged yacht. The cabin was only twisted wreckage, and the stink was stronger here, a compound of burned wood and plastic, varnish, wet burned upholstery. Rick had really admired this one. Worth what? He shrugged. "Hundred thou, maybe two." But he didn't care for the name carved on her raked stern, *Spray*, and under it the braided sideways figure eight that stands for infinity.

"I think that's a bit much," he'd said. "Just a little pretentious, wouldn't you say?" Rich man's toy. Good. The more expensive, the better.

Time to get on with it. Starting toward *Caminante*, I saw a quick flash of light that came from inside the cabin. Looters, before the bodies were even cold. I ran along the dock and bellowed, "Hey, in there! You!" and pounded my feet—when you're my size, you learn to compensate. I beat on the hull with my fist, feeling bold enough with the two sailors farther along the dock as protection.

"You! Get your body out here!"

"Just hold your horses." A man's voice, calm. A flashlight came on, lighting up a pair of legs in light blue denim climbing the little wooden ladder inside, and boat shoes. When he came out on deck he said, "Now let's not get excited." And he turned the flashlight on his face for an instant with a quick grin—see?—like a little kid posing for a picture. "It's just your friendly insurance man."

He jumped down onto the dock, righting himself as it swayed underfoot, and held out a card. The two men out on the end were coming toward us with what's-going-on-here scowls.

My friendly insurance man held his flashlight on the card so I could read it. "Gage Pfeiffer, Marine Surveyor," and then shook my hand. "Gage Pfeiffer. I'm a marine-insurance assessor, investigating the extent of the damages we've got here." He had a flat midwestern twang from somewhere north of Texas.

The two men came up to us and I said, "It's all right. He's the insurance investigator." The shorter one, scowling under his billed yachting cap, nodded once, very captain-like, and they went on inshore.

"I represent Tay and Barrett," Pfeiffer said. "They wrote the policy for Tenhagen on that boat there, the *Spray*."

"Already?" I said. "You sure don't waste any time."

"Had my scanner on. And they called me right away, like always. I was in the shower, naturally. And who might you be?"

"Martha Brant. As a matter of fact . . ." I got out my business card that says I'm an auto-claims investigator for T. Ambrose, and gave it to him, halfway expecting him to be amused.

"This is a boat, Ms. Brant."

"So I noticed, Mr. Pfeiffer."

". . . T. Ambrose," he said. "Your boss Leo Jablonka?" I nodded. "I know him. How's old Leo doing nowadays, anyway?"

When I told Pfeiffer that I'd been aboard the boat with Rick and Judy earlier, and the extent of their injuries, he got a lot less cheerful. We both knew that personal-injury cases were in another class altogether from property damage, and Pfeiffer's company—or somebody's—was looking at a major claim.

"I was just about to head up to the hospital," he said. He made the right noises, sounding genuinely sympathetic, but I could also see him calculating.

He was wearing a jacket with lots of pockets, and from one of them he took a little silver tape recorder the size of a cigarette pack, and asked if I minded answering a few questions.

"To begin with, I'll need their current addresses, and yours."

Gage Pfeiffer had an effective interviewing style, low-key but serious. He appeared to be in his late thirties, or maybe a vigorous forty. Plain brown hair combed straight back; two deep grin lines carved in either cheek, and he moved with no wasted motion; otherwise he was contained and still. Only his eyes kept moving, zip, zip, taking in everything under the raised grooves of his forehead, as if he were forever asking, "What? Are you sure? What does that mean?"

When I got ready to take my pictures of the *Caminante*, he said, "It really isn't necessary, you know." Then he pointed out the best angle he'd found to show the damage, and even suggested I go up on the landward dock to show the relative positions of the two boats. He had a Polaroid clipped to a strap that ran diagonally across his chest, so that he could have both hands free. He was a real pro.

Then we climbed aboard the *Caminante* and down into the little cabin, sliding in the chili on the floor and trying not to bump into one another. You could see all right once your eyes got used to the dark, there was enough light coming in through the jagged hole in the hull. It was just below deck level, and about the size of a bathtub; the place was really torn up. Just a few hours ago Rick had sat at that table slicing celery for the salad into thin green crescents, those familiar hands so steady and precise. . . .

"Funny, the way it caught them both together," I said. And at different heights. Maybe Judy was sitting on his lap. I could tell they hadn't been together very long, they were still so aware of one another.

Judy had watched me the whole evening, miserably jealous behind her company smile. She was about twenty-three. Her midriff under the tied-up shirt was smooth as a plum as she bent over the table with her mouth puckered up, serving the chili, her hair like dark mist that ate the light. When she and Rick slid around one another in the tiny cabin, changing places, their jeans whistled together. And now she was up there on the operating table with her skin peeled back, while they fixed her smashed ribs.

It was awful, rummaging through their gear. Rick's good boots, oiled and set up out of harm's way, the French chopping knife that had been his grandfather's, the opened rose he'd carved on the little headboard above the funny triangular bed in the bow. Everything in the world Rick cared about had been right here. I was crying then, the tears kept running down my face and I couldn't stop snuffling.

"Here now," Pfeiffer said. "You don't want to do that."

"It's only the smoke. Makes your eyes burn. Wind really carries the stink, doesn't it?"

Finally we found a denim drawstring bag under the foot of the mattress. Judy's billfold was yellow, one of those massive things like a portable office, all flaps and snaps, with a calendar and a ring for a pen. Pfeiffer helped me up on deck again, and we climbed down onto the dock and scraped off our shoes.

The cool night air pouring down the harbor washed over us, and opposite, on Lido Isle, those million-dollar houses with their two-story entrances sent shivering columns of reflections slantwise across the dark water. A car moved across the Lido bridge, above its arched underside outlined in red lights to warn off night boaters.

"Would you mind?" Pfeiffer said, holding out Judy's driver's license, his tape recorder at the ready. "Reading it. You sound better than I do."

"Sure." Whatever could help. . . . Judy's last name was Christensen. Address in Fremont, a town southeast of San Francisco. I thought, her family doesn't even know yet.

Heading back along the floating dock, we had the floodlights of the yacht brokerage in our eyes, rimming the moisture-coated masts and railings and the worn cleats on the ramp with fiery halos. Rick had said they rigged up towels to make it dark enough to sleep, but that was okay: made it safer. Hah.

"How do you think it happened?" I asked.

"Oh, I know how it happened," Gage Pfeiffer said. "It was definitely a gas leak. I'd say the hose was probably leaking for quite some time, dripping into the bilges. Tenhagen came in, turned the light on, probably—the socket arced, and he blew himself up. Or, you know . . . it could've been that electric heater; a spark from the switch. It was all scrunched . . . took me a while to even figure out what that mess of wire was."

"Wait a minute. Tenhagen; you mean the guy that owned the boat?"

"That's right, Arnold Tenhagen. They were pretty positive when I left, but they still wanted to check the dental records. He was about unrecognizable, but it—he was wearing a ring with the right monogram."

Tenhagen would've died instantly as the gas seared his lungs, Pfeiffer told me, so technically the cause of death was probably asphyxiation. "We'll know better after the autopsy."

We shook our heads and I made sympathetic sounds; but I was angry, too, thinking about rich men who were careless with their expensive playthings. What was that line about dying with the most toys? "Pretty gorgeous toy to die for," I said, "not to mention in."

"He was a good guy," Pfeiffer said. "I knew him, somewhat.

What burns my—burns me, is that it looks like it was done on purpose."

"What do you mean?" My heart had started that hard slow pounding again. Pfeiffer looked at me with his eyes narrowed, as if he could hear it, debating whether he should tell me and how upset I'd be, but really wanting to talk about it.

"Well, I just—you look to be mighty tired." It sounded like "tarred," and I didn't understand him right away. "I've been debating whether even to tell you right now, knowing it'd bother you."

"I'm fine; don't you worry about me. Tell me what you found in there."

"Fire started from the center of the hose," he said. "Where it just had no business being. You can tell, all right, if you know what to look for: there are these little arrows, plain as anything." He got out the Polaroids he'd taken.

"Looky here," he said. They were murky close-ups: part of a blackened hose, the cabinet around it mottled and streaked—I couldn't honestly say I could distinguish his telltale little arrow marks, but he was certainly convinced.

"You mean it was a setup?" I said. "Arson?"

He nodded. "Cover of the hose burned away, of course, so there's no way to tell—I figure there had to've been holes poked in it."

"On purpose." The compressor sounded different now, it had a diabolical hum cleverly designed to speed up your heartbeat— I felt weird, light as a helium balloon but more fragile, and figured I was on the edge of hysteria. Hold on to your string, baby. I smiled at him to reassure him. "But can you prove it?"

"Easiest thing in the world, about. What's hard is finding out who did it. And hardest of all, trying to make it stick."

"But then, that's not just arson. It's murder."

He patted my arm, looking worried. "Listen, it's real late, and we're both tired. We can talk about this all some more later."

"So then where are the police? I don't see them swarming all over the place."

"Been and gone. Hey, don't you worry. Last thing we need is for somebody to be running around down here creating havoc with stuff like this. Or even believed to be doing it. Can you imagine what it would do to our business?" He tried to make a joke of it, and saw he'd failed.

"What I'll have to do starting tomorrow is cover the waterfront, literally," he said. "Talk to people and just check over every possibility. Maybe he had an argument with somebody down here. Maybe some fool holding a grudge, got drunk and—hey, listen. Tay and Barrett have a number of boats covered down here, they represent a tremendous liability. No way are they . . . am I going to tolerate some crazy arsonist getting his jollies on my turf."

"How big is the policy?" I asked.

"Hundred thousand max. All it covers is physical damages." Something in my expression must have struck him. "For God's sake," Pfeiffer said. "The man didn't blow himself up deliberately."

"I don't know that."

"What we've got here is a 'fire of suspicious origin.' These things can be contagious, spread like the damn measles. Which will not be allowed. I am going to solve this to my own satisfaction. Oh, it's under control; yes, ma'am."

I knew he was making sense, but I was just too tired to follow anymore. The compressor sounded odd now, feeble, like an old man trying to clear his throat. "Hey; life goes on," Gage said, patting my arm, and went to look at it.

A scalloping of ash rode the water, and a cold little wind had come up, pat-patting the water against the boat hulls like many hands making tortillas. On the landward dock, two workmen carried out a big sheet of plywood and began boarding up the blown-out windows. Their movements were synchronized and they hammered away without talking, you could tell they'd done that job before. The glass crunched under their feet.

They were the ants of society, and Gage and I were, too; all of us cleaning up today's mess bit by bit and knowing that tomorrow there'll be another mess, and another. The boats would be hauled away and repaired, or sold, or whatever; Rick and Judy would lie up there, and live, or die, and hardly anybody would care, or even notice.

I thought about the night I'd met Rick. It happened on the Santa Cruz Boardwalk, and at the absolute lowest point of my life. I was having a shouting match with a stoned "friend," and I must've been winning, because this guy had me backed up against one of those palm trees along the beach and was slapping me around, while everybody else just stood there and enjoyed the show. Between the booze and the pills I was pretty far out of it—what I remember best is bright white car lights scorching over me and lighting up people's faces.

And then somebody yelled, "Hey, cut that out!"—a lanky guy straddling a bicycle: Rick. He wound up taking me back to his place, trying to balance me on his bike, with the blood flowing down his face—nothing bleeds worse than a smashed nose. I've never known anybody else like Rick, before or since.

Now I had the feeling I was saying good-bye. That damn hatch cover could've gone anywhere, it was a freak accident. Divine intervention—not God, too far away; fate, more. Luck. Some minor-league demon. It's a contest; you know that fate's going to catch up with you sooner or later, but you always think, not yet. And what could I put up against that?

Then for an instant the world stopped and I was transfixed as if struck by lightning—there was no flash, but everything became more intensely *itself*, so sharp and strong it hurt to see. Some crazy person out there had done this and I was going to get him, no matter how. It had to happen; I couldn't lose. I felt wonderful. I felt at peace.

"Come on," Gage said. "I'll walk you to your car."

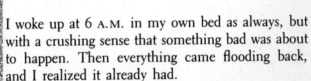

3 I woke up at 6 A.M. in my own bed as always, but with a crushing sense that something bad was about to happen. Then everything came flooding back, and I realized it already had.

The dream was still with me. In it I was going flat out, driving a stagecoach with no doors on it, pushing myself to the limit to get away from this charred lump that was chasing us. But no matter what I did, it managed to pull up and keep even with us, skimming alongside a little above ground level and looking up with a pitiful pirate face: eye patch and a look of desperation, imploring; and half its head was gone. Was that supposed to be Rick, or Arnold Tenhagen? Maybe the demon was friendly; or else just a neutral horror I had to take with the rest.

I was halfway afraid to find out about Rick, but I got up and phoned the Intensive Care Unit anyway. Yes, Rick Tyler was still "there."

"Has he been conscious at all?"

"Oh, no." The ICU nurse sounded offended. Enough that he was alive; unreasonable of me to expect anything more.

Judy had come back from surgery around four-fifteen, and it didn't sound too good, because the nurse began scolding me for not producing any of her relatives. I'd spent half an hour on the phone with Judy's grubby little black address book the night before, waking people up in three states trying to locate some of Judy Christensen's kinfolk. With no success. Somebody named Corinne had been upset, at least; told me Judy had moved out from Colorado a couple of years ago, and said she'd try to locate Judy's people and call me back.

Probably the nurse was worried about the bill, I figured, they were trained that way: a hospital is a business, like any other.

Think about arson. I knew that about twenty percent of the fires in this country are deliberately set. Maybe to collect the insurance, which would be Gage Pfeiffer's department. Or to cover a robbery attempt. Or even murder—maybe Tenhagen had been dead beforehand. Or revenge. A business rival. Jealousy—of a lover, or even of his boat. Greedy relatives. Maybe only the boat had been targeted, and they got him by mistake. To begin with, I'd have to find out everything I could about Arnold Tenhagen.

But first I had to clear the decks at work. I dropped off my film at the lab and got to T. Ambrose by seven-thirty, but even so, Leo Jablonka's big faded blue Chrysler Imperial was already parked outside. Leo was the current T. Ambrose, and he had two other branch offices, in Riverside and Pasadena, so that we sometimes didn't see him for several days.

We work in an inconspicuous cube of beige stucco on the back of a parking lot, behind a three-story office building in downtown Santa Ana. Since we handle auto claims for insurance companies, and not for the public, the less visible we are, the better.

I was still new enough at T. Ambrose to get a little buzz when I walked in. But not from the decor—the open central area had boxes of paperwork stacked around, and unshielded fluorescent ceiling lights sharpened the dingy traffic paths in the orange industrial carpet fanning out to our individual cubicles.

Leo heard me, and came out of his office. "Moz." He was holding a form I recognized, a new accident memo.

"Leo."

Leo's about sixty but in great shape, built like a former Olympic wrestler: freckled bald dome with short gray hair that he gets trimmed every week, grizzled eyebrows, and a full, carved mouth generally tucked in tight. I've never seen him in anything but a white shirt and tie. He seemed a little pale and weary, but I thought then it was just the light coming in the high windows—a gray, still morning with heavy cloud cover, the typical coastal stuff.

I tackled him head-on, trying to assess his mood; told him what had happened, and Gage Pfeiffer's conclusion that it was arson. Leo stood with his fists on his hips, scowling under those heavy eyebrows.

"If Pfeiffer says arson, I'd believe him," Leo said. "Good man, one of the best around. So, okay. What do you want from me?"

"I need to take some extra time to look into this. Find out who did it." He halfway smiled, letting me read his mind; the sarcastic "Is that all?"

"Fine with me. Work it into your schedule. The preliminary report on our big trash-mash is due tomorrow, right? Oh; and here." He handed me the accident memo. Leo put a twenty-four-hour turnaround on our new cases, meaning I had to interview the insured today. Thanks a lot, I thought.

Halfway to his office, Leo turned that radar look on me again.

"I know exactly what you're thinking," he said. "But believe me, you can't do anything Gage Pfeiffer and the police can't do better. Go ahead, though, I understand. Friendship."

Which left no doubt where I stood. I'd only been at T. Ambrose for three months, after learning the ropes at big, boring

Imperial Surety Corporation, where you could hardly go to the rest room without a time stamp. I had a lot more to learn, which Leo and I both knew, though he never even hinted that to the other two adjusters. Horlick was painstaking but slow as molasses, and Bob Fryer the machine-gunner worked like a Trojan but cut a few too many corners. I was intended to be Leo's happy medium.

And it was true that being a "breed," plus small and harmless-looking, I could wiggle myself into some places where your average beefy Anglo male couldn't get through the door. I don't know how many different languages I've been addressed in, by somebody assuming I was a sister; and I never knew any of them. Embarrassing.

We'd already had a couple of big cases where I'd shown Leo what I could do; but I knew I was still on probation. This job was my big chance, and I was going to hang on to it. I'd come too far to boot it away now.

According to the accident memo, the insured, a Mrs. Paula Yeo, had been making a right turn when she hit a teenager on a bicycle in a crosswalk. Oh, great. No bodily injuries reported, luckily . . . just pray that she speaks English.

My phone rang. It was a reporter from the *Orange County Tribune*, Tessa Kocher, who was doing a story on the explosion. She'd already talked to the hospital, and wanted some background on Rick and Judy.

"Where were they from?" asked Reporter Kocher.

"Monterey."

"And they got here—when?"

"Day before yesterday. They were both so excited to be here—sailing into beautiful Newport Harbor that they'd heard so much about. Happy, full of life . . . and now . . . well, you know. I understand it was definitely arson."

"That's a pretty serious charge."

"It's a pretty deadly activity. What kind of maniac do you think would do something like this? If he's crazy to blow up boats, Newport's the right place. This could mean that nobody down there is safe anymore."

"I'm sure the authorities will be investigating the case thoroughly," Tessa Kocher said, trying to disengage tactfully.

"Yes, but . . . you people could help, you know. If the *Tribune* were to offer a reward for any information about the arsonist . . . He ought to be stopped before he kills again!"

"Well, I'll certainly pass your suggestion along to the proper channels."

I bet. "What have you found out about Arnold Tenhagen so far?"

"He's from Newport Beach. Lives . . . lived with his wife, Vera, up on Sea Hawk Ridge. It's really not my story, actually. Listen, thanks so much for your help."

After I hung up I had an uneasy feeling that Gage Pfeiffer wouldn't much like my popping off to the paper like that, and Leo even less. But I hadn't told her anything really; she probably wouldn't even use it.

I grabbed a couple of files, set my phone answering machine, and headed out. With Leo watching.

"Moz," he barked. "You know the dumb-ass things people can do when their emotions are involved. And you're no different. Hell, *I'm* no different." Which let me know that Leo had probably messed up himself, once upon a time. "So watch the legality angle. I want you to make sure you don't do anything that reflects on this organization." Organization: I'd never heard him use the word before.

"You mean that might jeopardize your license," I said, making it a joke; but Leo's frankly speculative look reminded me that he'd gotten along without me before, and would be willing to do so again.

Out in the reception area, Arlene, our secretary, was crouched over her new PC stalking a spreadsheet, her platinum lion's mane almost touching the screen. She was wearing her tight white jeans, an electric-blue shirt with big ruffled sleeves, and two dangles in the left ear—I figured she had a hot lunch date, and it wasn't the guy she was living with.

"So you're off," she said. "Was Leo referring to any dumb-ass thing in particular?"

"Kind of complicated. Tell you about it later." Arlene shrugged, turned back to her keyboard, and pounced.

Where to find out everything about your local celebrity sailor and his flashy boat? At the Balboa Library. The Balboa Peninsula, without which Newport Harbor wouldn't exist, is a four-mile leg of sand pointing downcoast, with its knee bent seaward toward Catalina Island, and its toe at the harbor entrance. And edge-to-edge it's all prime real estate—you can rent by the week in summer, and swim before breakfast. Bring money.

The library is situated right where Balboa's calf bulges, two blocks to the water in either direction; and sure enough, it had a fat clipping file, plus a whole collection of boating books. The librarian looked fairly nautical herself, with sun-streaked hair short enough to stay out of her eyes, and wearing denim pants whitened on the seat.

She'd heard about the accident already, and we exchanged the usual murmurs of regret—"Can you imagine?" and "Absolutely terrible"—as she flipped through the file drawer.

And there it was: a wad of clippings from last year, with photos . . . the battered boat arriving on its trailer, and a shot of the newly refurbished *Spray* under full sail, with the Balboa Pavilion in the background.

She was a 40-foot auxiliary ketch built on the East Coast in 1936 by Cox & Stevens, and a marvel. Tenhagen had had her trucked across the country and restored here in Newport—a pretty penny that must've cost him. Every detail was right, down to the curve of the railing. She was alive, a living entity.

And here was an inset photo of Tenhagen himself, squinting in the sunlight. He had a strong, shrewd, expressive face; at fifty-four, he'd certainly been to the corner and looked around twice. A wide closed-mouth grin, as if he felt good enough to break out laughing, but wouldn't let himself. Thinning hair combed straight back, ears sticking out like Clark Gable's, and an open, boyish look . . . that must've been an asset.

Because he'd been very successful. A poor kid whose father was a milkman, he went through school on scholarships. Built up his own business, manufacturing electronic testing devices, from scratch, and then bought out his partner . . . would that parting have been harmonious?

His wife, Vera Tenhagen, was on the County Museum Board, and was also a "nationally honored local horsewoman" and part owner of the Twelvetrees Stables in Orange. There was a photo of Arnie and Vera at a museum benefit; they were exactly the same height, and both were showing a lot of teeth. Two children were still at home, the article said, Deirdre and Keith; their oldest son, Martin, had an executive position in St. Louis.

I thought about the seared lungs, and my left forearm started to look like a drumstick, a bit stringy—horrible; we're all of us just meat. But alive: there's the difference.

Arnie—I felt I was beginning to know the victim pretty well—had certainly had the opportunity and resources to tangle himself in some fancy webs, if not weave a few of his own. . . . I was already feeling sympathetic, which was exactly what Leo had warned me against. Bear in mind, Moz, he could've been a real son of a bitch. You don't get to the top with niceness. Figure just for starters that maybe he brought it on himself.

I photocopied the two longest articles to read later, and made a note to stop by Dickerson's Boatyard, where the *Spray* had been renovated. The librarian's eyes were filled with questions which, miraculously, she managed not to ask. Instead we had a little chat about other boating mysteries: the sinking of the marvelous all-steel *Good Will* on the Sacramento Reef with everybody aboard lost; Beulah Overell and her boyfriend, who blew up her parents for their money, while Mom and Dad were eating dinner moored right out here in the harbor; and the boat that was lost off Baja California in the sixties with Supervisor Caspers and his sons on board. She was quite a student of marine disasters.

That gave me a thought. Why exactly had Tenhagen gone down to his boat last night? His wife would certainly know. I left my business card with the librarian and went to look up the

Tenhagens in the phone book—behold, they were listed; and found a pay phone.

Which was certainly crude and insensitive, since less than twenty-four hours ago the woman's husband had been burned to a crisp. But we had our mutual griefs; and she could tell me things no one else would know, whenever she might be available. Besides, I was sure some friend or not-too-close relative would be on hand to field the condolences.

"'Ello, this is the Tenagain residence. Who is it, please?" A weary woman's voice, Spanish-inflected.

I introduced myself and explained about Rick and Judy. "I'm investigating the insurance coverage on their behalf. So would you please take a message for Mrs. Tenhagen? I very much need to speak with her, when she's able. Of course I realize the terrible circumstances, but I believe this is so urgent, I'm sure she'll agree—"

"Mm, mm," she muttered, and then suddenly came to life. "You are investigating this boat business? How it happens he died?"

"The insurance is only part of my concern, actually. . . ."

"What insurance is this?"

"Marine insurance," I said, feeling queasy. "On the boat." If Gage Pfeiffer had already contacted any of them, which seemed unlikely, I was going to be in the soup.

"Investigating," she repeated, and then, closer to the phone, "This is important. Give me again your name and your phone number, I write it down and somebody will answer your call. Needs to talk with you."

"Martha Brant; five-oh-four . . ." I'd finished giving my number and was in the process of disengaging when another woman's voice came on the line, and she was furious.

"This is Deirdre Tenhagen, and I'm absolutely appalled—" Tenheggen, she'd pronounced it.

"I beg your pardon, I—"

"Scavengers! I can hardly credit this." A younger voice, alternately nasal and totally un-nasal, like somebody with a head cold. Or who'd been crying a lot. "That anybody could be so unbelievably dense and thick-skinned as to trouble us at a time like this—"

"I certainly didn't imagine I'd be speaking to you personally."

"If you're presuming to try to hassle my mother with—who did you say you are? Couldn't it've waited, for God's sake?"

"Martha Brant, and as it happens I understand your situation rather well. Two of my dearest friends were badly injured in the explosion last night, and may not live."

"Ah." She heaved a great sigh, Another wretched chore to cope with. "Of course we're terribly sorry about that, too, we do realize . . . surely you can understand. You'll have to talk to the insurance company . . . I suppose I can get you that number." She fairly hissed with loathing.

"I've already done that. But I do need to talk to Mrs. Tenhagen personally about why this happened: to find out who did it."

"Who did it! It was an accident."

"No," I said. "It's pretty definitely arson."

"What?" Silence; it was registering. "Are you saying it was deliberate? Oh, no. Oh, no. What are you trying to do to us? . . . I absolutely can't talk to you any more now. I can't stand this!" And she hung up.

I didn't mind; I was just starting on the Tenhagens.

Nobody was home at Dickerson's Boatyard when I phoned, and Arnie Tenhagen's partner was not available, his secretary said. I recognized the hiatus that comes with a sudden death, the shifting of gears as everybody touched by it absorbs the shock, and the nasty reminder of their own mortality.

When I swung by to take a look at the accident site in daylight, the parking lot of the yacht brokerage was nearly full. Disaster seemed to be good for business. In a big brown van parked next to the street, a guy had his head tilted back against the seat, sleeping with a black cowboy hat over his face. Out on the waterfront, several spectators were sharing their opinions, pointing at the boats and arguing.

I went next door to the Snug Harbor and climbed the wide brass-edged stairs to the second floor, which was overlooking the scene, to find out when the bartender and waitress who'd worked last night would be in again. I handed over my business card; but when the barkeep reached to stick it up beside Gage Pfeiffer's, I took it back.

Afterward I roamed along Pacific Coast Highway, which runs right behind the harbor, and found a hole-in-the-wall café where Tenhagen might even have been a customer—people don't take the time to go into the Snug Harbor for just a cup of coffee, I figured.

The Crow's Nest Café had eight stools and two little tables, and all of it, even the woodwork, was permeated by decades of burgers and fries. And it was dark inside. Ah; the lights were turned off. Saving electricity?

The only person in the Crow's Nest was the waitress, a long, tall Sally slouching around with a cast-aside manner, as if trying to make herself invisible. She fumbled the coffee cup as she was filling it, slopped some in the saucer and poured that back in the cup. Either terminally shy or mildly retarded, I decided. She was about five-ten, good body, broad shoulders—she had a model's body, actually.

I laid out my card and began to ask about the boat explosion. She kept her head down and turned away, and then I saw why. She had a purple welt on her cheekbone and her upper lip was swollen and split, where her boyfriend had no doubt popped her one in a moment of passion. It made me ill, I wanted to get out: she reminded me too much of myself.

"I wouldn't know, I wasn't here," the girl said suddenly, a little louder than necessary. "I was home in bed last night. Sick." I paid for the coffee and left, I didn't even pretend to drink it. When I pulled out of the parking lot, the brown van was still there, and the guy under the big black hat was still asleep.

I picked up Mrs. Yeo's accident report from the Costa Mesa police and headed back to the office. It was empty and quiet. In my desk drawer the little red eye was winking at me, signaling a phone message. There was only one.

"Hello. This is a person—I'm calling about Arnold Tenhagen." A young male voice. The caller took a couple of raspy breaths, struggling for control. He said the name just like Deirdre did, too, "Ten-heggen" instead of "Ten-hah-gen," but I didn't notice that the first time through.

"Not bad enough he's dead. But they actually went ahead and killed him? I can't believe this is happening! Okay; I been thinking about it all day, and here's my conclusion. He's gone and I can't bring him back, there's no way. But I know who they are, and I know why they did it. And if you or the law, either one, let them off the hook, I'll go after them myself. So you better hurry up and get them. Or I will."

 Wow, what a break! Anonymous Caller must have been close to Tenhagen: he sounded really torn up. How did he get my number? Well, how did the *Tribune* reporter get it? I'd been spreading my card around town all day, for one thing. I felt great, for about thirty seconds. Then I began to realize that he hadn't told me much of anything. Not who "they" were, or even a hint about why they did it—not one concrete detail.

Maybe Anonymous was just some paranoid nut who saw conspiracies everywhere. Or someone who worshiped Arnie from afar. . . . He definitely sounded involved, I'd swear the emotion was genuine; and besides, he pronounced their name just like the family did. So he had to have a connection. Some vibes here disturbed me, hints of a secret gay life maybe—cruising, Hollywood Boulevard and leather bars? That didn't fit my picture of Arnie Tenhagen at all.

He was playing some kind of game with me. Well, it was working. If he really did know who did it, and why . . . maybe the call was intended to be a test. Not a shred there to identify him. Hey, Mr. Anonymous, ring my phone again. I reset my machine, and took off for the hospital. I could only hope.

Hospitals are different when you come in through the front door. I was no longer an acknowledged participant in the life-and-death drama, merely that necessary evil, a visitor. No, I couldn't see Rick or Judy. I wasn't "family." The X rays had verified that Rick's skull was fractured. Judy had several broken ribs, a punctured lung and other internal damage, and was "not very comfortable," as the nurse put it.

In the waiting area outside Intensive Care I found an older couple who looked familiar. Rick's mother, Fran—we'd met once—was a tall, quiet woman, with chestnut hair tinted to cover the gray, and with Rick's careful, vulnerable ways. Tom, Rick's stepfather, jumped up and pulled his green polo shirt smooth over his belly to straighten it, glowering protectively under thick black brows. He took me in as Fran reintroduced us, and I saw the "Oh-oh, another one of Rick's hippie friends" look; but Fran hugged me like a long-lost relative. I was glad they'd come. Now they could handle any life-and-death decisions.

Rick's condition was unchanged. "I get to see him for five minutes every hour," Fran said. "He seems to be resting all right."

"He's in a coma," Tom said. "I don't know why they pussyfoot around like they do." He wrinkled up his ridgy brow and asked me about the accident. Fran listened and kept shaking her head.

"Terrible. Just a terrible thing," she said. "Unbelievable." She wanted all the details from my evening with Rick before the accident, she was already treating it like his last supper. She'd come to visit Rick once when I was living with him, and we were all pleasant and fake and horribly uncomfortable. She'd been scared to death I had a lock on Rick, and I know she was relieved when we split up. Judy would've suited her fine.

I turned the problem of locating Judy's kin and her address book over to Fran. "I couldn't possibly," she said, looking unhappy; but she took it.

Next morning at the office, the phone machine gave me some bad news and some good. There was nothing more from Anonymous on the tape, but Vera Tenhagen would see me tomorrow at 10 A.M. Then I read Mrs. Yeo's police report—Leo would know if I hadn't. I never even tried to lie to him.

The insured, Paula Yeo, had been making a right turn from Fairview onto Fair Drive when her vehicle collided with a bicycle being ridden by a fifteen-year-old girl, with another fifteen-year-old on the handlebars. Damage to bike's front wheel, right front fender of Mrs. Yeo's Datsun. Extent of bodily injuries undetermined. Approximate time of accident, 5:15 P.M. Maybe the sun had blinded her. Nobody answered at the Yeo household, which gave me a momentary reprieve.

Before I left, I spent some time on our notorious trash-mash case, which involved a loaded cement mixer on Beach Boulevard that lost its brakes and creamed five vehicles waiting at a signal, a couple of which in turn hit three parked cars. We'd gone out right away and shot a dozen rolls of film. It was going to be a dandy to untangle.

By the time I got down to Dickerson's Boatyard, the morning overcast had burned off and heat waves were beginning to shimmer above the few open areas of cracked gray-white asphalt. These people had worked with Arnold Tenhagen on *Spray* for months. They ought to know something about him.

Alongside the low building a shirtless Viking type bending over a whining power saw straightened up, squared his shoulders and sucked in his gut when he saw me. His nose was a solid white triangle of zinc oxide smeared on to prevent sunburn, and he had blond neck-curls and thick blond mustaches growing out onto his cheeks. He shouted across the yard—"'Ey, Ben! Company!"—to another man up on the deck of a scoop-sided racing hull.

Farther back I saw a jeep pulled up into the shade of the building; and a big blue van was parked in the greenish aquarium light of a rippled fiberglass roof.

Ben Dickerson waited with one foot up on the gunwale, giving me the once-over. A compact, wiry man weathered the color of the teak deck he was working on, Dickerson looked to be maybe a tough fifty, with dark hair and tight beard both threaded with gray crinkles. When I introduced myself his eyebrows went up, revealing white slashes where the sun never reached, fanning out from his eyes.

He climbed down and rubbed his palm across his shirtfront before taking mine in his stubby hard fingers, all callused.

I introduced myself. "I guess you've heard about Arnie Tenhagen."

Ben nodded. "Oh yeah. Wasn't that a terrible thing? My Gawd, what a shock! Eddie and me, we've been thrashing it over all day, just trying to take it in." When Eddie came over, I saw that his zinc oxide had been wiped off.

"And just what might your connection to this be?" Ben asked.

I gave each of them a card, and explained. "Purely a freak of chance I wasn't in it, too." So I had to tell it one more time. The phrases were getting stale with repetition and they all sounded fake now; they stuck in my mouth like wax.

Ben whistled solemnly. "Damn lucky," he said.

"What kind of a guy was Tenhagen?"

"Salt of the earth," Ben declared. "You couldn't ask for a finer guy to have dealings with. Am I right, Eddie?" Eddie nodded. "I took a run over there right when I heard," Ben said. "A thing like that—you have to see it with your own eyes to believe it."

"Gage Pfeiffer says it was arson."

"He did! Yeah, I know who Pfeiffer is; and I say that's bullshit," Ben said. "I saw that boat. The inside of it is charcoal. How could he or anybody tell how it happened?"

I shrugged. "Technical stuff. He has the evidence. Anyway: you both knew Tenhagen pretty well. How was he doing, business-wise? Have any money problems? Who wasn't he getting along with?"

Oh, no, nothing like that. To hear them tell it, Arnie T. was smart, generous, but at the same time tough where a man should be tough; honest, and all-around wonderful. When I looked skeptical, Eddie came to life, leaning in with his thumbs hooked in his pockets.

"You strike me like a person who's got something to prove here," Eddie said. "What's your game, anyway? Trying to save your company money, am I right?"

Ben shushed him, and suggested I go see Arnie's good friends, John and Sandra Healy, to get another opinion. "The three of them took a cruise through the islands last winter, Fiji and the Solomons," Ben said. "Sandra Healy's got a real soft spot for Arnie. . . . Did have." Suddenly he teared up, snuffled and poked at his nose. "Damn. You just never know, do you."

"Isn't that the truth," said Eddie.

"Somebody suggested it could've been caused by the repair job on the boat," I said.

Ben was flabbergasted. "Now just a damn minute!" His voice rose like a steam whistle. Then he reined himself in. "I want to tell you that I've been working on boats for more than thirty years now, and never once has anybody had the gall to say a thing like that to me."

"Hang on, Ben," Eddie said.

"I stand by every piece of work I've ever done. I've said it before and I'll say it again: I've never fixed a boat that I wouldn't trust my life to after!"

"I believe you. It's obvious to me that if Arnold Tenhagen chose you for his job, he thought you were the best around."

"You damn right." We shifted into the shade of a boat, and Ben explained at length what they'd done to the *Spray*, the new deck planking all entirely caulked, new flooring inside, and the rest. Eddie was getting restless, I could see Ben preparing to end the conversation, and I'd gotten exactly nothing.

"Tenhagen pay you all right?" I asked.

"Oh, hell yes; no problem with that," Ben said. "That boat was his baby. He wanted everything authentic."

"All the original hardware," Eddie said.

Ben was scowling. "What?" I asked. "You just thought of something." He and Eddie exchanged a look.

"He had a little theft kind of trouble," Ben said. "Had some valuable antique navigation instruments on board, a compass and an old sextant. Somebody broke in and stole them." His scowl deepened. "Funny part, none of the other boats around were hit."

"Could the instruments have been seen by anybody passing by?" Ben shook the thought away, disgusted. Of course they would've been concealed, locked inside. "Meaning it was somebody who knew they were there," I said. So he and Eddie obviously qualified as suspects. "But that could've been it, right there. If he had his suspicions, that'd be enough reason for some people, wouldn't it."

"There's a thought," Eddie said.

"Didn't seem to bother Arnie all that much," Ben said, "he just let it pass." Over on the building the phone bell started ringing. "He was getting ready for his big cruise—you tell her about it, Eddie, while I go get that phone." Ben jogged away stiff-legged, and Eddie straightened his shoulders, assuming the social burden.

"Yeah, he was talking around about it some. Which I could understand, the lure of the sea. I know the feeling, I share that same philosophy." Eddie had two modes: aggressive, leaning forward to attack; and defensive, like right now, with his arms folded in a high, tight hug.

"Myself, I've got to be in the open air," he said. "I can't stand being indoors. None of these nine-to-five desk jobs. Hey, those neckties'll strangle you. Man wasn't meant to live like that." He inhaled deeply with his head thrown back and his eyes closed and then held the pose, being a sun worshiper. "Most people miss out on the important things. Tell you the truth, I believe I was born in the wrong century. . . . You live around here?"

"Inland. You?"

"Native; Newport Beach product all the way. Born up at Hoag, went to Harbor High with Stud Jenkins—Olympic water-polo team? Old Stud and I started skin-diving together off Laguna, when you could still find something to shoot out there."

Ben trotted toward us with a little smile. "That was the vet," he told Eddie. "He says to tell you your kitty-cat is okay, back in circulation. Full of sardines and ready to boogie."

"I wouldn't've taken you for an animal lover," I said to Eddie. He didn't answer, just looked sullen. Obviously Ben enjoyed rubbing him the wrong way now and then. Ben stood sideways to me, ready to get back to work. I'd used up my little welcome.

"One last question." I directed it to both of them. "Ever see Tenhagen and his wife together? Were they getting along all right?"

"Far as I saw," Ben said. "He used to work down here with us when he could, like on Saturdays, and she brought us all our lunch a few times. Seemed like a real nice lady."

"Speaking of which: did he have any, you know, outside interests?"

Ben was indignant. "Even if I did know that, what makes you think I'd tell you?"

I wanted to hit him. "Because your reputation is riding on this, for one thing! Not enough some dumb jackass blows everybody sky-high—" I heard myself screaming at them both standing there solid and healthy, breathing so easy, turning and reaching—two minutes after I left, their lives would be back to normal; but ours, never. They had that sick, helpless look. "Hey, we've got a hysterical woman here." Like they were watching somebody having a seizure.

I covered my mouth with both hands and turned away, and stared hard at a funny wedge of black shadow till the shaking stopped and I was sure I wasn't going to break down. Then I apologized.

"Think nothing of it," Ben said. "It's the strain you been under. Nobody ought to go through an experience like that."

"Right; you should take it easy on yourself for a while," Eddie chimed in.

"What you need is a good rest," Ben said. "Get away from all this—"

"No way. I'm never going to quit."

"If I think of anything, I'll sure let you know," Ben said, walking me toward my car. "Now that I understand where you're coming from. And you might want to keep me posted as to whatever turns up, same way."

If Ben had blasted old salt-of-the-earth Arnie, I couldn't figure why. I leaned on my window frame and he looked down the neck of my shirt, friendly-like, making sure it wasn't empty. I imagined him munching along my neck with that scratchy beard, and that bothered me, too. "Marine adjuster said the leak made no sense, right in the middle of the hose like that," I said. "How would you cause that kind of a leak, if you were going to?"

"Mm—stick it with anything sharp. Like an ice pick. I'd think your real question would be, why?"

Eddie stood holding his saw and watching me as I backed around, and I wondered if worried was his normal expression. He sucked in his stomach again and waved. Ben was already halfway back to his boat.

I liked Ben Dickerson. Most people I know spend their days pushing paper around or massaging a computer keyboard, or talking things to death; but Ben was an artisan, he actually made something real. Boat-building you'd have to learn on the job from an expert, those were skills handed down from one person to another all the way back to . . . Noah, maybe.

I stopped to call Gage Pfeiffer, and he suggested I drop by his office. "I may have a little something for you," he said. So it was back to Santa Ana through the gathering smog.

Gage's office was about ten blocks from ours, in a Spanish-style building in an open square with a big central fountain filled with a clump of huge, spiky agaves. The door to number 17 stood wide open, and the terminal on the secretary's desk had a screenful of amber characters, but she was nowhere in sight.

"Eleanor's on a break," Gage said. "Come on in." His own office was just behind, a plain little room with his desk situated to look straight through the reception area to the patio, and only one picture on the wall, a color print of a big white powerboat. He left his door standing open, too.

"I believe I've found us a possible witness," he said.

"Terrific! . . . Possible?"

Working his way along the harbor as he'd promised, Gage had learned secondhand that a boater moored in the same area reported seeing somebody on the deck of the *Spray* early on the morning of the accident. Only problem: said witness had just left for Baja on a deep-sea fishing trip, and wasn't expected back for several days. "Not a thing in the world to do about it but wait," Gage said. "How's your boyfriend doing?"

"Not boyfriend; old friend." Gage, having found out what he wanted to know, looked pleased with himself. He'd checked on Rick and Judy, and knew as much about their conditions as I did.

"Well, we'll have to keep our fingers crossed. . . . I'm single myself, now," he said, swerving back to his original subject. He looked at me, inquiring. Not subtle, but it got results.

"Yes, I was married once, too, for a little while," I said. "Wasn't everybody?" Which took care of that. Gage tucked the subject away, I could almost hear the drawer click. Then his expression got a little bleak.

"I saw the statement you gave to the *Tribune*," he said. "About it being arson. That wasn't very smart. Just damn lucky they didn't use your name."

"Why? I took you at your word. You mean you were wrong? I should've gone to the fire department instead, get their okay?" I hadn't been there, and didn't want to go. Naturally, they'd tell me to mind my own business.

"Hell no, I wasn't wrong. That isn't the point. You haven't worked an arson case yet, I guess. It's next to impossible to get a conviction."

"I can't believe that!" But it sounded familiar, I'd heard it before; only then it didn't matter.

"Believe it. If I were this close to you and I saw you do it, that in itself wouldn't be enough. Takes two witnesses. Thing is, you need to get the motive. Say some guy has a grudge, maybe he's been talking about doing it beforehand, threatening—"

"Then I'll find it." In the silence I could hear the dry rattle of computer keys. Gage's secretary was back.

"Say: my stomach's telling me it's lunchtime," Gage said. "Wednesdays I always eat Mexican. Care to join me?"

"Sure. A man of regular habits, I see." On the way out he introduced me to Eleanor, a no-nonsense woman around fifty with cropped gray hair and colored pictures of her three grandchildren on her desk. We got into Gage's snappy little white Saab, and he showed me the European safety features: padded dashboard, collapsible steering column.

On the way, Gage told me five or six stories about boaters' stupidity; like the day he started back from Catalina in a pea-soup fog, and a guy roared up in a 34-foot Hunter and asked Gage if he could follow him back to San Pedro.

"Now, this is one of the top criminal lawyers in the county, mind: I recognized the guy. And he was out there without a compass."

And arson. They always looked for money problems right away, Gage said; for example, the man in terrible financial trouble whose hundred-thousand-dollar powerboat burned, far enough off Catalina that it sank in deep water. "He said the engine caught fire. Clear day, calm—oh, no, he couldn't put it out. But he and his buddy stayed around in their little skiff and watched it burn for three hours, till it finally sank."

"Anyway, you got him."

"Nope. Best I could get was a settlement. We compromised."

We pulled up at La Rancheria, a restaurant converted from

an old adobe farmhouse, with wisteria vines like rope twisting up the veranda posts, and mossy terra-cotta pots of fuchsia that had just been misted, their rosy two-toned ballerina bells glittering.

Gage got us a table under a big pepper tree, and I tried to pretend there wasn't any man-woman stuff going on.

Gage seemed to be the settled type, and obviously looking around. Not me—just the idea of marriage makes me sweat and quiver. I know it's still the preferred way to have a kid, and that aspect does have a certain attraction, in spite of my own disastrous background.

Ada, my fair-skinned English mother, is living in Seattle with her sixth husband, Carlton—"I and Elizabeth Taylor; we always have to marry them," Ada says, frequently. Carlton's a southern gentleman who pretends to get up when you come in the room, drives Ada's white Caddy with vodka dings (also Ada's), and wears handmade Italian shoes she provides out of the proceeds from her beauty salon. What can you do? Men come and go; a kid is forever.

Gage hadn't heard anything about the theft earlier on Tenhagen's boat.

"I figure the thing had to have been done for money, someway," I said. "Being as he was rich. You?"

"Family's not what I'd call rich," he said. "Just well-to-do."

"Maybe he was in over his head; set it up to collect the insurance, and made a mistake."

"Mm . . . hard to believe. Arnie had too much experience. Kind of brilliant, actually; invented things. Held a couple of patents."

"Plenty of money there. Maybe someone in the family wanted to get their hands on it." I was thinking about Anonymous's call, which I had no intention of telling Gage about. Wouldn't he just hoot?

"Why would they want to kill the goose that laid the golden egg?"

"I just wonder," I started, my throat tight, "how it is you can find all the reasons against doing something, and nothing, none of them for?"

Gage looked at me and pushed a glass of water closer. "Here." I drank it and looked across at the wisteria till my eyes cleared.

"Sorry," I said. "That was uncalled for."

"No problem." Our food came, chicken enchiladas with sour cream and a side order of chiles rellenos, and we fell to.

"Promise me something, anyway," he said, a few minutes later. "That you'll lay off with the arson talk till we've got it nailed down a little better."

"If you'll tell me why."

"Because, for one thing, how are we going to accomplish anything with you giving it all away? That's the problem with using women for claims work: they tend to get too emotional. I'm sorry, but it's true."

"What do you mean, too emotional—" I almost shouted it, and then I had to smile. Stuck there without my car, I couldn't even stomp out in a rage. Cool it, I told myself. This guy is essential.

"That didn't come out quite right," Gage said. "Not one of my better days."

"Nor mine." Then we got into quieter territory, or at least he must've thought so; where did you grow up and so forth.

"I'm an Okie, myself," he said. "Born and raised out in the sandhills. Five Nations country. Oklahoma means 'red people' in Choctaw. Did you know that?" I didn't bite.

"So I joined the Navy, and fell in love with the water," he said. "Hard to believe, isn't it. Stuck out there on it, sleeping on a shelf with six inches of clearance—and just never went back. How about yourself?"

"Only child. My mother moved around a lot. I went to grade school for a while in Culver City. That's in LA, downhill from Westwood. The little old bungalows with open porches across the front are still there, and the driveways with two separate strips of concrete." I didn't volunteer any more about myself. I wanted him to ask outright.

"My wife left me last March. Said I was overwhelming her, and she needed more space to develop in. I still cain't figure that one out."

Still hooked on his ex-wife. "People don't necessarily give the real reasons," I said. "Maybe they don't even know them."

"I guess it was a combination of things. We don't see each other at all. The thing of it is, I'm not the man-about-town type. These single bars don't interest me." Right then the waitress's arm came between us, refilling the coffee cups, so I didn't have to answer.

"Actually, I wish her luck," he said, and shrugged. "What else?"

Blam! A bird flew into a plate-glass window eight feet away and everybody looked up. I was halfway out of my seat.

"Bird," Gage said. "Sky reflection confuses them. It's probably in the bushes. You want to go see?"

I shook my head, settling back. "There're a lot of birds around my place," I said. "All the trees. Tanagers lately. Must be going south for the winter."

He picked up his fork again and then stopped. "We might could find it."

"No," I said. "Either it flies, or it doesn't. Like the rest of us." I hadn't meant anything special by that. But the look Gage gave me was so serious, it hurt.

5 Gage and I parted in the parking lot behind his office building and he went away whistling some country song. Then I recognized it—"San Antonio Rose." So he'd decided about me: just plain Mex.

Which would be better: if the arsonist turned out to be some nut getting his jollies, a common criminal, or one of Arnold Tenhagen's near and dear? Which would mean less hassle, clean up this mess, and get Rick's and Judy's bills paid the quickest? Stupid question; you couldn't choose how you'd like it to be, only find out which it was.

To start with the most obvious, Arnold Tenhagen had been making plenty of money, which somebody else would enjoy now—probably his kids. Could they be Anonymous Caller's "they?" Well, I'd be getting to them. But first I went around to see his current business partner, Roger Murch, to start building the financial picture.

I found T/M Technology in a jazzy new office complex west of Orange County Airport. A cluster of one-story mirrored boxes latticed with redwood and reflecting rolling lawns and tender green, young eucalyptus trees bending under puffy clouds—you'd expect to see a flashy dance sequence roll out, or a hot-air balloon settling, it was much too gorgeous for mere accountants and lawyers.

T/M's carpet was greener than money, and through an open door I could see a man drawing what looked like machine parts on a computer screen. Murch's corner office, glass to the floor, was surrounded by waving branches, and nobody outside could see us.

This was about as far removed as you could imagine from Arnie's sailing world. He had everything, I thought, and then I could hear Ada being mother-dear: "Now, Moz, you know what they say—material goods don't necessarily make people happy." We must've been in the chips at the time.

Roger Murch was an indoor type, sallow and pudgy, a sharp guy who probably resented having to talk to me because he'd liked Arnie Tenhagen a lot. He drily explained T/M's business, high-tech quality control involving some sort of nondestructive electronic testing of materials and equipment, implying that I wouldn't understand and wasn't really interested. Which was half true.

"Arnie was a very organized person," Murch said. "A planner. He customarily took a global view of the possibilities; which has been a real asset for us, naturally. A very imaginative guy."

"How'd he get along with the employees? Any problems there?"

"None at all. We were all stunned—horrified. I haven't quite absorbed the shock of it yet. . . . He had everything he handled, his end of things, brought right up to date. We're having surprisingly few problems keeping things running."

"Sounds too good to be true."

That startled him, which I knew only because his pupils dilated suddenly: otherwise his expression didn't change. "If you'd known the man, you wouldn't think so. Frankly, I get the idea you're looking for some kind of dirt, something underhanded; in which case I pity you. You're really grasping at straws."

Just to reassure their business associates, he'd already done a preliminary audit of their books, he said, and found nothing unusual.

I believed him. "You know," I said, "I'm on his side, actually." It was true, which surprised me; and it wouldn't be an advantage, either, since my job was to find the worm in Arnie's apple. Murch pointed my way out, and that was that. I could always have Equifax run a background check to find out what Arnie's actual financial situation was; but right now, it looked like a waste of money.

So then, maybe A. Tenhagen was killed for love. I went back to the office and left a message with the Healys' answering service—they lived on their 46-foot yawl *Vagabunda* and didn't have a telephone.

In the meantime I got hold of Mrs. Paula Yeo, and she certainly did speak English, a torrent of it. She explained how those rotten kids just popped up from nowhere, this great hulk of a girl with her friend riding on the handlebars and weaving back and forth so much she couldn't possibly see where they were going.

"The policeman gave them both tickets," said Mrs. Yeo. "And nobody was hurt; does it say that? It ought to be there in the report. I almost had a heart attack, I'm still not over it. You better put that in, too."

I soothed Mrs. Yeo somewhat, without making any promises, and signed off, with her still muttering about her insurance rates going up now. "I swear, the world has it in for single parents," she said. Her statement went in my to-do pile. If the girls agreed, and their parents signed, this one could be settled fast.

John Healy had the courtly tones of a gentleman, and invited me to their boat at five, when his wife would be there, too.

The *Vagabunda* was tied up at a slip about two miles farther up the harbor toward the entrance; a desirable spot, since it meant they could be out in the open ocean that much more quickly.

John Healy looked the complete gentleman sailor, too—lean and brown, about fifty, the steady good-guy Paul Newman type and at least as good-looking. He waited for me at the top of their boarding steps, and asked me to take off my high-heeled shoes, to spare their varnished teak deck. In my stocking feet I slipped at once, and he caught my elbow and righted me.

Wife Sandra was out, but would be back shortly. We went below and sat down at the table in an elegant cabin twice the size of Rick's, all hardwood-paneled and fitted like a jewel box. The portholes were oval and their brass frames shone.

I saw right away that Healy and Tenhagen had been close friends. He was grieving and prickly, defending Arnie as if he were still alive.

"I don't buy that arson theory at all," he said. "You'd have to be stupid to turn on anything electrical without checking for gas, and that's one thing Arnie wasn't: stupid." He thought it more likely that Ben Dickerson had made a mistake . . . maybe when he was setting a screw he'd drilled through and nicked the hose, set up "a leak situation."

"It'll never be proved, of course: but *he'll* know. It's something he'll have to live with the rest of his life. I can tell you this much: Ben Dickerson's probably washed up around here. He might just as well pull up stakes and leave."

By this time Healy had thawed enough to make us some coffee. I could see that he was attracted to me, and also that he didn't take me seriously, as he would've someone nearer his own age. He bent to pour the boiling water into the white cone in each cup, smiling as it sank through the coffee. "When something like this happens, it tends to sharpen your attention," he said. "I expect you've had much the same experience."

He sat down and turned his cup around, inhaling the steam. "There were so many things Arnie wanted to do yet," Healy said. "He had sort of a childlike streak in him, a kind of venturesomeness. . . . I know he regretted a little that he hadn't lived in the early days, when there weren't all these electronic navigation aids and a man was thrown back entirely on his own abilities. You take his boat, now; the name?" He looked at me inquiringly.

"Tell me about it."

The original *Spray* had been an old 37-foot wooden boat rebuilt by Joshua Slocum, an aging New England sea captain who'd made a dozen voyages along the coasts of the Americas and crisscrossing the Pacific, but couldn't get a proper ship anymore. Slocum, fifty-one when he started, sailed the *Spray* around the world singlehanded.

" 'Two feet shorter than this one,' Arnie'd say. 'Only took him a month to get around Cape Horn.' Tip of South America; Straits of Magellan? Terrible place: ships' graveyard. Of course we've got the Canal now. After Slocum got back, he wrote his memoirs." Healy went to a cupboard and brought back a book with a worn green cover. "You might enjoy reading them sometime."

"And was Arnie thinking about duplicating Slocum's voyage?"

"Ahoy, the *Vagabunda!*" A woman's voice came from outside. Healy went up the stairs and I followed in time to see him reach down to take his wife's burden, a basket of folded laundry.

"Well, hello there!" Sandra Healy said, squeezing my hands. Weathered face, the same network of sailor's squintlines, and a Cleopatra fringe of corkscrew curls, a natural perm growing out; jeans frayed white at the hem and Birkenstock sandals slapping as she whirled around, stowing things away while we talked. Or mostly she talked, being clearly the more dominant of the two.

"Ten-heggen" was the traditional pronunciation of the name, but they'd given up on correcting people years ago, Sandra said. "Probably only a few of us said it properly. Relatives and their truly oldest friends."

I asked them about the theft of equipment from the *Spray*. Neither of them had heard about it. "Sounds like more of Ben's carelessness," John said.

"Any of the family seem to be in particular need of money? His children, his wife?"

"The iron butterfly?" Sandra said. "Hardly. She had her own money, inherited quite a chunk of it a while back."

"What are their kids like?"

"Typical Newport Beach products, probably," John said. "Achievers—" Sandra's voice overrode his.

"Meaning pampered darlings, such wonderful taste, enormously self-concerned. I understand there were problems with the youngest, Keith. He was evidently quite thoroughly into drugs, they put him in Schick for the cure a couple of months back. I believe it took all right, at least I haven't heard otherwise yet." Drugs, money to buy them, stealing things from the family to sell. Could it be that simple?

Sandra watched me with a disagreeable smile, as if she were reading my mind. "You're pursuing all the obvious, aren't you," she said. "I think you need to be looking for less tangible motives."

"Such as?"

"I'd really prefer that it was some kind of hideous accident," John Healy said. "It's either that, or posit darker deeds."

Our glances met and then skipped away, none of us with the will or the energy at that moment to sketch out those "darker deeds." So far I'd come up with a whole lot of nothing, and I was beginning to feel stupid and somewhat malicious. Poking around in people's lives, hoping to stumble on some clue—and what if Arnie and Sandra Healy did have something going?

Maybe Gentleman John was just a handsome hulk, burned out himself. You can't ever tell by looking.

How old do you have to get before you quit being victimized by lust? My dippy mother, Ada, with her latest husband, Carlton the sport, was obviously never going to outgrow it. And jealousy never dies. Or maybe Sandra had been nursing a hopeless passion. Hardly a major crime. There was nothing here, I should just get out.

"So, okay," I said. "If he was such a great guy, how come he's dead? Why do you think it happened?"

"I think we'd agree," Sandra said, "that what we did see was a man in a state of transition. John?"

He nodded. "Mm . . . maybe a general dissatisfaction with the direction his life had been taking."

"I'd put it a little stronger than that," said Sandra. "Say rather, he wanted to get off the merry-go-round entirely."

"You think," he said. "I don't. I categorically disagree."

Suicide? The thought had never occurred to me. "You mean maybe he—but, oof! what a way to do it. You think he was depressed enough to—"

"That's nonsense," John said. "Arnie was a sound, successful, well-balanced man in the prime of his life."

"A very responsible person," she said. "Also a realist."

"You could count on him all the way," he said.

"Epitaph for a winner," Sandra Healy said, looking away from us. Her eyes were filled with tears. They both had loved Arnie, in whatever way—and because of that I understood him a little better.

When I got up to leave, John Healy offered to lend me Slocum's memoirs, and Sandra switched faces again. "That's not necessary," she said, taking the book out of his hands. "She can easily find it at any library. You should try the Balboa branch."

I did, and they had it. I negotiated a library card and carried off Slocum's complete works in one volume, including photographs of the boat and a skinny guy with a scraggly beard going gray. Silly idea. Well, I wouldn't waste much time on it. Hm . . . Keith Tenhagen, stealing his daddy's goods to feed his habit? That couldn't last long. Maybe he'd been dealing. Maybe he still was.

The hospital lobby was already becoming wretchedly familiar, but that faint sharp smell still made the hairs along my arms prickle.

Rick's parents, Fran and Tom, were graciously introducing some new relatives-of-disaster to hospital ways. Fran beamed at me and the faucet came on, a gush of technical information about Rick's condition—yes, our boy was still unconscious; but I had trouble paying attention.

"I want to see him," I said.

"Only family," Tom said promptly, and "A shame, yes," Fran said. "They're so rigid. You know, big organizations . . ."

"Tell them I'm his sister." Fran and Tom exchanged a look. "Half-sister. From an earlier marriage."

Tom clamped up his mouth like he'd been offered a forkful of squid; but Fran said, "Why not?" surprising herself.

Rick lay wedged on one side, inert, breathing steadily. His left eye was somewhere behind a purpling bulge flush with his nose. At the head of the bed the monitor bounced its green track across the screen, that precious sign you would fall on your face and promise anything for, bribe the Lord of the universe to keep it wiggling. I went to see Judy.

She was curled up at the center of a web of tubes, one of them a fat vibrating spiral attached to a green machine, *squiiish . . . thunk*; a respirator, forcing air into her lungs. Her fine dark hair was stringy and matted, and among all that glossy plastic she was only a sad, sick animal, far removed from us and horribly perishable. Outside Fran waited to hear me say something cheery and upbeat.

"Obviously holding their own," I said, not believing it. Rick was in there suspended in limbo, and I hadn't done anything yet to buy him out.

Even though it was after hours, I went back to the office,

hoping to find another message from Anonymous Caller. That long string had been tugging on me all day. The winking red eye only recorded clicks and patches of dial tone from impatient callers. I sat down and wrote up Mrs. Yeo's claim.

I'd reset my recorder and was just leaving for home when the phone started to ring. Probably Fran with bad news, I thought, suddenly too tired to cope with it; so I just turned up the volume and waited through my little message.

"Hello. It's me again." And damn, it was: Mr. Anonymous. After an uncertain pause he blurted, "I want to know what you found out so far." He sounded calmer this time. Should I break in and risk his hanging up?

"Hello!" I burst in, sweet and breathless. "This is Martha Brant. I'm so glad you called me back, I need your help."

"My help? What for? You—you're the one doing the investigating. Did you know they took his ashes out and threw them in the ocean this morning? Couldn't wait to get rid of him." The hysterical grief was past. This time he just sounded angry.

"Which 'them' is this?"

"His kids, of course. They're going to get everything, aren't they."

"You think they did it to get at his money? I hear they've got enough as it is, they're all quite well off."

"Yeah? Well, I hear they've got some pretty nasty habits—oh, I could tell you plenty; and he wasn't putting up with it. They're such spoiled babies."

"Like how? So tell me about these habits." I noticed voices in the background now, a television maybe, and a kid yelling.

But he went on in his own direction. "For one thing, they could've figured out when he was going to be on his boat and timed it just right; you know, the device. That's what really gets me, the sneaky way they did it:—bam! No warning, no time to prepare yourself or nothing. Listen, if it can be proved they did it, would they still have the right to his money?"

"Depends, I guess. We'd have to find some pretty strong proof, really good evidence to prevent it. You know, it looks like you and I have got the same interests, we're trying to accomplish the same thing here." I told him about Rick and Judy, how I'd been afraid his call was the hospital saying one of them was finished.

"Listen," I said. "What we ought to do is get together somewhere and talk about this whole deal—" Whop! He'd slammed down the receiver, and I was left with the dial tone.

He'll call back, I told myself. I know he will. I sat looking at the phone and waited. I didn't even look at my watch and set myself a deadline, for fear that might jinx it. Called the same time of day twice. Right after he finished work, I figured. It was quiet enough to hear the cars that passed by outside at intervals, and my stomach growling. Overhead somewhere the building snapped, settling.

The phone started to ring and I grabbed it.

"Sorry about that," he said, and his voice was deeper, more authoritative. "Something came up. I'm getting fucked over again, I know it. But that's okay. I'll figure out how to handle it. I have before. So what happens now?"

"Maybe nothing. Maybe life goes on just like always, and they get away with it. So? Unless we care enough between us to try and nail them." He'd called me back to give me this chance, some reason we should cooperate, and I was blowing it, I could feel it slipping away. "You must have known Arnie pretty well," I said, groping.

His answer was a snarl of frustration and despair. "None of your business."

Before he could hang up again I gave him my home phone number and asked him to call me anytime.

"Okay: I'm going to check you out. Maybe we'll be in touch."

He was going to check me out? Was that nerve, or what? Two points: he pronounced the family name right, and he knew Arnie had been cremated; which meant that he had some kind of connection to the family. . . . He knows one of the kids, and has it in for him. Arnie's young gay lover, grieving and jealous of the Tenhagen money. A poor relation, or an old family friend who got dumped while Arnie was making his climb. Or maybe his dad was a former partner of Arnie's who got cheated out of a patent or something. Oh, my imagination was in high gear, without one fact to hang on to.

I reset my phone machine, locked up the office again and headed home, feeling a very small glow. For one thing, I'd managed to establish some rapport with Anonymous; and for another, I just felt he hadn't done it. Item: he didn't know exactly how the explosion had been caused. Or else he really did, and was playing games with me; which made him a whole lot smarter than I was.

It was almost dark when I coasted down the alley and into my usual parking spot, alongside the old three-car garage packed with my landlady's antiques and therefore unusable, so that my apartment above it was wonderfully quiet. Starting up the outside stairs on the side away from the alley, I heard what sounded like a van upshift and accelerate down the alley. But that didn't really register till quite a while later. The stucco wall alongside was still warm to the touch, and halfway up I stopped to soak in the tranquility.

In the distance a television news broadcaster burbled away. The only other sounds came from a flock of invisible birds in conversation, the giant pepper trees hissing in the evening breeze, and the scrape and rattle of the eucalyptus. The house of my landlady, Mrs. Chaney—"You can call me Gloria," she always said, but I never could—was fifty feet away, and so walled around by shrubbery that I felt almost as if I were living in a forest.

Only a few people have ever been up here with me, which is deliberate. Their auras tend to hang around, which makes me more and more cautious about whom I invite home. I'd planned on Rick being the next. I'm in the phone book, all right; but you have to know the place to be able to find it.

I opened a can of clam chowder and settled down with Joshua Slocum's troubles and adventures. . . . The age of the big sailing ships was beginning to die out when Slocum finished rebuilding his boat and started off to sail alone around the world, lashing the wheel while he ate or slept. All that water, and no place to pull over.

Slocum had incredible troubles getting through the Straits of Magellan. About a month it took him, with the storms and getting off course; at nighttime the boat being knocked around by huge waves foaming over rocks that weren't supposed to be there. And when he did make land, he had to spread tacks on deck to keep the Indians from sneaking aboard and killing him while he slept. He had some great times, too. He hit the Cocos Islands, six hundred miles southwest of Java, by dead reckoning.

He found a whole other world with its own rhythms, a different kind of time, even . . . that must've been partly what Arnie had been after, and Rick. I'd never been out of the harbor, but still I could feel the pull of it from here. Sailing around. It took Slocum three years.

While I read, a ghost came and sat alongside me, his warm thigh pressing the length of mine and an arm flung across my shoulders. Arnie, or maybe Gage? This involuntary celibacy was for the birds; but I needed only one. . . . When I looked up, it was 12:45 A.M. I slid into bed, lonesome for somebody, but I didn't know for whom.

And then I slid out again, to call ICU and check on Rick. No change.

In the night I half-heard glass smashing in the alley, and I figured it was the rowdy teenage bunch Mrs. Bradley had been complaining about. Either that woke me, or a quiet nightmare in which Rick was a skinny helpless kid, a naked ten-year-old and he needed something important, like food. I was trying to keep track of him in this crowd, only we got separated, and I kept running and running—it was very hilly; San Francisco, I think—but I couldn't find him anywhere.

When I got down to my car next morning, the window on the passenger side was one big impact star, and a beer bottle was lying on the grass, brown with two thick red Xs on the label; Dos Equis. The bottle was unbroken, the top still on, and I thought, those kids really must've been wasted. Throwing away a full bottle of beer.

**6** On my way to meet Vera Tenhagen, the rich lady on the hill—no, just well-to-do, Gage had said—I felt my palms beginning to sweat. I could have worn my proper little Jones New York suit of cream wool, but instead I put on a not-too-old pair of classic jeans with spike heels to get myself up to eye level, and a burnt-orange shirt that looked like silk but wasn't. Good color on me, makes me look pale and exotic.

"Get in here out of that sun!" Ada, my fair-skinned English mother, used to holler. "Why can't you play in the shade?" Her first marriage, a brief liaison with her "pygmy Omar Sharif" from Quezon City, produced only scrawny little Martha Rosalind—without me, she could've forgotten the whole incident. I'm afraid that the only memories I have of him, I've invented. Ada used to smear this icky stuff on my face, egg white mixed with lemon juice, trying to bleach me out. A real confidence-builder.

At the entrance to Sea Hawk Ridge the uniformed guard, blond and blow-dried, sneered at my dusty maroon Toyota and made me spell my name. Then he punched out a phone number and talked to somebody, and finally he raised the barrier.

I chugged up the long grade getting madder by the minute, passing those great big houses and lavish grounds, beautifully groomed by dumb peasants for hypertense owners who stand and point out spots they've missed, and then slide on down to the health club for some overdue exercise; thinking how it takes maybe ten thousand grimy little households in Garden Grove and Anaheim to make just one of these places possible. Not to mention the Pakistanis bent over their sewing machines, and the Brazilians ripping out their rain forest.

Which was an attitude I had best suppress for the moment—after all, if you were born up here, wouldn't you fight to hang on to it? Also, I had to admit that what bothered me was the possibility that the people who lived up here were naturally superior; the horrible thought I've been fighting all my life: that maybe the rich really are better than the rest of us—brighter, stronger, better-looking, more capable and therefore obviously the best-suited for running the world. After all, they're doing it, aren't they?

Toward the top the houses got even bigger and farther apart. Ada would love this—no, she'd be eaten up with envy. We'd lived rich for a while. Uncle Brucie's place was easily twice the size of these. He and Ada were always fighting, screaming and throwing things . . . I used to run away and sit in the bushes, and watch for the peacocks to come around—awful noise they made, it hurt your teeth. All the time we were there I had a knot in my stomach, waiting for something bad to happen. Which says it all about my childhood. "Normal" meant we were already into the disaster.

From the street the Tenhagen place didn't look all that imposing. Hidden behind blank white walls, it ran along the top of the ridge—a half acre, I found out later. Why would Mrs. Tenhagen even talk to me? "What do you want with me?" she'd say. "You have no business up here. Go away and leave us alone." I closed my eyes and did some deep breathing to center myself, and thought about Rick.

The Mexican woman who answered the door was no taller than I, and not much darker; bleary-eyed with weeping, calm now but exhausted. I wondered if it was going to be a damp afternoon all around. She brightened when I told her my name. I shook her hand automatically and then felt silly, that certainly wasn't done up here; but she held on to it and moved closer.

"Your friends, hurt so bad. They are still alive?"

"Well, so far. Listen, I'd like to talk to you sometime. Do you always answer the phone?"

"Yes. This terrible thing, you investigate it?"

"That's right. Mrs. Tenhagen is expecting me." She said something else to me in Spanish, just as a young woman appeared at the other end of the long hall and called out, "Socorro? I'll take care of this."

"Sorry," I said, "I didn't catch that." The light of Socorro's interest withdrew like a turtle lowering its lids. She turned away and I followed her stately stride. Knotted calves in service-weight stockings; feet in blue-and-white Adidas that were probably Tenhagen family castoffs. A navy polyester uniform topped by a navy cardigan, and the long black hair worn in one thick braid looped at the back of her neck like a figure eight and doubled under.

Deirdre Tenhagen's springy step met us sooner than halfway, and she took my fingertips, releasing them at once. In her late twenties, Deirdre was a head taller than I, and very pretty (what do they do with the ugly ones, I wondered—drown them?) but too thin. She had the artfully simple helmet of hair, gold-brown, capped in eyebrow-length bangs, that all society types wear to the grave; shoulder-length now and shortened by an inch every decade. Unexpectedly her father's full-lipped smile appeared, although barely civil, revealing beautiful teeth. Of course.

She apologized for her rudeness on the phone; more convention, she didn't want either of us to be there. "Don't mention the arson thing," she said quietly.

"Why not, if it's true?"

"Uh-uh. She can't handle it right now. Just do as I say." When Deirdre raised her hand, beckoning me to follow her, I saw the short-clipped nails of a nail-biter trying to cope, and I wondered why she hadn't covered them with fakes. Probably anorexic, I thought. Would that be Anonymous's big secret? Maybe he was just a nosy neighbor kid— "Hey, she's a secret vomiter!"

. . . Waiting around to fall into a good marriage, and getting anxious. A little wrinkly under the eyes, a bit long in the tooth altogether—she'd better get moving. My automatic reaction shocked me, the realization that I was as brainwashed as the rest of womankind. No matter that Deirdre would probably agree.

"—Goolagong," she said suddenly.

"What?"

"That's who you remind me of; the Aussie tennis player, Evonne Goolagong. —Nothing personal."

Everything's personal, I thought; and if you weren't such a smart-ass already, I'd explain it to you.

"Oh, excuse me," Deirdre said, "I hardly know what I'm saying. We're just exhausted. Frankly, I'm all cried out."

"I can imagine."

"Even Socorro. Her people heard about it right away, over the news, I suppose, and started calling almost immediately."

"To find out what happened," I said.

"I expect; I wouldn't know, she wasn't speaking English. Oh, Soky can well enough, when she wants to. . . . She's been with us forever," she said. "She adored my father." A shadow of anger crossed Deirdre's face, a common-enough reaction to a major loss. I wanted to talk to her about what had happened, but right then I didn't have the nerve. I could picture her laying that stare of cold steel on me, and nothing more.

We moved across hardwood floors and Oriental rugs as we

passed various rooms and two patios, one sun-dappled under a swaying eucalyptus, the other all in shade with a tiered fountain sending up a spiral of water. Two young Mexican girls were cleaning the glass in the French doors, one on either side. Knowing Vera T's interest in the museum and things historical, I'd been prepared for pegged floors and pink marble washstands and maybe an authentic spinning wheel, but the whole house was cool and uncluttered.

Deirdre stopped short. "Arson. That's a shocking accusation." I opened my mouth to answer, but I didn't get a chance. "You don't know for sure, do you?" she demanded. "I mean, you can't prove it."

"I can't; but I know somebody who can. You don't need to worry, I'll be tactful."

"Good." She led me into the living room, its long outer wall of glass looking past a terrace and swimming pool to a magnificent view of Newport Harbor. A windowed corridor that led off to the left and another wing shared the view.

This room was all in white, the carpet woven in a corded diamond pattern, with couches of honey-blond leather. The coffee table, a free-form slab of glass, rested on a pedestal of immense quartz crystals. And the background music was a single classical guitar. Perfect.

But the view was the heart of it, the grand dogleg of Balboa Peninsula wrapped around the harbor with its islands, Lido and Balboa, and to the left the tip of the peninsula and the two jetties at the harbor mouth, with a three-masted sailboat just going out. The pale wash of sea darkened to a band of blue and an inkstroke at the horizon, beyond the coastal overcast. The house faced almost due south: sunset, if there was one, would be upcoast behind Palos Verdes.

A big brass telescope was aimed beyond the peninsula to the open ocean, where several little white triangles tipped upcoast, and a powerboat drew a line of white wake past two boats with their spinnakers up, being pulled along by those big-bellied sails striped red and yellow and black.

"Go ahead, take a look," Deirdre said, indicating the telescope. "I'll be back in a sec." And that's what I was doing, bent over and working along the waterfront to see if I could spot the *Spray* from here, when Vera, the Widow Tenhagen, walked in.

She had long, strong hands, and her gaze was glittering and steadfast. "You're looking for the killer boat," Vera said. "You can't see it from here." In the hallway Deirdre stood rock-still. Then she introduced us, quite formally, and went away.

Vera was holding a glass half-full of something cloudy, and before she took my hand she flipped away a strand of auburn hair falling over one eye. She had a diamond jaw like Claudette Colbert, but she wasn't pretty and fluffy like that at all; in fact, the opposite. Horsewoman: yes, I could see her dominating one of those beasts. "Please, just call me Vera," she said.

I would've said she was in her mid-forties, except that I knew her oldest son was over thirty. She wore an expensively simple shirt of ivory cotton, and silk shantung trousers of sea-foam green, beautifully cut to show off a good body, well-proportioned and taut. Clothes, room, life—everything about her was planned, disciplined. I was relieved to see that she wasn't prostrate with grief at the moment, although her eyes were dark-ringed.

"You have a wonderful view," I said.

"Yes. My husband loved it." Vera took a deep trembling breath. "We were one of the first to build up here. 'It may not be the biggest,' Arnie said, 'but it'll damn sure be the best.' He wanted to be King of the Hill. And he was. How are your friends doing? When I talked to the hospital this morning, they were holding their own. Has the medical insurance come through all right?"

"I'm not sure; I'll check. They never would've been hurt if I hadn't invited them down and put them there at that exact moment. I know it was just a terrible coincidence—but you can see why I've got to do this. Find out exactly how this happened."

Vera just stared at me. "Oh, I know you're even more anxious than I am to have it cleared up," I said. "I mean, my God—"

"Do you think that'll bring him back?" she cried, and closed her eyes, shutting me out.

"I know how terrible for you— But we can do this much for them. We owe them."

A string of guitar notes filled the pause, the opening of a Bach chaconne or some such.

"That's Segovia, isn't it," I said.

Vera looked at me, a little surprised. She was quite calm now. "Yes, I think so," she said, and lifted her glass to drink. It was a heavy crystal tumbler, and I had a flash that if she dropped it, on that terrace outside, say, the thick gleaming shards would rebound upward in slow motion, turning with the melody. "Lemonade," she said. "Would you like some, Martha?"

"Yes, please. And I wish you'd call me Moz, my friends all do." Vera went out herself to get it, even though there was an intercom within arm's length.

When she came back with the lemonade, she was noticeably shorter, having changed into flat shoes; literally putting herself closer to my level.

"Let's get some fresh air," Vera said. "I'll show you the grounds. And of course I'm going to help you in every way I can."

She led me past the swimming pool and along a series of terraces down the hillside, brickwork paths and reflecting pools she'd had put in, wonderful little nooks with leaf-framed views. I made the appropriate admiring remarks as I sipped my lemonade with the sprig of mint and tried to sandwich my questions tactfully betweentimes.

"What was your husband doing at the boat that night?" I asked.

"Working on the cabinets. Arnie enjoyed doing some of the finishing work himself." She said he'd used the electric heater to counteract the dampness. "Sometimes he worked so late,

he'd lie down for a minute and fall asleep, stay all night."
Could be a neat way to make room for someone else in your
life, I thought. But he had died alone.

I asked her about the theft from the boat. "There was a boxed
compass from the early 1800s, really a nice one," she said.

"Did you report it to the police?"

"No. Arnie said to let it go, not to bother."

"That seems strange. I'd think it could easily be traced. Was
he trying to protect somebody, maybe?"

"The thought never occurred to me."

"These two men who worked on his boat, Ben and Eddie.
What's your impression of them?"

"Oh, Arnie's known them for years; Ben, anyway. Eddie's
kind of a sad case—he started out on his big cruise all the way
around Baja, and lost his boat in a storm in the Gulf. Wound
up on the beach in one of those little villages. Some of our local
sailors found him in absolutely wretched circumstances and
took pity on him, gave him passage back."

"So much for dreaming big. . . . Can you tell me who
might've had reason to think of himself as your husband's enemy? Just anyone that comes to mind." Ow, a mistake. I'd
promised not to mention the arson, and Vera would still be
thinking "accident."

But it hadn't seemed to register. "Enemy?" she said. "I can't
imagine what . . . I wouldn't've believed he had one."

"Was he possibly involved with someone else? Please, I can
be discreet."

Vera was halfway smiling. "You mean, another woman?"

"Or . . ." Her smile broadened for a moment. So confident;
it would be that much worse for her if she were wrong.

"I'm sorry, Martha—Moz," she said. "Truly. I can't think of
a thing that would help."

And she told me the family anecdotes that went with each
spot: here was the tree Martin fell out of when he broke his
wrist; there the terrace where they had their Fourth-of-July bar-
becues.

"We had everybody over on the Fourth," Vera said, "all our friends and all the children's. There'd be little fireworks up and down the beach outlining the shore, and the big shows off Huntington and farther up the coast—sometimes you could see clear to Long Beach. One year we had a Dixieland band and absolutely everybody danced, all of us together, and happy—it was just so right! It made you want to live forever."

It would all be ready for the grandchildren when that time arrived, she said. Her view was a little longer than Ada's, who planned ahead about fifteen minutes, on the average.

Glancing up once, I caught Deirdre watching stony-faced from a window. She withdrew quickly, more to prevent Vera from seeing her than me, I felt sure.

Only Vera and Socorro had been at home the night of the accident: Keith, in his senior year at USC, was away at school; and Deirdre, who worked as an aide to the local congressman, had her own apartment in Park Newport, a couple of miles away.

If it turns out to be one of her kids, it'll kill her, I thought. Deirdre was watching us again. Vera's back was to the house, and this time Deirdre twitched the curtain into place to make sure I didn't miss her.

We came back around to the pool, and Vera said, "Next time you come, we'll have a swim. I suppose there'll have to be a next time. Even though this all seems totally irrelevant to me now." We fell silent, standing together facing the great wash of pale-blue ocean stretching away to the horizon. She had managed to put this little barrier between Arnie and the sea, but it leapt out and caught him anyway.

"Mother?" Deirdre called. "You have to come and rest. You promised." But Vera wasn't finished. She took me into the study, all maps and sailing charts and a big relief globe, to show me her prized Chinese horse. A marvelous little beast of almost-white jade, the horse sat on a pedestal near the window where it caught the light, its neck arched and looking around at us. Ming dynasty, Vera said. Arnie had given it to her for their silver wedding anniversary. "The first and only marriage for either of us," she said. "Rather a rarity in itself, nowadays."

Vera was so obviously exhausted that it made me angry. I wanted to get away. Why was she bending over backward for me like this? Why didn't she tell me to leave, why hadn't she just pointed me at her insurance company? The obvious answer: she was working overtime to deflect suspicion from somebody.

In a color photograph on Arnie's desk, Vera with her arm flung over the neck of a big mottled gray horse laughed and shouted at the cameraman. "Buccaneer," she said. "Isn't he beautiful? A hunter; I made him myself, from green stock. When we had to have him put down, I almost gave up riding."

One wall was covered with black-and-white candid photos of the children growing up, done by professionals. I remarked at Vera's good fortune, having three handsome children.

"Oh, yes; especially because—four, actually: our first was stillborn. You can imagine how thrilled we were when Martin arrived." Little towhead Deirdre and the others with big front teeth, and then young teenagers with the braces—they'd had years of orthodontia, she said. What nasty things could those darlings be into nowadays? Nothing Vera would know about, probably. They'd be careful to protect Mother.

Whatever it was, I'd bet then that Vera could survive it; she was certainly much tougher than Deirdre gave her credit for. She'd created this world for them, the serenity and order so totally opposite from my own childhood, and I felt the bite of envy— Something was distracting me. The way the light fell through the doorway onto the polished floor had a peculiar look, reflecting the faintest silhouette. Somebody was standing outside, listening.

"You must have a lot of good memories," I said. I eased around to get a sharper image without Vera noticing; from where I stood, I couldn't see out directly without making a lunge, and a big fuss. The profile of the head, a thick knot of hair low down, made it Socorro.

Vera took my hand in both of hers and held on tight while

she talked, to hide her trembling, I thought. "I have wonderful memories!" she said. "Nothing can ever take them away." When I looked back, the image was gone, Socorro had moved away.

When I left, Vera took down my phone numbers at work and at home, and promised to call me if she got any ideas at all. "And you keep in touch with me too, Moz: I insist. No matter what you turn up. I can stand it." She strode away without looking back.

Class. I pictured Vera moving like a widowed queen through her silent maze . . . that house had so many diagonals, nooks, and tangents that you could lose yourself, make a secret world and hide in the heart of it, undisturbed. I didn't want to leave. In a crazy way I felt I belonged up here, like the princess who was stolen and raised by commoners.

Deirdre came toward me with that doing-her-distasteful-duty expression, and I woke up. Vera's grief and misery weren't over by a long shot, I figured; there could be even worse to come. I was the outsider here and barely tolerated, because they didn't know yet whom they were dealing with—Moz the hybrid, tougher than all of them, with the energy and drive they lacked. And I was going to do for them what they couldn't do for themselves. Socorro watched me from inside the kitchen door, waiting.

 **7** But I didn't get a chance to talk to Socorro, because Deirdre was already rushing me out. I tried to slow her down a little.

"You said that Socorro's relatives were very concerned about the accident."

"Right. We've gotten tons of flowers, of course, including several arrangements from them— Here, I'll show you." She veered down a side hall opposite the kitchen. "Mother couldn't stand them, she gave most of them to Soky." She knocked twice with a knuckle on a closed door and then opened it immediately.

Socorro's room was dark and close and sweet-smelling, jammed with floral arrangements: a cartwheel of salmon gladioli, a burst of yellow roses, twisting sprays of orchids— white, pale green, speckle-throated. I nodded, embarrassed at the intrusion even though Socorro wasn't there, and pulled the door shut again.

Just beyond it, the hall ended in another door. "That go outside?"

"Mm-hm." Then Socorro could come and go unnoticed; and so could other people. As we turned back toward the main hall, Socorro passed along it with her eyes fixed on the floor ahead; holding herself aloof, taking no notice of their world. Only a pose, I knew now. She ought to be able to tell me plenty.

When we passed the kitchen door again, Socorro and I exchanged a look and a nod. Only a flick of cosmic chance had landed us on opposite sides of that door, guest and servant. . . . She kept pace with us on the other side of the wall, reappearing in the dining room opposite us, picking a leaf off a six-foot schefflera. I raised my voice and said to Deirdre, "I'll probably be in touch again soon. I may need more information." Socorro faded away, and Deirdre opened the door for me.

"Does Socorro have any children?" I asked her as we stepped outside.

"What a bizarre idea! Soky's never been married, we've had her with us forever, or all her adult life, anyway," Deirdre said. "We're her only family—that's sad, probably. But she's got *mucho* relatives in Santa Ana, which is where all her money goes."

A cluster of people was just getting out of a cream-colored Mercedes sedan. They glanced our way and then conferred, and a matched couple in their sixties, all cashmere and camel's hair, were escorted around the side of the house by a pale-skinned, somewhat fleshy man around thirty and obviously a Tenhagen, whom I took to be older brother Martin. At the same time the driver strode toward us, flashing that wonderful Tenhagen smile.

Keith Tenhagen had Vera's jaw and Arnie's grin, and muscles. He ran his fingers through hair sun-streaked like Deirdre's, and that old animal magnetism blazed off him; he radiated it. And knew it. "She's here to investigate the fire," Deirdre said, introducing us.

"How's it going?" he asked. "Have you found out anything useful so far?"

"Oh, yes. I'm making progress slowly." I took back my hand, shocked at myself and determined to hide the yearning fifteen-year-old who had just resurfaced. The best defense an attack. "You look familiar to me, somehow. Have we ever met before?"

"I'd certainly remember, even if you didn't," Keith said. "You from around here?"

"Los Angeles. You?"

He nodded. No, his was definitely not the hysterical voice on the phone. He asked me about Rick and Judy, and as we talked, I saw Vera's influence. He was interested and perceptive, even though bursting with nervous energy like a race horse waiting for the gun. There was the slightest reddening around his nostrils. It could just be the sun; but if he was doing coke—and this early on a weekday, with the relatives about?—then his Schick interlude was just money down the drain.

Deirdre stood off to one side, quite aware of the nonverbal dance going on and disgusted by it. "Oh, brother," she muttered once.

"I still can't believe this is happening," he said suddenly, waving his arm in an arc. "Sun's shining, little breeze kissing our faces—how is this possible? You'd expect the whole world to turn belly up."

"Don't start, don't start," Deirdre said, "or I'll never be able to stop. It *is*, it's done, and we've got to accept it. Daddy loved that boat—"

"'Daddy loved that boat,'" he repeated, as if mocking her. "Anyway, he died happy. Only one thing would've been better: if he was actually out sailing her when it happened."

Deirdre looked aghast, tried to smile and blurted, "Do you think there are sailboats in heaven?" Her face twisted into a grimace with "Oh, you jackass!" as she hugged him to show it was all right, pushed her face into his shoulder and rapped his bicep, emerging with a stiff, manic smile.

Keith turned back to me with the same frozen grin. "Listen: I intend to help you out every way I can," he said. "This is a terrible situation for all of us, for everybody involved." One of his feet was jiggling in a separate rhythm, as if involuntarily.

"So tell me what theory you're working on." He flinched as he asked me, jerking his jaw down. "What's your approach in a case like this?"

"Just following down every detail. In a good percentage of cases it turns out to be somebody who knew the victim."

"Out of the question here." He gave me a spacey little-boy smile, "oh, how ridiculous," and a dimple winked in his left cheek.

Saying good-bye, he took my hand and leaned close, being dramatic. "I am going to see more of you, you hear?" He kissed my hand and then held it against his cheek. "Ve are going to meet agayn." Deirdre rolled up her eyes.

Going back down the long curving grade, it all played over in my head, a furious counterpoint of melodies twisting together. Ben said Arnie was getting ready for a long trip; Vera said not. Socorro listened behind doors. Sandra Healy thought Arnie could've done it himself—and darling Keith, the bonny prince of the household, maybe had an expensive habit to feed.

But underneath everything, another theme was playing, the ultimate tango. I hummed along, and in a minute I recognized it—"Kiss of Fire." I haven't believed in love at first sight for quite a while; but lust, oh yes. Once again flesh and spirit were heading in opposite directions. Smart, Moz. Attracted to spoiled rich kid who does dope and maybe stole from his father and then blew him up to hide it? Not too interested in proving that, are we.

I whizzed downhill along the grade made for big powerful cars, coming down on the stone gatehouse too fast and my brakes not all that great. Be quite a mess if you missed your turn. *Ka-runch!* I could picture Keith on a monstrous high saying "What the hell," and just letting go. I braked and down-shifted and squealed on by. The guard pretended I wasn't there; he didn't even look up.

Gage Pfeiffer was halfway right—how could I expect to accomplish anything if I let my emotions take over? And that irritated me more; I hardly knew the man, and here I was letting him stand in for my conscience. . . . Take a good look at dutiful daughter Deirdre. She was the kind who'd march right ahead, one foot in front of the other, wherever she chose. With a greedy boyfriend, maybe, who was looking for an instant heiress? I had a whole handful of possibilities, and not one of them solid.

More like a handful of worms. Here I was, digging up reasons why each of these perfectly decent people could be evil and rotten, prying up rocks to see what was twitching underneath. It made my stomach hurt.

No change: that's what the hospital said, no change. Tom, Rick's stepfather, was going crazy from the inactivity. Fran sat hunched over a crossword, looking hunted.

"Moz, you know this area," Fran said. "Can you recommend a decent, clean, cheap motel?" Tom was going home on Sunday; he couldn't stay away from his job any longer. Fran's job would just have to get along without her, she said, poker-faced.

"This is bankrupting us," Tom said. "You haven't found out anything yet about who did it, have you." It wasn't even a question.

I told Fran to look out along Harbor Boulevard, farther inland but not too close to Disneyland.

"Maybe I should talk to a lawyer," Tom said. "Aah, I hate that shit."

It had been getting more overcast all afternoon, and by the time I got home the clouds were low and wet-looking and the wind felt like rain. When I pulled in to park, something reddish-brown was lying up against the side wall of the garage. It was a dog, and I knew right away it was dead, though there were no visible wounds. It was a mix, part setter: barrel body and short legs, longish silky fur and floppy ears; the kind of dog kids would call Brownie. No collar or license. Maybe it was hit by a car, I thought, and crawled around here to die.

My first impulse was to go tell Mrs. Chaney, the landlady,

but I stifled it. Mrs. C. has a cuddling-size poodle, Toto, which she never lets outdoors, a quivery little yapper that looks as if she was stained with coffee and dishwater; and right then I didn't have the strength to listen to her rave about maniac animal torturers or bubonic plague. The wind rose in the trees and a couple of spatters hit me, the rain was starting. Too late today to call somebody to come get it. . . . I went upstairs for an old bath towel, and covered the dog.

The phone rang around ten, just as I was getting out of the shower. It was Anonymous.

"I've been checking you out," he said.

"How?"

"Never mind. I've got my sources."

"Well, I'm real curious about that," I said. "Obviously you're familiar with somebody in the family."

"How's that?"

"For one, the way you say the name, 'Tenheggen.' And you were the one who told me Arnie had been cremated. And if you know them, then they know you, right?"

"Lots of people know them," he said. "I bet hundreds."

"You were a personal friend of Arnie's?"

He snorted. "Well, I'm not an enemy. I of all people wanted to see him alive," he said bitterly.

I was sitting on the floor in the dark, leaning back against the counter and watching the light from Mrs. Chaney's new and hideous thousand-watt yard light twisting in brilliant green snakes down my window. "Actually, I was wondering if maybe you did it yourself," I said.

"That's not even funny. Listen; I've got something, some evidence in a way, for you. You want a look at it?"

"You know the answer to that."

Anonymous had it all worked out, where we should meet; on the corner of Bayside and Goldenrod, in Corona del Mar.

"Why can't you tell me about it right now?" I asked. A band of green light coming through the rain lay across my ceiling and down the wall, and I watched it shift and change as if it were alive. Like an intestine digesting something.

Because it wasn't that simple, he said. Something I had to see for myself. "I give you the pattern, you'll still have to work out the details. Put together the big picture. You interested or not?"

"I'll need some time to think it over."

"Well, naturally you'd be cautious, I can understand that. Listen, this is a public place, perfectly safe. You'll see."

"But why should I trust you?"

"Same way here. Don't you think I've got the most to lose?"

A gust of wind-driven rain pounded the glass. It wasn't raining yet where he was, which probably meant he lived farther inland; otherwise, he was careful not to give away anything personal. We made conversation about the weather and earthquakes, when the big one was coming. I did stop to wonder if he'd had anything to do with the dead dog; but what would be the point?

Still some stuff to do on his end, he said; he'd call back in a day or two. He yawned hugely, I could hear his jaws crack.

"Man, I'm dying for sleep," he said. "Now get out there and do your homework. Oh, you can wait till morning. That'll be okay."

When I left next morning, the rain was a steady drizzle, and I avoided looking at the sodden towel-covered heap. At work it took me most of an hour on the phone to find the public agency responsible for collecting dead dogs.

Leo stuck his head in my office, found me on the phone and nodded once, approving; he didn't know I was setting up a meeting with Socorro. Thursday was her usual afternoon off, and she wanted to see me tonight in Santa Ana, in the junior-college art gallery.

"I will find my nephew there," she said. "But please, you don't say anything about this to the Tenagains, no part of it—" The last words were hasty and muffled, and I said, "What?"

"I know I don't say it right. The kids, they laugh at me. But you get my meaning okay. Seven-thirty; you be there? I go now." Tenagain. Ten-heggen. Was Anonymous one of Socorro's Santa Ana kinfolk?

My next call was from Deirdre, who directed me to meet her

at Hof's Hut, a coffee shop near the Orange County Airport, in half an hour. "I promise I won't keep you long," she said.

Deirdre was just closing her umbrella at the top of the steps, and she watched me zigzag across the parking lot, dodging the puddles. The waitress led us to a table by the window, and Deirdre said, "We're just having coffee this morning." She arranged her umbrella and sat down.

"My mother quite likes you," Deirdre said, "and that impressed me. I trust her judgment. My father adored my mother, he'd do anything for her, he tried to protect her from, oh, any kind of ugliness. 'Don't let your mother find out,' he'd tell us. 'We can take care of this ourselves. She doesn't need to know.' Which is what makes this all so incredibly ironic. Particularly when it comes to Keith's reactions."

"Mm?" I wasn't going to help her any.

"I'm going to be up-front with you," said Deirdre—a real yellow-alert statement. "Keith's a wonderful person, but the truth is, he's not all that swift. I love him dearly, I can say it because I've always been big sister, looking out for adorable little Keefie tagging along behind." The waitress brought our coffee, and Deirdre kept quiet till she left.

"Loaded with charm, an absolutely beautiful little boy—but then you expect it to work for everything; why not, if it always has? And my father was a very demanding person, oh, in the best ways; but he expected maybe more than Keith was capable of."

To please his father, she said, Keith had tried to carry a double major in college, business administration and electrical engineering, and had caved in under the load; had been on probation, and was only now beginning to get his act together. "So you see, all of a sudden the pressure's off. Sure, Keith is relieved; but it's too much so. I can see that he's scared by it, and overwhelmed. Just by way of explaining his weird behavior yesterday."

"Did you think it was weird?" I said. "I just assumed—the terrible shock of it. You mean that subconsciously he might have been wanting an out, and suddenly he's got one?"

"Exactly." She nodded once over the rim of her cup. "All this is in strictest confidence, of course. He hasn't been much help with the legal end of it, either. So many details!" The lawyers, all the business with the various bank officials . . . I waited to see where she was leading, Deirdre not being a ditherer by nature.

"The essential thing is to spare Mother," she said. "If you have any more questions at all, just come to me with them. Socorro's been given her orders; I'll be perfectly happy to help in any way I can, but I'm going to insist. Here are my numbers"—she snapped out her business card with her home phone number already written on it in ink—"and feel free to call anytime. Now: what have you found out so far?"

Wonderful; she had our roles all laid out. I was the private eye, and she was going to play boss-lady client. Good enough. I could use that. "I'm very much concerned that it was someone we may not have thought of, someone related to the family in a tangential way," I said, trying for an English-detective tone. "A bit of family background would be useful."

"I doubt that." But she gave me the outlines, much the same information I already had. Besides her job with the politician, she was attending UCI, working toward her master's degree in social ecology; and she lived in Park Newport, a classy condo complex, with Daddy certainly making the payments on the place.

"How did your father feel about your living away from home?"

"He was totally supportive in every way, including my career choices. It's demonstrable how important paternal encouragement is in producing high-achieving daughters, and he was behind me a thousand percent." Tears glittered in her eyes; she looked exasperated with herself, and talked that much harder.

"If somebody's mad at the Tenhagens," I said, "your mother may be in danger, too."

"Oh, I can't imagine that. In any case, we have an excellent alarm system. Of course you have to activate it first, as I keep reminding her. She tends to believe other people are as nice as she is."

"Good thing you've got Keith for masculine support. I assume he doesn't need to work."

"Of course he does. He's expected to get a job, establish himself in a career like everybody else. People have some pretty funny ideas about money."

"True. I imagine it gives you some problems too. Speaking of which; how's your love life?" I asked, figuring, Why not? She'd set the candid tone: You can ask me anything because we're perfect.

She smacked down her cup with a sneery smile. "God, you are a study," she said. "I suppose it just reflects the kind of people you deal with normally. To answer your question: Just fine, and nothing whatsoever to do with this. Miss?" She called for our check.

So what was that all about? Far from persuading me of Keith's innocence, it had the opposite effect, which Deirdre must certainly realize. Was she giving me a nudge?

Little old Corona del Mar, manicured and expensive, sits on the ocean-front bluff overlooking the mouth of Newport Harbor, the tip of Balboa Peninsula, and the rocky coast south of Laguna. The drizzle had thinned to an intermittent mist as I drove its tree-shaded streets and checked out our meeting site.

Bayside runs parallel with the bluffs about four blocks inland, following a little canyon that has been completely tamed. A green shoestring park lies along its inland side for several blocks, with big trees widely spaced and asphalt paths for the joggers, and overseen on its inland side by remodeled older houses with varnished siding and nicely furnished decks.

The ocean side is a steep slope about four stories high, covered with shrubbery. People in the houses at the top can look through the trees and down on their inland neighbors, if they're interested.

As our meeting site, Anonymous had picked the corner of Goldenrod where it slants down to meet Bayside. We were to meet not in the car, but out on the street. I parked up on the rim of the canyon and walked in and out of the little streets that dead-end at the edge, and then across the geranium-lined Fernleaf footbridge overhead that carries local strollers and bicycles over the road and the canyon, trying not to visualize a sniper kneeling and sighting between the salmon-pink blossoms.

Cars passed by regularly: there would be enough traffic to chaperone us; it looked as safe as a supermarket. The sky already seemed lighter, as if maybe it had finally drained itself; you could smell wet soil and musky geranium leaves, and all the foliage was clean-washed and dazzling. Anonymous didn't wish me any harm, he was only insecure and grief-stricken and on the outside, and in his naive way he thought of me as a person of authority, somebody who could help. Gage Pfeiffer would say I was crazy. So? He didn't need to know.

Fran was alone in the little waiting area outside Intensive Care, sitting close to a table lamp crocheting away at something with sky-blue yarn. She took off her glasses and stuck in her hook, and I knew her somber look was not a joke. "What's wrong?"

"You haven't heard, then. Judy died this morning, a little after five."

"Oh, no. I had no idea . . . what happened?"

"What they've been afraid of ever since the surgery. A blood clot that reached her heart."

I was stunned. Since the accident I'd hardly thought enough about Judy to inquire; because she hadn't mattered that much to me. And now she was done.

"Heartbreaking," Fran said. "Such a waste. And all alone, no family with her . . ."

"You did everything you possibly could to reach them," I said, knowing it wasn't true. We should've tried other things, like contacting the police in Colorado Springs. Another stone on the pile.

Fran had sent Tom out to see Ben Dickerson about storing Rick's boat. "For when he's well again." I could hear her saying it. Making a little white magic.

"I've been thinking," I said. "You don't want to sit around alone in some motel, waste your money besides—come and stay with me. I've got room."

"Oh, I couldn't possibly do that," Fran said.

"Of course you can. Why not?" We set it up for the following Monday. I really didn't want her to move in with me; I enjoyed my privacy. It would be like putting on a hair shirt. Exactly: a kind of penance, and a living reminder of my number-one duty.

How to tackle Socorro. I'd halfway convinced myself that her relatives were involved, that it was a simple burglary or some such. Picture those kids growing up poor in Santa Ana and hearing about all that Tenhagen money secondhand: what a temptation. I was ready to blame it all on the dirty Mex, the old Frito bandido, and not much liking myself.

First surprise: the college art gallery was jammed, a mostly blue-jeans crowd about fifty-fifty Mexican and Anglo, chattering, laughing, and munching corn chips with guacamole. It was opening night of an exhibition of six Chicano artists, one of whom, I realized, must be Socorro's nephew—the second surprise, and embarrassing. I'd been assuming he was a janitor.

Socorro wasn't there yet and I circled the walls to look at the pictures, not knowing the nephew's last name, or hers either. I kept expecting bright, hot Aztlan murals, with cornstalks and two-headed snakes, and white-shirted peasants with rifles. Instead I found charcoal drawings of pretty Arabs—were they boys?—and fuzzy four-poster beds; black-and-white photographs of B-movie parking-lot murders, and interesting junk in boring assemblages.

Francisco Godoy, maybe forty-five, with coarse black hair tucked behind his ears and thick glasses, stood spraddled-legged and rocked slowly back onto his heels as he shook people's hands and smiled at their compliments. In the painting behind him a line of old men stood in bright sunlight waiting for something, tough and wary and still, all their wrinkles and warts as sharp as the crunched 7-Up can in the gutter.

"It's cheerful and grim at the same time," I said.

"Is it?" Godoy said. "You know, this is just about my most popular painting. I did it about seven years ago, and I've had people tell me they've come back to see it several times, whenever I have an exhibit. And yet nobody's ever made me an offer for it."

We were talking when Socorro came in. "Ah: you know my aunt?" Frank's eyebrows went up as she introduced us, but I could see he'd been told about me beforehand—they exchanged a look, she was asking his opinion.

Socorro was the real surprise, stately and composed in a long-sleeved black dress with a wide collar of pineapple lace, and heels. "Ah! Cómo está?" While Socorro made polite conversation in Spanish with a couple of friends, Frank talked to me.

"That lady is the salt of the earth. She helped my mother raise us kids, nine of us, and her a woman alone. She gave her life to us. If it wasn't for her, we'd still all be picking tomatoes in El Centro probably."

Socorro turned back, switching into English, and she and Frank exchanged news about Chuy, Benita, the Lopezes. Frank put his arm around Socorro's shoulder and said to me, "Anybody ever gives this lady a problem, they'll have to answer to me. We'll take care of her forever."

"You see enough already?" Socorro asked me. "Now we go and talk, okay?" She led the way outside and down the sidewalk, which had become a windy tunnel between two big buildings. An onshore wind with more rain in it was rising, and smoky-pink clouds boiled past about eight feet above the rooftops.

"You don't say anything about this tonight to Mrs. Ten, all right?" Socorro said. "Frank's paintings or nothing."

"Whatever you say. But I'd think she'd be really interested."
Socorro shrugged. "Better not her fussing." Not that Socorro
wasn't proud of Frank, her sister Benita's second son, who'd
already painted three murals in Orange County and was just
starting a fourth, on the side of a market in Anaheim. Chuy was
in real estate, somebody else in the post office, and one of the
girls was studying computers. Abel had had some problems, but
they got him to go in the Navy. And where was Abel right now?
On a ship somewhere by Iran, because of the oil.

AHbel, she said; like "Sahntahna," all one word, instead of
the Anglo "Santa Ana." A different place. When I was the new
kid in junior high, I ate lunch with the Mexican kids; we were
all outcasts gazing from afar on the favored ones, the natural
winners (Anglo, naturally), who looked great and had all the
right moves. I sat with the Mexican girls while they laughed
together and flirted with the boys and teased each other in
Spanish; I, a stone washed over by that warm broth, twice a
stranger.

"What you find out so far?" Socorro asked.

"For one thing, that Keith is maybe taking dope."

She nodded. "Yah. She spoiled him, always. Everything for
those kids."

"That's an expensive habit. You're not saying that his mother
gives him the money for it?"

"Not direct, no. But things, they go . . . he takes things from
the house, to sell, I think, and she never sees nothing, it don't
happen. She's like that."

"And stuff from his father's boat, too?"

"I didn't hear that. Could be. You trying to think he do this
to his father? No. I don't think Keith can kill nobody. He's not
strong like that."

I asked her about Deirdre, who her friends were. "Okay,
Deedee. Don't have a boyfriend, only working with her boss;
days, nights. . . ." That's how it is, Socorro said with her eyebrows and a shrug.

"You don't know nothing either, do you," Socorro said.

"Here it's already a week he's dead, more. What you been doing, anyway?"

"That's why I'm here." We came up to a monstrous old Caddy, about a '60, fat and shiny black with those dinosaur fins jutting. "Wow," I said.

"Yah—the boys, they love it. Always trying to talk me out of it. I tell them no way." She unlocked it and motioned me into the spacious back seat. "Mister Ten, he give it to me, when it makes a little bit old."

"A generous man." Socorro had been with the family ever since the children were born, and it was apparent that she'd adored Arnie Tenhagen. I felt a headache beginning. "Do you think he could've killed himself?" I asked.

She made a rude noise. "Who says this?" And no, Arnie didn't have any other women that she knew of—not that she would've told me anyway, I could tell. I tried being chummy, just girls together.

"So how about Mrs. Ten? What's she really like?"

Socorro clamped down on the inside of her bottom lip, thinking. "Writes on the paper everything we do, today, tomorrow. Pays on time, no problem. We eat good, same as them. . . . She wash her teeth all the time."

"What?"

"Yah. Every time she eat something, one little bit—shoosh: in there, clean the teeth again. Pull these strings through. I think she has a little worm turning around in her head. Wear them out, the teeth." She laughed. "So? She can afford to get new ones."

Thirty years Socorro had worked for the woman, and this was the most she could say about Vera? My headache was getting worse; it felt like a piano wire being twisted around my naked brain and turned tighter and tighter. "You don't like her very much, do you?"

Socorro considered that. "I can stand her, no problem. Little bit strange . . . it's real funny up there, him and her. Nothing out plain—no hollering, no fight, never. They just get real quiet."

"For how long?"

"Two days, three; then it's over."

"What did they fight about?"

"I told you, I don't hear." She brushed it away. "That is all past, it's nothing. Why you think somebody would go to kill Mr. Ten? You got no idea, huh?" She sat back and turned away, looking out the window. Another dead end.

"So tell me," I asked. "Since the night that—you know—has anything unusual happened?" And Socorro came to life.

"Day before yesterday," she said, and stopped.

"Tell me about it."

"Phone ring, I pick it up. 'Ello?'—pic! nobody. Little bit later, ring, pick up, I wait, they wait—pic! Martin get it, same thing. Then one time it rings, I see by the little red light she answers in her workroom. And I hear her. She yells. 'What are you trying to tell me!' Then, not so loud, 'You must be crazy.'"

"And when she comes to the kitchen, her face, ah! all gray, gray. Sick. She walks out in the hall, dining room, comes around again. 'Don't answer this thing anymore,' she says. 'Till I tell you. I'll tell you when.'"

"Some creep," I said. "Trying to scare her. Maybe told her he'd hurt her, or her kids." Maybe Anonymous, I thought. He was the telephone specialist.

"Yah, sure," said Socorro. "So why then she doesn't call the police?"

"How do you know she didn't?"

"She didn't tell nobody nothing. I'm there all the time, I can hear." There was more; I could see Socorro wanting me to ask.

"What else?"

"Little while after, one more time it start to ring, just bip! and stop right away. I see red light is on, means somebody's talking. She's the only one there, no? Not too long—five minutes, maybe four." She leaned back, her eyes holding mine. "That's all. Don't see her no more all day; she stay in her room, talk to me on speaker. Innercom."

We sat staring at one another, and the wind made a roaring

sound where one window wasn't rolled up all the way. "What do you think it was, then?" I said. "Who?"

She hates Vera, I thought. Thirty years with the Tenhagens, to keep Benita's kids out of the fields. It was dark in the back seat and cozy, with the wind outside rocking us like an upholstered capsule in space; except that Socorro sat hunched forward a little and she never blinked. A fierce pain drilled into the back of my skull, dead center, because Socorro was a witch, an honest-to-God *bruja*, one of Don Juan's companions, and probably she could even outfly him—take three running steps and she'd soar, change into a big owl you wouldn't be able to hear going over, or else turn invisible and shoot into somebody else's brain and they'd be suffering, instead of me.

I couldn't believe this was happening. I put my hand on the door handle to open it, and then took it away. "What's going on here?" I said. "I thought you cared about this guy, you wanted to help."

Then I understood—Socorro would volunteer nothing, it was up to me to figure out the right questions to ask. Her face curled up into a wide slow grin and she sat back, satisfied. I rested my throbbing head on the cushions and closed my eyes.

"Okay. You say Deirdre spends the night with her boss. How did her father feel about that? Did he know?"

"Oh, yah. He hates this, he yell at her, anyway. 'You trying to ruin your life? That con artist is as old as I am, for Chris' sakes!' You know, like that." So much for totally supportive Papa. "You think Deedee. . . ?" Socorro sneered and lifted one shoulder, dismissing the idea.

"I don't know if you make out this thing," she said. "Maybe yes, maybe no. It's not finish yet, and if it's you or somebody else can do this, I don't know. But it don't stop now for nothing."

"You mean you think somebody else will be . . ." I was afraid to say it outright, I was getting flat-out superstitious. Anyway, Socorro scowled at me; that wasn't what she'd meant.

"But you do have some idea why he was killed."

Her mind was seething with the dreadful possibilities, I could see it; but she sat there like a—boulder. "I promise," she said.

"Promised who?" No answer. ". . . Him," I said, and saw that it was true. She'd promised Arnie. "Oh, shit." Socorro smiled in spite of herself.

"It's coming," she said, "if I help, or don't help. Like poison, like a fever that goes and goes; you know? In your hand a little bit wood, it got to go bad inside till it can come up. You're a smart kid. You figure it out." She slid forward and opened the car door, and we got out on opposite sides. Still.

Maybe Anonymous was one of the Godoy clan, and Socorro really didn't know anything about what he was doing. But if he had called Vera direct, why would he bother with me?

Say Vera did know something about Arnie's death and wanted to go it alone, trying to protect somebody. Crazy—he'd be even more dangerous now; because what did he have to lose?

In the night I lay awake and thought about Judy hanging on Rick's shoulder and watching me, so jealous. Those were the last few minutes when she'd really been alive. Well, none of us know how much more time we've got; except for the suicide. And the murderer can only know for his victim, not himself.

"They never expected me to show up," Vera said, leaning close. "While I'm here they can't talk about me, the old dears. Not on duty, anyway." The corner of the museum workroom where we sat was obviously Vera's domain—desk immaculate, shelves orderly, and the "old dears" were staying well away, ensuring our privacy. "If they expected a total collapse, I'm living proof to the contrary."

Vera looked fit, though pale, in dashing high boots and black-and-green plaid. "You're looking very well," I said. "That plaid is wonderful on you."

"The Gordon dress plaid. My mother's people were Gordons." I waited to hear why Vera had summoned me. Vera sat back and folded her hands.

"Well; what have you been doing with yourself lately?" she asked.

"Not much. That's funny. I assumed you were the one with news. An anonymous phone call, say."

"*Au contraire,*" Vera said, clear-eyed. "You've been quite busy, according to Roger Murch, and others. This arson charge is the worst. I can't tell you how many of our friends have asked me about that. It's very serious. There are criminal implications—"

"I know it."

"To begin with, we have no indication whatsoever that this boat business was deliberate. I've discussed it with the Newport Beach Fire Captain, and he says there's no real proof of arson."

"Oh, but there is. Gage Pfeiffer says—"

"Yes, the insurance person. Who has his own agenda, obviously." She raised her eyebrows. "Moz, I'm afraid you're becoming intrigue-happy."

"Not without help. Deirdre seems to be a little worried about her baby brother." I told Vera about our meeting at Hof's, where Deirdre had tried to explain brother Keithie.

"Good," Vera said. "Deirdre's got a strong sense of family. I'm proud of her." She pushed a plate of crispy little cookies toward me, as if we'd finished with the subject. We were drinking hot chocolate from china cups with violets on them, thin enough to see the pattern through.

"You do know that Judy died?"

"Oh, no, I hadn't realized—that's terrible! I'm so sorry. This horrible mess . . ." She leaned on one elbow and closed her eyes for a long moment. Then she straightened up. "It's just dreadful."

"That means he's killed two people already."

"What 'he'? There hasn't been a thing so far to indicate that it was anything more than a . . . terrible accident." A woman with a chic cap of white hair opened the door opposite and stared at us. Vera ignored her.

"Maybe you've heard the other rumor," I said. "That Mr. Tenhagen . . . did away with himself."

"Suicide?" She looked amazed. "That's preposterous. Whoever gave you an idea like that?"

"Oh, a friend of his, who I know meant well."

"It was Sandra Healy, I'll bet. That twit. You can always count on her for something really off the wall." Vera stared into her cup, revolving the dregs.

"Look at us," she said. "I'm the one with all of it on my back, and you just keep stirring up the mud. . . . Do you know what else we've just discovered? Arnie's handgun was stolen. He always kept it on the boat for protection, locked up, of course, and it's gone. They assured me they looked very thoroughly. Now, I call that common theft. Tampering."

First an accident, and now tampering. It was embarrassing to see Vera shifting around, grabbing at anything. "I don't think you're taking this seriously enough," I said. "Don't you realize that this person might come after you next?"

Vera smiled and shook her head sadly. "Moz, Moz. . . . I understand what you're going through. After all, think what I've lost. But we can't just believe a thing because we want to." The woman put her head in again, and Vera stood up. "They're waiting to start their meeting in here. I guess we'd better let them."

Before I could leave, Vera insisted on giving me a tour of the museum's new Asian exhibition, artifacts dug from a Bronze Age hillside village in what had become Vietnam.

"Their culture developed centuries before ours," she said. "We might all do well to acquire some of their wisdom and perspective." Her look deplored my lack of Confucian balance and inscrutable Charlie Chan tact. We stood in front of a case that held the skeleton of a full arm, with mud still caked on the whitened bones and a massive bracelet near the shoulder, and she kept talking about ceramic techniques, which was a little unnerving.

She finished up in her favorite Rancho Room among the relics of Orange County's ranchero days, saddles and bridles from Don Antonio Yorba's horses, a ten-foot copper still the priests used to make brandy, yellowed wedding dresses for little women my size. Vera fell into the patter she used with the schoolchildren two days a week, rolling her *r*'s nicely on *reata* and *corral*. "Life was a lot simpler then," she said.

"I guess." If you were in the big house, and not out in the fields.

At the entrance, Vera took my hand. "I think you're totally wrong, but I'm going to honestly examine your theories," she said. "I keep remembering little things. . . . Oh, God, is there no end to it! Moz, thank you for being so honest with me. As usual."

What was she doing? First the idea of suicide was preposterous—exactly how I thought she'd react—and a few minutes later she was going to "examine my theories." Why? Just an indication of how worried she really was that Keith could be in it right up to his eyeballs. Or maybe she flat out knew he was.

I picked up a report at the Santa Ana Police Station and took it back to the office, frustrated with all the waiting and wild to meet Anonymous and get on with it.

Finally the call came. "What do you think?" Anonymous asked. "You take a look? Still interested?"

"Certainly. I can handle it. Take me about half an hour to get there. You?"

"Tomorrow afternoon, broad daylight."

"Why not right now?"

"Because I'm busy today is why; I've got obligations. Listen. So you shouldn't be surprised . . . I look strange. You'll see. Some people think I'm kind of weird, till they get to know me. Then they realize I'm okay."

"Ah, come on—how, weird? In what way?"

"What I've got to get out of this isn't for myself, anyhow," he said, zigzagging again. "There are others that rely on me. A man's got to take care of his own."

"Oh, for sure." I remembered the domestic sounds, television, conversation, a little kid crying. Money makes the world go round. It has to be blackmail, I thought. Maybe he's got something on one of the Tenhagen kids—I couldn't pass up a chance at that. I assumed he wasn't dangerous; called at regular times, led a regular life. . . . I didn't want to think about it anymore, I wanted to get on with it. We agreed to meet the next afternoon at three-fifteen.

The rain had stopped finally, but everything was saturated and the intersections were still brimming over. At the hospital Fran told me that Rick was being moved to UCI Medical, which used to be the County Hospital. Some kind of pressure was building up and they were considering operating on his brain. On the way home I lost my brakes and slid into a telephone pole, putting a nasty ding in my right front fender.

If something happened to me, nobody would know for weeks, I thought. I hadn't been to any of my AA meetings lately, and my sponsor, Lucy, hadn't even bothered to call and ask why. I was opening a can of soup, chicken rice, in my clammy kitchen, and felt low enough to be thinking maybe I ought to get myself another cat, when Keith Tenhagen called.

"Grab your oars and paddle on down, and I'll buy you some dinner," he said. There was a burst of laughter in the background; he must be in a bar. He sounded bright, eager, happy—probably he was stoned, probably he'd forget about me as soon as he hung up, and be gone by the time I got there. "Where are you?" I asked. "Give me half an hour."

I put on a knit dress, the tomato paisley that always made people (meaning men) turn and look after me. Strictly business, I told myself. Perfect chance for some subtle interrogation. Sympathize with the boy, find out about his money problems, and how things really are at home. As I headed for the beach I could feel the old adrenaline pumping.

It was a jazz place on Balboa Peninsula, the Studio Café, at the foot of the pier. I had to park two blocks away, and by the time I got there my shoes were soaked and probably ruined. Keith was leaning back with his elbows on the bar listening to two other guys talking and looking only mildly buzzed. When he saw me his face changed. He looked happy and shy, as unsure of himself as Deirdre had said.

We found ourselves a table back in the corner where we could talk over the taped music. First crisis: he wouldn't believe me when I ordered Perrier with a twist of lemon, thought I was being funny, and got me the house drink, a big balloon glassful blue as a Swede's eyeball.

"Actually, I'm serious," I said. "I happen to be an alcoholic. I can't handle it." I should've been prepared. A lot of people get defensive when you won't drink with them, take it as a personal criticism, and that was Keith.

"How do you know?"

"Oh, for a while I thought I was accident-prone. Too many ugly things kept happening to me." Like waking up next to a guy I wouldn't spend ten minutes with sober, and not even knowing what town I was in.

"A strong and independent lady like you? I find that hard to believe."

"Believe."

He shrugged and smiled. When he finished his Scotch and water he switched glasses with mine, making a face at the blue stuff but carrying on bravely. We discovered we both had Django Rheinhardt records. We talked about movies we liked, *Mad Max* and *Blade Runner* and *Fritz the Cat*, and whether Bakshi would ever make another one. We'd both been skindiving in the Gulf with all those bright little fishes and the dolphins leaping in schools, and that hot offshore wind at night whipping the sand, and the tide dropping like water being sucked out of a bathtub.

Before our ribs came, he'd told me essentially what Deirdre had: that he'd been relieved as well as shattered when his father died; in fact even exhilarated, which scared him.

"Right about then I decided maybe I've got a problem. To figure out just who the hell I really am." He was anxious for me to understand.

"I thought it would be better, now that the pressure's off, but in a way it's gotten worse, like now I'm never going to make it. Expectations; they're in my head, okay? Only, before I had a chance to work my way out of it, I was on solid ground. And now it's all smoke."

"Hey, you know better than that. You can handle anything in your life, if you really put your mind to it."

He smiled and patted my hand, dismissing the subject. He was not interested in any kind of reassurance. I had a hunch he was worried about his coke habit, but I didn't want to risk bringing it up. "How's your mother getting along?" I asked.

"Not too well, in my opinion. Oh, she's being bright and gentle, and so calm, and so strong—like she's sleepwalking, most of the time. I don't know . . . she just smiles at you with this utter serenity, like she can walk over the abyss, go straight across if she just pretends it's not there."

Did he know about Vera's threatening phone call? I couldn't ask him directly, for fear of exposing Socorro. "Mm. Somebody out there lurking—who knows what he'll do next? Enough to scare anybody."

"She's not scared in the least. She's made up her mind just how everything's going to be, and she's driving me crazy. Listen, she never criticizes or complains, never even asks me to do something. But I always know exactly what she wants. And if she's disappointed, her face changes just in the subtlest way, she's probably not even aware of it. Like fingernails down a blackboard. It gets to me."

He signaled the waitress for another refill, and caught me watching him. "Keeping count?" he said with a nasty smile.

"Why should I? It's your life."

His laugh sounded bleak. "Don't remind me."

I changed the subject to my mixed-up mother Ada. It was a very mixed evening all around. On one level Keith and I were getting along wonderfully, we were in sync and the chemistry was there. When I complained about my feet being cold, he'd slipped out of his loafers and wrapped his feet around mine, the two of them like a big warm sandwich, rubbing and stroking first one foot and then the other.

And above the table we were carrying on well, too, avoiding the fluff about schools and vacations and status parties that people use to impress one another. But the dummy couldn't let it go. He'd ordered a bottle of burgundy, and he kept both of our glasses filled, switching them when his got empty—not saying anything, but with a sympathetic expression that implied a failure of nerve, that I'd broken the great social contract.

By the time we finished eating, the music was starting; a four-piece group: drums, piano, bass, and a sax. Keith swung his chair around next to mine so we could both watch, our shoes back on now but our thighs just touching. We were immersed in the music, taken over by it; our hands clasped, light and warm . . . his fingernails were broad and rounded, smooth with clear white moons, and, wanting not to, I imagined them stroking so gently, exploring the secret places, searching out those waiting nerve endings. The itch you can't scratch. That's Ada, too.

A point comes in a situation where you . . . not decide; in fact, it's just the opposite. And it happened then, the little *click!* that shifts you into another state and you just let go, let your mind roll back into the cave with the fire patterns moving on the wall, and go with the flow—another one of Rick's sayings.

At the bar a gorgeous tall girl with loose long silky hair stood bouncing with the music, her eyes half-closed. She was wearing suspenders and floppy knickers of that silvery astronaut's cloth that would make anybody else look ridiculous, and she had that casual arrogance I'd kill for and will never have; it must be genetic. Keith hadn't seemed to notice her, but he didn't miss much.

When the first set ended, Keith leaned closer to my ear. "What say we bug on out of here?"

"Where to? Oh, you're right; it is getting late. . . ."

He tilted his chair and braced his head against mine, his breath on my cheek. He knew a snug and cozy place with everything we could possibly want. He began to describe how to get there from here, illustrating the stops and turns with his free hand. I followed him onto the ferry and across the harbor with the lights moving on the water, Balboa Island and the right turn the length of it, and all the way up; turning in the gate with the lights out and coasting to a stop, and then in so quietly by Socorro's door. . . .

"You want to do it in Daddy's bed," I burst out. Had I actually said that? He froze and I felt one great whump! as my heart jumped, bracing myself for the crack across the face I used to get for my smart mouth— Keith set his chair down carefully, stood up with his drink and walked straight over to the girl in the knickers, and started up with her nice and easy, like they'd already met and he'd been waiting for her.

It was masterful. I had to admire his skill, even as I felt the fire rising to my hairline and looked around for something to throw. Two separate guys who'd noticed were each thinking about sliding my way to try their luck, I could see, but I sat there a minute longer and let the sting develop, nursing it.

Arrogant bastard. I could picture him on that boat with the ice pick, setting up the whole thing and then just walking away; and if I ever found any way to tie him to it, I'd love it, I'd laugh. . . . Somebody dropped onto the chair beside me, and I got up and stalked out. Who cares, piss on them all.

On the way home I bought a quart of buttermilk and drank most of it watching a Canadian horror movie called *They Came From Within*, about crawly little monsters that grew in people's stomachs and were vomited up, and then went looking for more victims. Maybe that was my bolt of Zen enlightenment for the evening; but if so, it missed me. Great job, Moz. You peeled him like a grape.

Gage and Keith. Gage was daytime and real world, solid and quirky and you'd have your work cut out for you. And Keith was nighttime, the tickle of danger and let's pretend. How could I be attracted to both of them? I must be sick. I slept badly.

Saturday morning I cleaned my apartment, getting ready for Fran and trying not to think about the stranger I was going to meet that afternoon. What if he was the one who'd set up the boat explosion, and called Vera . . . but those were sneaky things, not face-to-face dangerous. This was the breakthrough, I had to go with my intuition.

He was shy, and ashamed of his looks. I would subtly charm and reassure him, and get him to go have coffee up at that place on Pacific Coast Highway; it was casual enough and not intimidating. I would also put a message on my office phone recorder, and describe that tape of our conversations.

When I heard footsteps running up my outside stairs scratching on the cement, I panicked—dived for the door and locked it, and then peaked around the corner of the curtain. Gage Pfeiffer stood there holding a big brown paper bag.

Some way he must've found out about Anonymous. But how? I unbolted the door and threw it wide. "This is a surprise—what's happening? I know; you've heard from our mystery witness."

"This is strictly a social call," he said. He wasn't too winded—those stairs are a quick fitness test—but he was a bit flustered. "Here. I made you something." He pulled out a wood-and-glass affair that looked like a miniature front porch. "You mean you cain't recognize it? It's a bird feeder."

"Why, thank you. That's wonderful. You remembered about the birds." My voice sounded tinny; thinking of Gage in his garage, sawing away—he'd caught me off balance.

"I understand that your friend, Judy Christensen, died. That's a damn shame," he said, watching to see how I felt about it.

"Yes, it is. Actually, I'd only just met her."

"You're wondering about that witness. Still in Baja, they tell me. Fooling around down in Guerrero Negro, Black Warrior Lagoon."

In five minutes Gage was up on the roof, hanging upside down over all that concrete and screwing an eyebolt into the eaves to rig a pulley so I could bring the feeder down for refilling. He'd even brought along his tools, and a five-pound bag of wild bird seed. Oh, Gage was a planner.

I heard him singing to himself as he worked, about the Oklahoma hills and riding his pony in the Indian nation—trying me out as a little Cherokee squaw, maybe. I wondered if he'd ever get around to asking.

I really wanted to tell him about my meeting with Anonymous that afternoon. "You can't be serious," he'd say. "Why would you even consider such a thing?" Or even, "That's absolutely stupid." In fact, Gage didn't mention the Tenhagen case again, except indirectly. "Kind of isolated back here," he said. "You might want to be a little more security-conscious. Like, put a deadbolt on that door." He glanced to see how I'd take that; bossy or protective?

"There's a thought," I said. Gage was wearing old Levi's, standing in profile in front of the window, and I couldn't help noticing that neat male bulge you're not supposed to look at. It reminded me of the game Ada and her friend Maggie used to play, walking along the street. Whoever spotted the biggest one, the other had to buy her a drink. Once, when I was along, they forgot I was there, and Maggie was upset about it. I'd already been wild to know what it was all about, and their jokes just made me that much more curious.

"How about some lunch?" I asked. "I'll fix us an omelet."

"Sounds great. Hah!"

Gage stood motionless, and then bent forward slowly and began massaging his right shin. He'd run into one of the elephant trunks.

"Oh, I'm sorry . . . I should've warned you. How bad is it? Here; you better pull up your pant leg and we'll take a look." Easier said than done, with jeans. He had a sizable bruise on the shinbone already starting, but the skin wasn't broken. I sat him down at the dining table with his leg propped up on a chair, and put a plastic bag of ice cubes on it while I cooked.

"This omelet," Gage said. "Is it going to be European-style, or American?"

"I'm not sure. Define your terms."

"European is still all wet and gooshy in the center."

I laughed. "Then I guess it's going to be American."

All through lunch I could see Gage operating on two separate levels. He probably thought he was surveying the territory in the most cold-bloodedly rational way. "Just give us the facts, ma'am." But when I got up for something, I turned back and found his eyes following me with that terrible helpless yearning, and I was careful not to catch him unawares again.

While we ate, Gage told me about Leo's early life and hard times in Chicago. Leo grew up on the streets and had to hustle to stay alive. "Myself, I remember my daddy sitting and scratching his head, wondering how he was going to get us the shoes to start school in," Gage said. "One reason why I ree-lly enjoy the finer things now." He wiggled his propped-up foot with its beautiful brown loafer. "Good watch, new car every other year . . . Quality."

"Yes, I hear people and their quality talk. What they really want is the right label, to tell the world that the goods inside are grade A."

Probably I wanted to irritate him; but Gage just grinned at

me. "How'd you get such a chip on your shoulder where money's concerned?" he said. "Time you learned to lighten up and enjoy life some."

"How can you let yourself be manipulated like that? These advertisers are just making suckers out of all of us."

"Manipulate? You mean, as in using people? Isn't that what life is all about?"

"You mean it's okay to lie, mislead, con, finagle—"

"Well, naturally we don't call it that. It's the purpose to which it's put that counts. What else do you think would go on? We all take out after what we need, we cain't help ourselves." His Okie accent was suddenly much more pronounced, and I felt nervous for him. "We're all in the same boat," he said. "Of course, you've got to have your standards—"

"Ah."

"—And besides; you cain't rightly use somebody who's not ready and willing to be."

"Takes two to tango, you mean." Oh, "Kiss of Fire."

"Right on. Not my business to decide for you what you want." He gave me a look that left no doubt what we were talking about. Gage's eyes were a clear brown, like coffee with the sun shining through, and I wondered if maybe he was the one with some Indian blood. Which was ridiculous. Wouldn't he just laugh?

When I started to clear away the dirty plates, Gage got up to help. I put the dishes in the sink—I don't have a dishwasher, the plumbing wouldn't handle it—and he found the detergent, and then the dishtowel to dry them. It was all so domestic that I started to panic.

"I told Rick's mother I'd meet her at the hospital at two," I said. Gage immediately stood up to go.

"One thing," he said, and pulled a small brown book out of his shirt pocket. He extracted a white rectangle of paper with a peel-off label. "I had Eleanor make this up. It's my phone numbers, work and home. You can stick it on your wallet; that way if you ever need to call me, it's handy."

"Why, that's right nice of you," I said, and got out my swollen blue wallet. I held it open while he stuck on the label, both of us being careful not to let our hands touch.

After Gage had gone I stood and watched that silly bird feeder swinging in the wind, feeling a lot more solitary than I had earlier.

On any given day we'd probably disagree eighty-five percent of the time; but with or without labels, Gage Pfeiffer was the genuine article. If things were different, I'd be tickled to have something that substantial in the cupboard for later. Maybe he'd still be around when this was over; but in the meantime I was duty-bound to take Gage at his word: swim right into those clear brown eyes, and use him any way I could.

A cold wind drove streamers of ragged cloud inland, and I drove to Corona del Mar through speeded-up patches of sunlight and shadow. I got there at two-thirty, early enough to walk over the whole area. Two boys rolled across the Fernleaf footbridge overhead, one on a skateboard and the other on a bike, yelling just to hear themselves. The tree branches dripped and the ground squelched underfoot. The neighborhood was stirring, people coming out to get some air and stretch their legs, and everything looked normal and peaceful.

Three-fifteen; nothing. The clouds were slowing down. Too cold and tense to stand still, I jogged from Carnation to Heliotrope and back again. I figured there was a fifty-fifty chance he wouldn't show, that this was more than likely a test and he'd drive on by, just look me over. For a while I tried to examine all the drivers passing in either direction, and then gave it up.

Not very good-looking, he'd said. Deformed? By his voice I judged he was healthy enough, but probably not athletic. He lacked the self-confidence that people with physical skills generally have. Oh, I had plenty of time to intuit.

Three-thirty. Well, there was no rush. I'd decided to give

him till four to demonstrate my goodwill, in case he was testing me. But I kept moving, scanning the houses, cars, shrubbery along both sides of the little canyon, and especially keeping an eye on that rustic footbridge overhead.

My eyes moved to the high seaward side where several vehicles were parked alongside houses or at street and alley ends. No change there since I'd arrived. . . . A brown van half-hidden by a hibiscus bush—and then I saw him: in the driver's seat, shadowed, with a huge pair of binoculars trained on me, those big old black ones that are so heavy you have to brace your elbows to hold them steady. Startled, I kept my gaze traveling as if I hadn't seen him, and then decided that was dumb.

"Hey!" I yelled and waved up at him. "It's me!" The van was silhouetted against the glaring sky and I couldn't make out much. He half-lowered the binoculars. Behind them he was wearing big dark sunglasses, too. I got a glimpse of a slouchy leather hat, with a floppy brim hanging down, and a tuft of medium-colored hair, definitely not brunet. The lower part of his face was shielded, but the forearm sticking out was more than healthy; it was brawny as a weightlifter's, with one of those wide black studded bands. So much for clever deductions.

"See? I said I'd be here," I yelled up at him, spreading my hands wide. "Where've you been? I've been waiting."

"Been here all along," he hollered back.

Same voice: it was Anonymous. And damn clever, too—there was no way I could get up there very fast. He could take off any time he was ready, and I'd never get close enough to follow him, or really to see him even. "So come on down."

"I can't."

"Hey, you gave your word! Didn't you?" Run across the street and try to scramble up through the bushes? He'd have time for a good laugh before he left.

He roared back, "I said I'd be here, and I am!"

"Then I'll come up. Will you wait till I get there?" I pointed. "I'll go up the stairs and take the bridge. You'll see me all the way." It's not easy to coax somebody at the top of your lungs.

"No! It's too late for that. Just a second—" He pulled back inside, and I hollered,

"Oh, wait! Listen!"

His elbow came out again and he yelled, "Brought you something. A present." Something white flashed, a medium-sized package that he threw with a snap. It landed halfway down, disappearing into the brush. Five, even ten minutes it would take me to climb up there and get it.

"No please, wait," I wailed, but he was already starting his engine.

"See you around," he yelled. "Maybe. Use them wisely." He gave me a big grin. He backed up, completely hidden now by the bush. I got just a flash of the van as it headed away up the street, with the steady rising sound of his engine accelerating.

The bank was so spongy that it tore away in juicy smears as I climbed, with the mud over my shoe tops, slipping and grabbing at smaller bushes that pulled loose. The dripping foliage soaked me to the skin, and I was worried that some resident opposite might call the police about their landscaping being vandalized.

It was a squashy bundle inside a clear plastic bag and wrapped in several sheets of the want ads, the *Orange County Tribune* dated two days ago. I slid and scrambled back down the bank and ran for my car. It was starting to rain again.

Inside the bundle was a stack of photocopies, maybe forty of them, all copies of newspaper clippings, sometimes two or three on the same page; and every single one of them about a Tenhagen. A few of them included the date, and I found one that went back fifteen years; Martin, the oldest son, making Sea Scout. There were stories about Arnie's partnership with Roger Murch, sailboat-race results, murky group pictures, at least three different articles on Deirdre's debutante ball. . . . I drove home, shucked off my wet, muddy clothes, and set to work.

I read myself cross-eyed, every word on every page. The only items even faintly incriminating were from the police log, several heavily underlined listings in which unnamed juveniles had been cited for suspected shoplifting, drinking, and creating a public nuisance; probably Keith as a teenager, the dates were right. And self-destructiveness was not at all the same thing as doing away with Daddy; I could attest to that.

Deirdre was well represented, too; several articles mentioned her and her politico in passing, and a photo showed her bending over and murmuring in the ear of a male of fifty, blow-dried and slightly jowly, in a beautifully cut jacket. And this was it? So far, Anonymous looked to be nothing more than a dingbat celebrity-watcher, a Tenhagen groupie. What had he ever told me that proved he knew the Tenhagens personally? Nothing.

A memory of the brown van and the floppy leather hat stirred, and later that night it surfaced. Anonymous could have been the one at the dock the day after the explosion, asleep under the black cowboy hat; or pretending to be? I kept expecting him to call, so I could at least ask what it was all supposed to mean. But he didn't. Nobody called. The wind howled and shook the building and the forced-air heater kept going on; I was going to have some gas bill.

And then, *voilà!* Next morning was beautiful: the leaves and the concrete fresh-washed, lush grass growing as you watched, blue sky and a dazzle of light that made your eyes water. I pulled my door shut, juggling a basket of clothes for the laundromat, and turned to start down the stairs.

The damndest thing is that I saw it in the split second before I went—the gleam of something across the top of those cement steps, a fine line ankle-high, but too late to stop myself. Caught and falling free, I grabbed for the wall, but no use—I crashed, tangled in the clothes, and then my head blew up.

Something was beating on the inside of my skull trying to batter its way out, and my nose was running horribly, I kept having to snuffle. I was lying outdoors, on cement, oh, at the foot of the stairs—I pushed at my nose and my hand was smeared with red. "And the claret is flowing now!" Howard Cosell would say. I remembered . . . it was the line that tripped me—somebody had done it on purpose and maybe he was watching me right now. I lay still, pretending to be unconscious.

Nothing stirred. A fly came buzzing around my face and I had to brush it away, and when I shifted, the pain in my shoulder made me yelp. I was lying half in a puddle in very bad shape, and I needed help. If whoever had set the trap for me was fool enough to stay around, so be it.

"Hey! Help! Somebody?" No response.

I rolled onto my good side, away from the shoulder that had

to be broken, the slightest movement hurt like fire; got up onto my knees and with one hand started to crawl toward the house where my landlady lived, maybe fifty feet away.

It was slow going. The blood gathered on the tip of my nose and I watched it fall in a single splot, perfectly round with little pointy edges like some kind of seal, while the next one gathered.

"Help," I hollered, not very loud, feeling worse by the inch. I could hear Mrs. Chaney's dog barking far away, inside the house. I sagged back on my haunches and threw up onto the grass. Then I moved on another couple of feet, and lay down to rest. Along with all the pain and mess, I felt something else: a bubble of joy. This made it all true, I wasn't just chasing phantoms. I had an enemy.

"Good grief. Toto, get out of that! Moz? Moz, can you hear me?" I was looking at Mrs. Chaney's absolutely beautiful runover house shoes and maroon polyester pant legs.

"Somebody tried to get me," I said. She helped me sit up, and I told her about my fall.

"Took a header down them stairs, did you? Well, anybody wearing shoes like that . . . just a matter of time, I always figured—Toto, get back here. You want to get up? Best not. You just sit tight, while I go inside and call an ambulance. And we'll just get some of that nastiness off of you in the meantime."

"Wait a minute," I said. "That'll cost." My health insurance had a thousand-dollar deductible. Mrs. Chaney stopped stock-still and I could hear the wheels turning. If she called the ambulance, she might be liable for the bill. The leaves moved and I closed my eyes against the flashes of brilliant sunlight that pierced my skull, a punishment for my sins.

"I guess I could drive you in my car," she said. "Think you could stand it?"

"Oh, hell yes." I sat there in the wet grass while she got her purse and locked up the dog, and brought a wet washcloth to clean off my face. She got her car started, retrieved my shoulder bag, and then she helped me get onto my feet. We shuffled out to the alley. The light blazing off the car's hood made me gag.

Anonymous, I thought. That bastard. Gets me off-guard with all his friendship stuff, probably laughing his head off. Maybe he even hid this morning and waited to see me fall. That'd be the best part. Probably I led him right here yesterday; I never even thought about being followed. Outstanding, Moz.

There were no other patients in the emergency clinic except for an old man somebody had brought in who was vague and evidently suffering from malnutrition—I could hear the doctor behind the curtain with him, questioning him about when he'd eaten last, and what. When the doctor got to me he asked me a string of questions, apparently to discover how badly my brains were scrambled; tested my reflexes, and looked at first one eye and then the other with his little flashlight, back and forth and tracking them, and leaning rather closer to my face than necessary.

"No, I haven't been drinking," I said. "What about my shoulder?"

It turned out not to be broken, only dislocated. He had the nurse take off my shirt, and he felt around and then crouched, knees together, and squinted at each shoulder in turn, front and side. Then he gestured to her, nodding above my head: she held me from one side, and he wrapped his arms around me and snapped. The pain was so intense that I passed out again for a minute, and he looked positively offended at my scream. Down the way, the old man was gabbling, panic-stricken.

"You could've warned me," I said, when I could talk. "Is that what you call informed consent?"

"It wouldn't've helped," he said. He was almost smiling. I could see that the nurse didn't approve of either of us. They wrapped the shoulder in one of those instant ice packs, and then the doctor wanted me to go over to the hospital and check myself in, stay overnight for observation.

Overnight? It was only mid-morning, and Anonymous was roaming over the countryside, full of craziness. People needed to be warned, and I had to plan what to do next, as soon as the roar in my head subsided and I could think. Besides . . . "I can't afford to do that," I said.

"Can you afford the risk of a blood clot, or possibly paralysis from this trauma? We can't even know yet what damage you've sustained. . . ." I pointed to my great and good friend, Gloria Chaney, who would be available in case of need. He grudgingly instructed her in the danger signs: fixed or dilated pupil; I must be "rousable"; check me every hour. He directed the nurse to prepare the forms absolving them of any responsibility, and disappeared.

Ten minutes later I was still waiting, while across the room Gloria and the nurse exchanged horror stories about head injuries they had known. I got out two dimes and trudged across to the pay phone and dialed Gage Pfeiffer's number.

"How are you?" he said in that neat old drawl.

"Not too good." Purple was beginning to flood into my field of vision from the edges and the center of the room was a wave of teeny black and white checks. I braced myself against the wall and talked as fast as I could.

"I'll be okay later," I said. "It wasn't broken, only dislocated. This arsonist, yours and mine? He threw me downstairs. It was a trap."

"What was a trap? What happened to you?"

"Whole thing was a joke, only it's not funny, is it. I didn't tell you about the phone calls, I thought you'd laugh. You would've, too. But one thing's for sure: he's demonstrated he's out there, and it's scary."

"Moz, you're not making any sense. Tell me where you are right now." I figured I must've sounded drunk to him, and that was the final blow.

"I never do to you, do I. Just a dumb little broad." Mrs. Chaney was coming toward me with a Big Mama scowl.

"Hey, now, stop that kind of talk," Gage said, "and just explain—"

"I sure as hell will, and right now." I tried to hang up the receiver. Gloria did it with one hand and caught me with the other.

I rode away sagging beside Gloria, assuming she was enraged

at having this unexpected burden. Wrong again. Gloria, the soul of concern, helped me in through her front door and that elegant blue-gray living room full of Biedermeier and cherry wood, and down the hall to her spare bedroom, where the blinds were already closed.

"We'll just make you real comfy here," she said. "First you can have yourself a little wash. Think you can manage all right?"

"Absolutely. I'm perfectly fine."

"Good. I'll go up and get you your own jammies."

Her bathroom was cold and fiercely clean and smelled of Ben Gay. In the mirror I saw a young eggplant trying to push out of the right side of my forehead, partly hidden by my hair. I braced myself against the sink and dutifully washed off the rest of my nosebleed one-handed.

Gloria brought back my yellow satin pajamas, which meant she'd gone through my drawers, and my ratty old bathrobe, a maroon plaid, boys' size large. "What was it?" I asked. "Across the top of the steps?"

"I didn't find a thing," she said. "Not a trace."

"Then he must've come back and taken it down," I said. "While we were gone."

"Course he did," she said, buttoning the pajama top around my sore shoulder. "That's exactly what must've happened." She didn't believe me for a minute.

I slid between the smooth shadowed sheets, aching in several places I hadn't noticed earlier but oddly distanced from them. The pain pills were beginning to work. Gloria brought in a down comforter and added it to the pile of covers to counteract my chill. I had to think about all of this. . . . That antsy kid I'd been talking to, he wasn't harmless after all. He'd killed Arnie, and now he wanted to kill me. Because I was on the right track. How wonderful. . . .

I dozed, sinking into a buzzing tangle of disasters—one of them was Vera with an ax buried in her head. That woke me up: I had to warn her. Gloria Chaney's cool knuckles grazed my cheek.

"Yes," I said.

"Yes, what?"

"Yes, ma'am." She smiled and went away.

When I woke up again it was later, the light had shifted, and I realized she'd been in more than once. The room solidified, sharp edges of blinds biting off the daylight, and down the hall Gloria hissed at Toto, shushing her. "Here now! You stop that!" The pain medicine was wearing off, I definitely needed more, and something smelled wonderful. I had to warn them.

Chicken soup and hot biscuits. Gloria was ready to feed me lunch in bed, but I ate two helpings in slow motion, with my slippers under her walnut curvy-legged dining table with embroidered place mats. I knew there was a Mr. Chaney who allegedly raved about her cooking when he was home, but I'd never seen him. He mostly traveled around the country on business, while she dusted all that furniture and tended the property and her yapping beastie.

I finished one last biscuit with homemade plum jam, complimented her again, and we got into an argument. I had things to do, but she wanted me to go right back there and get into bed, I was still in shock, the doctor had specifically warned us and so on. She was quite testy. "You only love me when I'm sick"—it was on the tip of my tongue, but too close to the truth to be funny, so I kept still.

"You've been way too generous already," I said. "Coming to my rescue like that. I'll always be grateful." Ignoring her glare, I made my way carefully to the telephone and called Deirdre at her office. She always liked to run things. Let her be the one to handle Vera.

"This is Moz Brant," I said. "I was injured in a faked-up accident this morning, and I think it was the same person who—you know; your father. I'm about to call your mother and warn her, too."

"What? No, wait a minute. Moz? I hear you talking, so you're evidently not hurt too badly. Tell me what happened."

That was a trick, with Mrs. Chaney clearing the table with eyes averted and ears pricked, back and forth to the kitchen and taking it all in. I was as vague as possible, trusting to Deirdre's ability to interpret. She kept muttering "Oh, God," and "No, no, no."

"So not only does he know all about your whole family, he's definitely dangerous. I'm going to call the police."

"No, you can't do that," Deirdre said.

"Why not?"

"Because he's one of ours."

I moved, forgetting my shoulder, and groaned. "What do you mean, 'one of yours'? Explain yourself."

"Oh, God," she said again. "Where are you exactly? I'm coming right over. Stay where you are, don't do another thing about this till we've talked. You promise?" I promised.

When Deirdre arrived she assessed the situation, took my apartment key, raced up and packed a bag for me, and inside fifteen minutes had me strapped, snarling and sweating inside my yellow satin pajamas, into her leaf-green Porsche Targa.

"I'll drive gently," she said. "Now tell me everything." True to her word, she drove carefully, taking back streets and easing up to the stops.

"He's some kind of menace?" she said. "I won't believe that."

"He? Who is he? Come on: it's your turn now."

"First you have to give me your word that you won't repeat this to anyone."

"Are you serious? This guy is a killer."

"You don't know that for sure."

"And I thought I was crazy. Is anybody following us? Look for a big brown van, a Dodge, fairly new."

Deirdre watched her rearview mirrors for a bit.

"Nope." She was bursting with her story, I could see it.

"The absolutely most vital part," Deirdre said, "is that my mother must never know anything about this." She looked over at me. "My God, you look terrible," she said.

"Just tell it!"

"His name is Jordan," she said. "Mother doesn't know he exists."

"But you know him; you've seen him, met him?" We pulled into the entrance of Park Newport and circled around to the back row of condos that overlook an undeveloped canyon, with a bright wedge of the Back Bay visible beyond.

"Not to talk to . . ."

Deirdre lived inside a peach. Walls and carpet were all the same color, even up the stair-treads to the second floor, with touches of white, and a soft green couch. "It's my Roman phase," Deirdre said, opening out the couch into a double bed. "I loved the colors in Rome, all the earth-tones of the buildings and churches—the green is for the trees along the Tiber."

She propped me up on the couch and brought me another of those ice packs for my shoulder. "I always keep them on hand, Andy has a tennis elbow," she said. Andy would be her politician. "All right; Jordan."

She'd first found out that Jordan existed the summer that she was twelve. Martin, then fifteen, overheard Socorro having a sustained conversation with their father, which was in itself a novelty for them—that Socorro could have any extended opinions which could interest Arnie. Moreover, it was some sort of argument between them, which was unheard of. Socorro wanted Arnie to go and see somebody named Jordan, and Arnie was refusing—but in a halfhearted way that really puzzled Martin.

Intrigued, naturally nosy, and bored with the yawning spaces between their tennis lessons and the swimming, Deirdre and Martin began to pursue the matter, eavesdropping on any contact between Socorro and Arnie. Socorro approaching him about money, Jordan needing various things: "His equipment, it's too small now," she said once. "He needs better stuff; it's only right." And Deirdre had remembered then another, earlier incident, when she was little: Socorro standing her ground inside the door of her father's study, Arnie over by the window with his back halfway turned, and Socorro saying, "You should

go to see him. Jordan, he talks now, he does this a long time."
And Arnie angry, snapping back: "That's not right, you've mis-
understood. You're exaggerating."

A couple of weeks after Martin overheard them, Deirdre
heard more money talk between her father and Socorro, with
Arnie agreeing wearily to something, making a joke about the
rate of inflation and it being a cost-of-living raise. And then he
said, "You're right, of course. You know I don't begrudge him."
Both of them were talking in that hushed, curt way that said
louder than anything, "This is a secret"; even though Vera was
out shopping.

After that, Martin and Deirdre had to find out, nothing
could've stopped them. They kept Keith out of it; he was too
young, only ten, "and a real baby blue-eyes," Deirdre said.

She and Martin, cherishing the hunt, made themselves into
the household CIA, determined to uncover every part of the
conspiracy: digging into their father's papers, searching through
his files, listening to phone calls and conversations whenever
they could. They decided that Socorro must be part of some
scheme to blackmail their father, but most probably an unwilling accomplice—they both liked her—and that "Jordan needs
new things" was a code phrase for the payoff.

They ransacked Socorro's things, too. Vera handled all the
household accounts, paying Socorro by check the first of the
month; they discovered that Socorro also got money separately
from Arnie every month, a cashier's check from an account that
definitely wasn't Vera's, drawn on a different bank.

It was Deirdre who suggested they track down the mysterious
Jordan. They found an address on an old gas bill among the
papers jammed in Socorro's nightstand, told a couple of strate-
gic lies to screen their activities, and took the first and only trip
of their lives on the Orange County public transit system. They
rode the bus to a southeast Santa Ana neighborhood, a mixture
of older houses—"some of them quite nice, really," Deirdre
said—and bungalow courts built in the thirties. In front, huge
trees met over the street, making a solid tunnel of black shade,
and the block swarmed with kids, mostly Mexican.

"It was pretty hot that day," Deirdre said. "Some of the smaller ones were just in their underpants, crawling all over the front sidewalk. And this toddler, starkers, with his little dingdong hanging out. . . . Playing in the dirt, charging around on their tricycles, yelling in a language we couldn't understand—it was like being in a foreign country." And she and Martin were the ones being stared at, they were the strangers.

The address they had was in a court, two rows of attached bungalows of green stucco facing one another across a patio of bare earth, with an arch over the entrance and the windows crowned with plaster shells and crumbling mermaids. Martin was worried, he wanted them to keep walking on down to the end of the block, at least, while they decided what to do next—they could hardly step right up to the window and look in. But Deirdre took the plunge:

"We're only kids, and a little bit confused, we just need to know how to find the bus stop on Bush Street."

Peering through the screen door, they saw a crowded little living room with no rugs on the floor and a cluster of kids watching television, Jordan sprawled in the midst of them on an old couch. He was wearing just a pair of jeans, a turned-down sailor's hat and a pair of sunglasses, even though he was watching TV.

"You could see which one he was right away," Deirdre said. "Pale and sickly, with a sunken-in chest—in the midst of all those brown legs and arms, he looked like a ghost shrimp."

The kids hollered for Anita, and a teenage girl came to the door and gave them directions back to the bus stop. The clincher: as they were leaving, Jordan shoved one of the kids with his elbow and the kid yelled, "Nita! Nita! Jordan's taking up all the good room again!"

"So we knew everything was true," Deirdre said.

"What everything was true?"

"That our father had four kids, instead of three. And one of them was being raised with the Mexicans in Santa Ana."

It took a couple of days really to soak in, Deirdre said. They had uncovered something totally outside their expectations, and hideously, dangerously, adult. The first thing they did was swear one another to complete and total secrecy: no one must ever know they'd been there, or that they knew anything whatsoever. And above all, their mother must never find out.

"It came at exactly the wrong time in my life," Deirdre said slowly. "Here I was just going into adolescence—it colored my whole view of what men were like, the whole sex thing—it rocked me to the core. For a long time I thought I hated my father. I didn't, of course—but I did blame him: I had to figure he was the one responsible, because he had the power. Men don't get pregnant. And I never hated Socorro, that didn't enter into it. When you figure the position she was in, her limited background—she's certainly Catholic. And after all, Daddy did the right thing by supporting her and the baby."

By unspoken agreement, she and Martin never discussed it again; only from time to time they'd catch one another's eye reluctantly. "You learn to live with things," Deirdre said. Eventually the fact of Jordan's existence just dropped out of her awareness.

"All in all, I'd say truly that I had a very happy childhood. And when I got older and a few things happened, I made a couple of mistakes of my own, oh, minor—it helped me understand other people better. I learned to look beyond the surface to what was really happening. So that was a plus."

Wrong, I thought. What you really learned was never to trust anybody.

My head was throbbing, and Deirdre went to get me water and another pain pill. Funny; I was remembering the day we left Uncle Brucie's—I would've been about seven. It was hot, and Ada had me by the hand, marching us along this endless road that must've been his driveway, crying and swearing, and stopping every so often to rest her suitcase hand. "Don't worry, Mom," I said. "I'll take care of you."

The whole thing was bizarre. Why had Arnie kept Socorro on, living in his house, if this was all true?

"I don't think he's a ghost shrimp anymore," I said, picturing the muscular forearm stretched out of the van window. "So, what you're saying is that your secret half-brother, Jordan, is the one who killed your father and tried to kill me."

She was tense and pale, with a sprinkling of little freckles standing out on her cheekbones. "At least half-wrong, you're jumping to conclusions," she said. "That's not what I'm saying at all."

"Be serious," I said.

Deirdre stretched her arms up and grimaced, baring her teeth, and slammed her fists down on the padded chair arms. "Just because he's turned up now doesn't mean he's responsible," she said. "Where do you see any proof of it, where? Show me."

Of course. Unthinkable that Tenhagen blood, even polluted, could turn on its own. "You like somebody else better. Keith, maybe? He's been stealing family stuff to feed his habit, hasn't he; and Vera keeps trying to protect him. Are you willing to risk her having an 'accident' like your father's?"

"That's not the only explanation for the fire." She looked out the window, waiting for me to react.

"You mean, you think your father could've done it himself, too?"

"It's not impossible. If he believed that in some strange way he was protecting her. To keep the truth from coming out."

115

"But it's having just the opposite effect."

"Well, *he* couldn't know that." She wrinkled up her face, trying not to cry. "Hell, how do I know. Maybe he felt too guilty to go on, he couldn't face *her*. Jordan's called me, and he called you: maybe he'd talked to Daddy already. And then . . ." She shrugged. "What we've got here is a disaster of cosmic proportions," she said, trying to grin.

In spite of myself I felt sorry for her, and I had to resist. Are you suffering, poor baby? Nothing to compare with other people I could name. "Yes . . . there could be even more to his secret life than this," I said, so sympathetic.

"I have no indication whatsoever of that." Her chin came up. "My mother has beautiful memories of my father, and they're not going to be spoiled. I won't let this ruin our lives. We're going to handle it ourselves."

"Are you serious? Take a look at me! This guy is crazy. Do you want to be responsible for what he does next?"

"Your landlady—is it likely she'd called the police on her own?"

"Oh, no. When she went back up there, the line was gone; he'd come and taken it down already. In broad daylight; lets you know right there what kind of guy we're dealing with. So naturally she didn't believe me."

"You mean . . ." Deirdre's surprise turned to anger, and I watched her wrestle with herself. Now she thought I was crazy, too.

"Oh, yes, you did," I said.

"Did what?"

"Need to tell me about Jordan. We've got to find out what he's after. What's his game, anyway? What is all this stuff supposed to get him?"

"That's easy—he wants in. He knows everything about us."

"What makes you think so?"

"He must; through Socorro."

"So then how do you suppose he feels about all of you?"

"Like everybody—that we're rich, and he wants a piece of the action. You'd think Socorro could control him a little better. After all we've done for her."

"After what?" I tried to laugh, and Deirdre did have the decency to look a little embarrassed. "Besides; tell me how well your mother controls Keith."

"Yes, there's that."

I sank back on my pillows with a little groan and closed my eyes. Actually the medicine had begun to work, dulling the edges of the pain; but I wanted some time to think. Deirdre went in the kitchen, quietly closing the door behind her.

I heard the murmur of her voice on the phone, and it occurred to me that she'd brought me here at least partly to keep me under control. All of Deirdre's actions had a political cast, as if she'd stepped back and edited her life for publication, remaking her past for the record. And an unacknowledged bastard brother who'd killed her father—and his—would not look good in the papers.

Besides which, Vera probably knew the story already; who but Jordan could've made the mystery call? Everybody hiding things from everybody else. Just your all-American family.

I slept, thought a little, slept some more. Not a good way to kill somebody, falling downstairs. More likely it was just to scare me off. Like the broken window, and the dead dog . . . oog. I pictured somebody holding Brownie and clubbing him; I was hoping to have one of those paranormal experiences you hear about, pushing hard for the hand, body, face of the killer to materialize. They didn't.

I woke with the light from the kitchen falling on me. It was getting dark outside, and Deirdre had evidently decided it was time for me to wake up. She brought me a fresh ice pack for my shoulder and strapped it on carefully.

"Great to work at home," she said. "No phones, nobody knows where you are—think I'll try it more often. . . . In the first place," she began, as if we'd been arguing, "you have nothing to tell the police. There's absolutely no proof. This bunch of clippings you got—they're not connected to anything really, are they."

"You don't want it to be him."

"You bet I don't. And if I have to, I'll pay you or anybody to prove it wasn't. Only I won't let it come to that. This can all be worked out quietly."

"I wonder if Socorro even knows what he's been doing. . . ."

"Exactly," Deirdre said. "We need to talk to her now, tonight. You're right, it can't wait. And it'll have to be you; she couldn't possibly discuss it with me. My God, the woman practically raised us. She must *not* know that I'm involved. Come on, now, up. It's time you moved around a little, anyway."

Somehow I disliked Deirdre most when I had to agree with her. When I telephoned, they were just finishing dinner up on the hill. Socorro seemed unsurprised by my call, and perfectly willing to come out and meet me at Coco's.

Deirdre helped me dress, poking at my hair a couple of times with her brush.

"Tell me again; why am I doing this?" I said.

"Just to find out where Jordan is, and what's on his mind."

"Presuming she knows any of that."

"Get her to help us: you'll know how. Maybe she can scare some sense into him."

"You think that's likely, do you."

"We've got to start somewhere."

She delivered me to Coco's side door ten minutes early. "If you start to feel too rotten, send somebody out to get me," she said. "I'll be hiding out back in the corner, where she won't see the car."

I sat propped in a booth, watching my reflection in the black window, feeling more than rotten and wondering if Jordan was out there driving by, watching for another chance. To do what? He could've gotten me any time before now, if that's what he'd wanted. Also, I was mad at Deirdre for treating me like hired help, and at myself for going along with it, doing her chores so obediently. All running their private little games . . . I didn't trust any one of them.

I had my eyes closed when Socorro came in, so I missed her first look at me. "'Ey, Moz. You okay?"

"Not really."

"What happen to you?"

"Jordan happen to me." She gave me a level look. "Yeah, that cancels out your promise now, doesn't it. I know all about him, practically."

She settled herself on the bench opposite. "Ah. Then you better tell me this all you know." The first milestone: she didn't deny he existed. So there really was a Jordan.

I told it from the beginning, his hysterical call; in the middle of which the waitress came, and we ordered pie and coffee. She looked sympathetic and beamed at us, and I could hear her little inner voice saying, "Mother and daughter, oh how sweet."

Socorro listened without interrupting, verifying everything with her automatic nods, and I began to panic, this was all too easy. It was running away with me and I didn't know where to steer it.

"So; Jordan is Arnie Tenhagen's son," I said, "which Mr. Ten knew all these years, but he never even got in touch with him." Milestone two: true to her style, Socorro didn't say no, so it was another yes.

"How he did this?" Socorro asked, indicating my bruised face and scowling like a summer thundercloud.

I described my fall, the line tied to trip me—this time I didn't mention that it disappeared afterward. Socorro shook her head. "No no no no no."

"He tried to kill me. You can see he's out of control, and you better help stop him. Listen, I'm sure you did the best you could for him—"

"No," she said. "He can't do this."

"You always say that. 'Keith can't do this, Jordan can't do this'— Bad things happen, but nobody's responsible."

"Because it's true. He is cripple. So how he can get up these stairs? He couldn't even get on the boat, he's in a wheelchair. No way he could kill Mr. Ten."

"What?" I smiled at her, that was preposterous. "Oh, sure. And how long has he been crippled?"

"Always. Since he was born." She went back to her lemon meringue pie.

"That big strong arm sticking out of the window?"

"Sure. He does muscle works, exercises with all those things."

Well, there were special hand controls. . . . Socorro had kept quiet about a lot of things, but so far she hadn't lied. "He said he's got a wife and a kid."

"Yah, he can. He told it true." Socorro leaned back, visibly more relaxed. "Is somebody else," she said, pointing her fork at me. "You looking in the wrong place."

"But I bet he has friends who can get around all right," I said. She went on eating, her eyes on her plate. "Who wouldn't mind helping him get what's coming to him. You didn't know he was making any of those calls, did you? When did you see him last?"

"A month, maybe two. I don't see him that much."

"It's the money he's after, isn't it."

"He don't need it, he can manage. He has his own business."

"Oh?" I smiled, disbelieving.

"He does; he sells *discos*, records. It's a living."

"Right. I wonder how he feels about the family, Mr. and Mrs. Ten, and those kids with their shiny cars. . . . He'd have to be jealous, wouldn't he? 'My future is gone,' he told me. He must've had expectations. . . . Socorro: I still can't believe it. How could you stand for your own son to be treated like that? All those years on the outside, looking in—no wonder he went a little crazy."

The smile started slowly and spread across her face in a big grin, and she jauntily scraped up the last bit of lemon filling, just tickled with herself. Why so cheerful now? I figured it must be the relief of having it all in the open finally, if only here with me. She might even enjoy having Vera find out, if somebody else did the telling.

Always cautious, guarded; but even here Socorro had a dark presence, you could feel the dynamo humming inside the walls. I remembered her at the art show smiling and animated, ridiculing one of the goofy collages, and I could see what might have drawn Arnie. Along with that otherness, there was the old lure of the unknown—Hedy Lamarr and "I am Tondelayo"; so corny, but still true.

"You don't like your pie," she said. I'd ordered cherry and eaten two bites, feeling queasy.

"It's okay; I'm not—here, you have it." She shrugged and I slid it across to her.

"I haven't said anything about this to Vera," I said.

Socorro ignored that. "Always little bit strange," she said, "even when this big. Of course, plenty spoiled; that helps, no? Big dreams, stories he tells the others—*fantásticos*. And they're never sure, maybe he could be right. But a good heart. He's a good kid, you could trust him with anything. He didn't have nothing to do with this, none of it, for sure; I know it. I talk to him."

"You have, or you will?" She nodded, leaving me still confused. Her English seemed to expand and contract to suit the occasion. "If you haven't, you better."

"Yah."

"Tell me about his family."

His wife, Lupe, was a nice little country girl from Chihuahua, whom Benita had found for him; not pretty but a good worker and real sharp; under three years she's here and already she speaks better English than Socorro herself; a big help to him in the disco, and so good with the baby, Miguel, Mikey. . . . It was an odd way to keep a secret, telling me so much I could practically find him myself. Socorro's intentions seemed clearer by the minute; but I was being steely-cool, and not leaping to any more conclusions. Hah.

". . . You know I'm going to have to talk to him," I said. "And I don't intend to get any more bruises." She nodded. "So, will you see him first and find out what's going on? If he really hasn't done anything, then he'd want to help me, wouldn't he, instead of playing games?"

I paid the check and Socorro took my arm and walked me to the side door, and then held it open for me. Outside, Socorro raised her voice and called. "'Ey, Deedee! Come over here and help your friend. She needs you. Deedee?"

We started toward the back of the lot and Deirdre came trotting up to meet us, looking sheepish. "Next time maybe you talk with me direct," Socorro said dryly.

"Mother knows nothing," Deirdre said. "*Nada*; okay?" Not a question but a statement, more like a warning. Socorro just scowled, thinking about that.

Deirdre bounced into the driver's seat and slammed her car door. "What did she say? Fasten your seat belt—oh, here, I'll do it. Come on; did she admit to anything at all?" Toward the front of the parking lot, Socorro's big black Caddy was moving out onto the street.

"Yes, there really is a Jordan," I said. "I don't think she knew about the calls, but she's sure he didn't do any bad stuff, she says he couldn't." Deirdre watched me, holding her breath. "Get this: because he's crippled. In a wheelchair."

"Yow-yow-yow!" Deirdre shouted for joy, jolting me, and pounded on the steering wheel. "I don't believe it! Tell me everything straight through from the beginning, I want to know every word."

"Not till I've had another pill."

What I left out were the details about Jordan's present life, Lupe and Miguel and the *disco*, because it didn't occur to Deirdre to ask anything more about him. If she'd really been interested at that point, things might've gone differently. . . . But Deirdre only wanted everything zipped up and put back the way it was before. Just give me tranquillity, peace at any price. I recognized the feeling.

We sat in Deirdre's darkened living room with the curtains open on her view, the brush-filled canyon that was one mass of black with no edges for your eyes to catch on, and beyond it a dim wedge of bay with a few lights reflected from the rim of houses on the bluff opposite.

Vera had trusted Socorro with everything, Deirdre said; shopping, the kids—she'd been with the family since the first baby. Always busy with her own nieces and nephews, weddings, birthdays, christenings. And treatments; she told them which herbs would cure sore throat, stomach sickness, she was their *curandera*. Once when Keith was so sick with a strange fever the doctor couldn't diagnose—he wanted to put Keith in the hospital but they wouldn't let him—Vera and Socorro had taken turns sitting up all night with Keith, and he got better. Vera's right hand.

"I'll talk to Soky tomorrow," Deirdre said. "See if she can get Jordan straightened out. It's not too late. Nobody else knows about this but Martin."

"And Jordan, and his friends probably, and all Socorro's relatives. . . . Nobody, really."

"Nobody close to Mother. You know, she seems terrifically strong, and she is in most ways. . . . My father always protected her, and I feel like I'm carrying on for him. She had a period of illness a long time ago—just very occasionally she'd have this kind of shaking fit, trembling all over, out of control. Extremely rare, I only saw one once—but he dreaded that beyond anything, he just wouldn't permit her to be upset. And neither will I."

"If she saw this bruise, what would she think?"

"Oh, you'd make up something. Right now Mother believes that, at the worst, Daddy was killed by some random thief caught in the act. And that's good enough for me."

But not for me. I was awake a lot that night—a couple of times because Deirdre was dutifully checking to see that I was "rousable," as Mrs. Chaney had instructed her. Once I went into the kitchen to take another pill, and noticed that the phone had been removed. If I asked her in the morning she'd say, "Of course. I didn't want to take the risk of your rest being disturbed."

I felt minchy-mean and co-opted; I wanted out of this plushy peach cage. I was sick of the Tenhagens, the whole lot of them. Deirdre trying to persuade herself that Jordan wasn't involved— of course she believed he was. Why else would she tell me the whole story? I should've gone back up those stairs to see for myself. If there were any signs left, Mrs. Chaney could've maybe missed them: Deirdre certainly wouldn't.

And the beautiful fantasy, stouthearted Arnie alone at the tiller sailing into the teeth of the storm, had dissolved, leaving only a raw place in the back of my throat. He'd run away from the real storm, hunkered down in the harbor . . . spent his life ducking it; and now the rest of us had to take it for him.

No fair. I was just stuck, I had to go straight on through. What a miserable prospect; having to watch out for everybody, sitting with my back to the wall in a world full of enemies. When all I wanted was for things to be normal again. . . . Not exactly true, Moz. I had the scent now, and nothing could have kept me from the hunt.

Right then I wanted another pain pill, but I was afraid to take it. Easiest thing in the world to get hooked. It happened to Lucy, my AA sponsor, and Ada had been a mess for a while. I hadn't even been in to see Rick in a couple of days, and the key to that was, I didn't want to. Fran would be moving in tomorrow, and I'd have to hear every miserable detail. Before, I'd been afraid he'd die: now I was afraid he wouldn't, that he'd go on living like this, another Karen Quinlan.

Was the sky getting the least bit lighter, morning coming already? Hurry up and sleep, Moz, you need your strength. . . . I wanted a drink.

12 Deirdre dropped me off at my apartment next morning. "I'll take care of Socorro," she said. "And then let me know what you find out."

"Why don't you see what you can do on your own about Jordan?" Deirdre was good at giving instructions, not so good at taking them. "Without rocking the boat, of course. Want me to come up with you and look in the closets? You look pretty rocky—better get some rest. And watch your step."

Thanks a bunch. I already knew what I was going to do: find Jordan myself. Either he was who they said, or he wasn't. Subconsciously I'd accepted it, but us claims agents need things in black and white. And then, if this Jordan couldn't be tied to the explosion in any way, at least I'd be able to eliminate him as the Enemy. I wasn't cut out to be an urban guerrilla.

Going into the hospital, I got lots of sidelong glances. The lump on my forehead wasn't any bigger but it was a definitive purple, and I had one terrific black eye.

"What happened to you?" Fran said.

"Bit of a nasty fall—tell you about it later. How's Rick today? I want to see him."

"I can't think why, at this juncture," she answered, irritated. "He's become paralyzed on the right side. At this late date—Dr. Tedler was really surprised. He's fairly much convinced it's only temporary. Anyway, they're moving him today to the UCI Medical Center to do some tests."

I got out the extra key to my apartment. "I'm not exactly the safest company," I said. "Somebody set a trap for me, on my stairs." I told her what had happened to me, but it didn't seem to register. I could see that Fran was elsewhere; with Rick.

"I hardly think he'd come back, do you?" she said. "Besides; safety in numbers." Fran was doing something funny with her mouth, maybe rubbing her teeth together. "Rick always used to say you were a tough little thing."

"This is true."

At T. Ambrose that morning, Arlene had the skinned, yellowish look which I'd finally realized meant she hadn't yet put on her makeup for the day. She stared at me. "Oh, my Gaaaaahd . . . well?" I didn't say anything. "Of all the women I know, you're the last one I'd ever figure to get beat up by a guy," she said.

"I wasn't. I had this sort of . . . planned accident."

"One of our clients? What happened? Come on, tell me, tell me!"

"No, I'm not going to make any accusations till I have the proof. Don't worry, I'm working on it. And listen: *don't* tell Leo."

"You're in luck, then; he's got some crisis in Ontario, he won't be in for a couple days. The guy in the cement truck, I'll bet, wasn't it. He sounded like a mean son of a bitch. Where'd it happen? Jeez, he could've killed you."

I told her the minimum about my fall. My vague half-answers to her questions left her unsatisfied, and I retreated to my office. Leo might not be in, but his mark was, notes in that thick black felt-pen scrawl clipped to everything. The water was rising, and I couldn't get myself to care a damn bit about it.

Gage had left two messages on the tape. He'd talked to Mrs. Chaney, and also the emergency center where I'd been treated, but he couldn't find me. Would I please call whenever I came in, no matter what time? He even included his pager number, and his unlisted home phone. I phoned his office, and after a few minutes he called back.

"I'm down here at the harbor in the middle of something else now. If I come over there at ten o'clock, will you stay put till then?"

When Gage got to the office, he took one look at me, said "Whoa," and closed the door. The sight of my face seemed to satisfy him, someway; maybe he'd thought I was hallucinating when I phoned him. He eased into my visitor's chair—we were almost knee to knee. "Tell me what happened to you," he said. "From the beginning."

I did. When I came to the part about the vanishing snare, I could see that it stuck in his throat. "I know how it sounds," I said. "To be honest, I'm even beginning to doubt my own sanity. But I *know* it was there."

Our eyes held. "I believe you," he said. I knew he was lying. He wanted to believe every wild detail, but he just couldn't. It gave me a terrific boost, but at the same time I wished he hadn't said that. It was a commitment from him I didn't want.

He took in all the stuff about Jordan, processing it, asking questions. Gage really didn't want to know about Arnie's bastard son. He didn't care to get involved in people's messy private lives.

"None of our damn business, normally," he said. "But if it was done for revenge, and not the start of a plague of arsons . . ." He shook his head.

"Well, that's what I'm going to find out."

"I'll look after it," he said. "You really ought to go home and rest. You're not going to, though, are you? Well, take it easy—

you don't want to set up any aftershocks. If you stay quiet in the office you'll probably be okay, with the secretary right here."

"Oh, I'll be fine."

I phoned Socorro. "Don't call me. I call you," she said, sounding harassed. "When I got something to say."

First I went to a discount beauty supply place out on West First Street, where an old woman with flaming orange hair and domed purple eyelids sold me some goop she called "pancake" that was about the same shade as my skin. She let me sit in the back corner of her shop and watched as I spread it on to cover my bruises. Her mouth was pushed up like a turtle's and she shook her head at the wickedness of the world, not even interested in the details.

"Good thing the skin wasn't broken," she said.

There were five *discos* in the yellow pages, all clustered in central Orange County. I decided to start in Santa Ana. Disco Guadalajara, in a shopping center on South Bristol, was run by a weary, voluptuous redhead of about forty, all in black and wearing spike-heeled sandals, looking as if her feet hurt already. When I asked her to recommend a good singer for my friend's birthday present, she pulled out a record by Jose Luis Rodriquez.

"They call him El Puma. He's very popular. You can't miss with this one. I'll play you some of the songs; I've got one open back here."

"Thanks, but I guess I better think about it. . . ."

El Lobo Rojo was in downtown Santa Ana, on a side street half a block off Fourth Street, the main stem. Santa Ana is about seventy percent Mexican now, even though the City Council is still all Anglo, and downtown feels almost as if you were in Mexico, with songs in Spanish burbling out of the shoe and jewelry stores, and cafés advertising *mariscos* and *tacos al carbon*; and there was a big new video rental store with movies in both languages.

I followed the full-throated sounds of a Vegas-style ballad, "*Voy a conquistar-taaaay . . .*" up the empty sidewalk to the doorway of El Lobo Rojo. Alongside the door was a larger-than-life-size painting, the head and shoulders of a man halfway transformed into a strawberry-blond wolf with brawny shoulders leering out of a thicket of brush. The artist was either Frank Godoy or a good imitator, and I knew I was there.

A scarred wooden ramp painted dark brown bridged the threshold. The store was deserted. It didn't carry records, only new and used tape cassettes in wire baskets set at about waist height along a couple of wide aisles . . . enough room to maneuver a wheelchair. The door opening had evidently set off a signal somewhere in back, because the volume of the music dropped suddenly and a girl about twenty appeared. It had to be Lupe.

She asked me in Spanish if she could help me.

"I'm sorry, I don't understand. Do you speak English?"

"Oh, yes, a little. But this place is, you know, only Mexican music." She pushed the sleeve of her navy cardigan up and down as she talked, struggling with a heavy accent. She was short, just my height, with shiny black bangs and a ponytail that accentuated her wide cheekbones and sticking-out ears. In her white round-collared blouse and navy-blue skirt, she looked like a parochial-school student.

"I'm looking for anything by El Puma," I said. In the back room a kid maybe fifteen months old was babbling happily to himself and pounding a toy on the bottom of his playpen—that would be Miguel. I moved a little so I could see him through the open door.

He had bright dark eyes and that big-eyed look, cautious and expectant, ready to be delighted. Fine beige hair stood up in an arc along his hairline and at the cowlick; he had a grinful of baby teeth, and skin a little lighter than Lupe's, and was what Ada in her Texas period would've called "just a lovin' armful." Everybody should get a chance at one anyway, I thought. Then I realized I must be looking at Arnold Tenhagen's grandchild.

"You have already the song that is playing?" the girl asked.

"Oh, no, I don't. . . . To be honest, I'm looking for Jordan. Is he here?"

"Not ri' now," she said, suddenly wary. "What do you want him for?"

"You must be Lupe. Socorro was telling me—" Miguel was standing up now, hanging on to the playpen railing and yelling, "Ma-ma! Ma-ma!" rocking back and forth, and Lupe retreated, went to him and hoisted him up, hugging him and bouncing him as we talked.

"You better talk to him about this," she said. "I'll tell him when he comes back. You leave your number, where he can reach you and I will have him to call you up."

"Do you know where he is?" She didn't answer that. I got an idea. "I came because I want to help him out. I think he's in some kind of serious danger, and there isn't much time. You tell him to call me right away, at either of these numbers." He already had them, but she wouldn't know that. I held out my card, and she reached for it with a look of fear and revulsion.

"Your son, Miguel? He's very handsome. You should be proud." She only hugged the baby tighter, and watched me out of the store.

When I checked at the office, all I had on the tape was a collection of clicks, indicating callers who hadn't bothered to leave a message. I stayed till almost six, hoping Jordan would call. He didn't, but Deirdre caught me at the last minute.

"I haven't had time to breathe all day—well; any luck?" she said. "Contacting our mystery boy, that is."

"I thought you were taking care of that. What did Socorro have to say?"

"Haven't had a chance to touch bases yet, actually. . . . I've been thinking. When you do get to Jordan, let's not do anything precipitous to scare him off. We don't want to burn our bridges. I mean, we always want to leave room to negotiate, right?"

"I'll keep you posted."

Negotiate, eh? Deirdre adapted fast, I had to admire that much. Her unacknowledged brother on the outside all these years, like a kid looking in the bakery window, and Deirdre was going to arrange some little payoff to make it all right. Her arrogance brought me up sharp, like a good whiff of ammonia. The Tenhagen goals were not mine—they didn't own my loyalty, no matter what Deirdre presumed, and I didn't care which of them did what to whom. Still, I couldn't help feeling sorry for Vera—disaster was galloping toward her, you could hear the hoofbeats; and in spite of Deirdre the negotiator, I couldn't imagine any way of heading it off.

The night was overcast, a sagging belly of cloud stained dirty pink by the city neon. A strange car was parked in my spot alongside my apartment. Lord, Lord—I'd forgotten about Fran moving in. The last thing in the world I wanted was to be civil to another human being. I stomped up the stairs scratchy with resentment.

Fran, in pajamas and a man's velour robe of tobacco brown, sat on the end of my scruffy green couch with her glasses on, crocheting something blue and watching a football game. The couch sits in the middle of the room with its back to the dining area, dividing the space. The countertops gleamed, the rug had been vacuumed, and Fran had a pot of spaghetti sauce on low to keep warm.

"It's meatless, tofu," she said. "I didn't know but what you're vegetarian. Lots of Rick's friends are."

"Nope."

"Interesting way you've arranged your couch. I guess I'm just used to sitting with a wall behind me. This makes you a little uneasy."

"I like to think of it as creating dynamic tension," I said.

Fran rushed over to start cooking the spaghetti, set out two glasses and began opening a half-gallon of Gallo Hearty Burgundy.

"I don't drink," I said. "Rick probably mentioned it. I'm an alcoholic. I quit."

"Oh I forgot, I'm so sorry—" She tightened the cap again and looked around for a place to put the bottle.

"You have some," I said. "Go ahead."

"No, I'm actually too tired. . . ."

"It's perfectly all right. Go ahead, dammit; or don't. Suit yourself."

"Right," Fran said. "I will." She poured herself half a tumblerful, tightened the cap and set the bottle under the sink. I bet myself it would be gone tomorrow.

For dinner we had Rick's forthcoming angiogram, which would determine if a blood clot was causing his paralysis. Fran described the process in detail: how they would thread a tube in through the femoral artery in his groin and run it up past the heart and into his brain, and then inject the dye.

"It's quite a painful process," she said. "Gives you a terrible headache—if you're conscious. You know, I'm getting greedy. At first I prayed, 'Oh, please, only let him live, that's all I ask.' But now I want more; I want him to wake up and lead a normal life." She looked at my face. "Tell me what happened to you."

I did. Fran was fascinated. "Did you believe that whole story, about his being crippled?"

"I'm trying to check it out."

"Better than 'As the World Turns,'" she said. "By far. Real life always is. . . . We have to be sure to get the right person."

"That's the plan."

She looked over at the door. "We're pretty snug in here."

"Not much more we can do," I said, "short of running away, or jamming a chair under the doorknob."

"Good thinking," Fran said, and she got up and did it.

Fran insisted on cleaning up the kitchen, and I let her. Then she went back to her handwork—she was crocheting a set of round place mats, robin's-egg blue. "You know?" she said. "I've always thought of myself as a civilized person. But I'm beginning to understand people who pull out fingernails, give electric shocks, and those kinds of things. The one that did it—I'd like to see him—oh! I keep picturing all sorts of nasty, ugly things. You know how they talk . . . cut off his balls."

Ah, but I looked tired, Fran said, being a good guest. How

did I usually relax in the evenings? Sometimes I listened to records. So Fran insisted I put one on, and we listened to some Chopin waltzes. I'd been hoping Jordan would call, and he hadn't. I sat there twitching; I didn't want to listen to this now, I wanted to slop around, watch something like "Miami Vice" and pick my teeth if I felt like it.

"I'm going to really try not to wake you when I get up in the morning," Fran said. She wanted to get to the hospital early enough to see Rick before the test; and I began to understand that this angiogram was a risky business. Fran got out the blankets and a pair of sheets, and piled them on one end of the couch.

I took the hint, smiling through my teeth, and went off to bed, totally bent. And then, thinking about Rick's paralysis and the clot, I got scared. Maybe God had taken me seriously. We'd made a deal. It was time for me to produce.

When I got to the office the next day, Arlene had our monthly commission checks ready—our pay was partly based on the number of cases closed, and I'd be looking at a skinny check next month.

"You outside guys are just like big flies," Arlene said. "You only come in for the sugar."

Still no word from Jordan, and nothing on my calling machine but more clicks. But the phone rang almost immediately.

"Well, finally you turn up." It was Jordan. "I thought maybe you were hiding out or something. Listen; we've got some serious stuff to decide."

"You bet we do. Why don't you come on over."

"Okay, I think I will. You wait right there."

Sure you will, I thought. But about ten minutes later I hear a horn honking outside, BLAM ba-BLAM, BLAM ba-BLAM, just a steady racket. When I got to the front door, Arlene was already standing there, looking.

"Can you believe this?" she said. "What do I do now, call the cops?"

A big brown van sat with its nose pointed toward us. The

man at the wheel was wearing wraparound sunglasses and a floppy black beret like that old Che Guevara poster. "No," I said. "I'll handle this." When I pushed open the door he quit honking and waved at me with a big grin.

I walked up to the driver's side, feeling a little shaky and halfway expecting him to slam into reverse and take off. "Hi, there," Jordan said. "Moz; right?" I nodded. He had reddish-sandy sideburns and a pointed chin, and up close his grin reminded me of Keith's—

"Take off your sunglasses, okay?"

"You sure? It's not very pretty." He lifted them off. The right side of his face was dented in, a deep warp in the cheekbone that pulled the eye down; but that wasn't what stopped me cold. I couldn't see any trace of Socorro at all, but he was definitely a Tenhagen. The diamond jaw was a signature, a shout. He was Vera's.

13 I stared at him, amazed.

"Think you've got a problem," Jordan said. "What about me? I've got to see it in the mirror shaving every morning." He put the glasses back on.

"Whose kid are you, anyway? You look Tenhagen to the core."

"That obvious, eh?" He was really pleased. "You picked up on it right away. Yeah, and another thing." He swung the car door open so I could see his legs, limp and shrunken inside fresh-pressed khakis, and then he lifted one up by the cloth and let it fall back. "I haven't been climbing around on any boats lately that I know of. Or stairs, either."

"I never said that, exactly. . . ." He slammed the door again and scowled across at the building, where Arlene still stood watching us, shading her eyes with one hand. I waved at her and called over, "It's okay."

"Some nosy people," he said. "Come on, get in."

I went around to the other side and climbed up onto the seat. He started the motor and began to back around. "Where are you going?" I asked. He stopped the van.

"You want to invite her into the conversation, too? I just thought we could use some privacy. Fasten your seat belt."

"Oh, right." I heard a *clunk!* in my door. He'd locked it from his side, where he had all the hand controls to manage the van. He turned out onto North Main and headed toward downtown Santa Ana at an easy pace. The cab was a cozy nook all lined in honey-colored plush, even the dashboard.

"To tell the truth," he said, "I'm really disappointed in you. Here I am doing everything in the world trying to catch this guy, and you turn around and accuse me—me! When Socorro told me, I was really pissed. I try to help you out, and what does it get me? In the shit again."

"Oh, please. Who called who to start with? And all that monkey business with the bagful of clippings, throwing them out in the rain and the mud. . . . So what's the deal supposed to be here, anyway?"

"The deal, as you call it, is real simple: me just doing what any other guy would try to do, which is provide some security for my family. See, I already know I won't live as long as normal people, those who don't have my medical complications. I can't; so I've got to plan ahead."

We kept on rolling down Main, getting farther and farther away from the office. He seemed perfectly normal mentally, in full possession of his wits, and he obviously wanted to cooperate. I figured I had two choices. I could either tell him to turn around and head back, or go along with this and see where it got me. Which was no choice at all, actually. Right now he was in charge, and loving it.

"You know, you sounded quite a bit brighter over the phone," he said. "A person whose life's in danger, and you walk right into the lion's den?"

"Meaning this van?"

"Meaning Miss Deirdre's apartment."

"That's pretty funny, coming from you, who haven't given me fact one to go on. I still don't have any idea what your real connection to Arnie Tenhagen was, or if you just invented the whole thing—"

He swerved into the curb and hit the brakes, slamming me against my seat belt. Then he smacked the lever for the door lock, releasing my door. "You don't trust me? You want out? Great; go for it!" We sat and stared at one another. Gradually his breathing slowed.

"I never met him," Jordan said. "I vaguely remember seeing him once, or anyway—no, I'm sure it was him; but I was real little, that didn't count. I waited too long. I been trying and trying to figure—maybe he was waiting for me to make the first move. You know? It would've proved I was ready." Somebody behind him honked, and I motioned for him to start driving again.

"But how much do you know, for sure?" I asked.

"When I was little it was just something nobody talked about. Some kind of hot secret, too dangerous to say right out—you know, almost like what the big boys and girls do in the dark. Naughty. Baaad. Only it was me, this person."

Benita was Mama, and Socorro was Tia, Auntie, and nobody told him otherwise. "But it was a good secret, too, because it made them treat me special. It wasn't just the legs, or my face; it was the secret that made me different." He began putting together little hints, careful not to let anybody know that he was interested.

"For one thing, the clothes. The best stuff we ever saw came from up there, the castoffs Socorro brought home—bagfuls, terrific stuff, most of it brand new. We used to fight over them— God! did we. You know how it is in a house with that many kids, making sure everybody's hind end is covered for school. And socks? Forget it. Except me: I always had socks. 'How come Jordan gets to have the socks, and he don't even walk?'" he whined, imitating. "Not one bit of it ever went to waste; believe it."

We were on South Main now and almost to Costa Mesa, heading toward the coast. "But didn't you think—I mean, you obviously looked different from the other kids."

"As in 'weird.' Yeah, I knew that much—we saw an albino on the street once, and for quite a while that's what I thought I was." His smile was embarrassed, remembering. "Then they got me into this handicapped school, and I started to straighten out a lot of things, put the pieces together."

We drove in silence for a while, heading in the general direction of the coast. He cut left and went over the Newport Freeway, and then right again. Obviously he had a destination in mind. "Our first child was stillborn," Vera had said. "So you can imagine. . . ."

"When did it happen?" I gestured toward his legs.

"I don't remember, I was too little." He shrugged. "They never said." Because he'd never asked? Well, what difference would it have made to a kid, if it couldn't be fixed.

If it was true, then he had to be monstrously bitter, he'd certainly hate them. . . . I couldn't begin to figure yet what his big plan was, but I could see he had one, and evidently I was part of it. No wonder Socorro was worried. If her life's work, for whatever crazy reason, was keeping Jordan's existence a secret, she had a problem.

"Didn't you ever ask anybody who your mother is? Was?"

"You must be talking about Benita. She's the one that raised me."

Benita tried not to spoil him, Jordan said, but she ended up doing it anyway. "Actually, I had it made. I was good at reading—what else? I had the time—so I'd do their homework, Chuy's, Abel's, and in exchange they'd do stuff for me. Be my legs. Hey; I could maneuver those guys into anything. Sucker them into a fight, they'd be rolling around knocking into things—used to drive Benita crazy."

Jordan's dark frizzled sideburns, so different from the silky, reddish-sandy head hair, ended in an angle that exactly bisected the diamond jaw-point—he'd spent time and thought on that face. He caught me staring at him and gave me a knowing little male smile that should've been a joke, but wasn't.

We turned onto Jamboree, and he headed across the San Juan Creek bridge. Something is funny here, I thought. If he goes straight ahead a couple of miles, he'll come to Deirdre's place at Park Newport. Did he know . . . was that where he was headed?

At the end of the bridge he turned right instead toward East-bluff, the big residential section on this side of the bay, and then swung right again onto a little old two-lane road running along the foot of the bluffs. The road rounded a curve and we were alongside the Upper Bay and suddenly out of sight of any traffic; isolated, in another world.

The tide was out and the rich black mudflats were alive with hundreds of feeding birds, gulls and sandpipers scrabbling in the ooze, ducks in the open water and cruising the network of channels. The bay, shaped like a big hot-air balloon, empties into Newport Harbor, and we were moving along the shoreline where it begins to narrow, with a sheer bluff of dark brown rock opposite.

We jounced along over the potholes for a mile or so, with pearly gray water still as the sky on one side of us, and eroding chaparral-covered bluffs on the other.

Then Jordan pulled off the cracked paving onto a graveled turnout beside the water, and turned off the motor. His window was open, and the dusty-sweet weed smell flooded in, and creaky bird-sounds loud in the sudden quiet. Eastbluff, civilization, was at the top of the bluffs, and in those big houses silhouetted at the top of the opposite bluff. We were completely alone.

"Now," he said. "Let's get serious." He shifted his torso with those powerful arms and crossed one leg over the other with his hands like a bundle of laundry. I felt a flash of revulsion at the helpless dead flesh, and knew where the fear and loathing came from. What if that were me?

"Okay." And then neither of us spoke, each outwaiting the other in a stare-off. He leaned back with his brawny arm along the back of the seat, very casual, looking out across the still water, gray under a gray sky. I unlocked my seat belt and moved away, knowing already that he wasn't a casual person. Impulsive, maybe, but everything he did had a reason.

"Is that better?" he asked. He dropped his hand on my shoulder, a nice friendly pat, and then slid it around my neck and gave a little squeeze. "You wanna feel thee power in my feengers?" he said, playing Frito bandido.

I shrugged it away. "This is what you call serious?"

He backed off, smiling. "You've met the kids," he said. "Tell me about them. How's Keith? Looking bad, I bet. Strung out."

"No, not actually. He seems to have things pretty well under control." I didn't want to tell Jordan anything. What did he have in mind? "Which reminds me," I said. "What was the point of that mountain of clippings?"

"Simple. I just want my fair share. Figure out how much they've spent on those kids over the years. On the lawyers alone. What I'm after is a straight-up accounting."

You too? I thought. The whole world's gone money-crazy.

"Did you know that Martin's gay?" Jordan said.

"Really?"

"Sure. That's why they got him to go away to St. Louis. You meet this dude that Deirdre's mixed up with? What's he after, anyway? Wants to marry her, I bet."

"I really couldn't say."

"Deirdre sounds like a real witch," he said.

"Sort of. Very self-assured. Smart. Hey; what about you calling Vera, a couple of days after it happened?" I asked, remembering the phone call that Socorro said had spooked Vera so badly. "What was that all about?"

"Not me. I never spoke to the woman in my life." The quick one-sided smile was Keith's, or Deirdre's, and even his smallest movements and gestures were definitive Tenhagen. I didn't really need any more proof. I was convinced.

He sat staring at the water, watching a file of seven ducks evenly spaced move down the exact middle of a narrow channel, leaving a single perfect V of wake.

"Isn't that nice?" he said, nodding toward them. I was beginning to wonder if he was playing with me, just pulling my strings. But Jordan seemed to be living outside the usual time frame. His childhood would have been like that, too; endless hours of sitting and dreaming . . . of his rich father on the hill, and their grand reconciliation?

"You know why it happened right now, don't you," he said. "Them killing him, I mean. Because he was about to recognize me. So totally greedy . . . Keith with that drug habit, his mother thinks she wants him to quit but still she all the time gives him money, supposedly for other stuff. . . . It didn't need to've happened. He was surrounded by enemies. If I'd made my move sooner, I would've been there and then it'd be too late, they couldn't've got away with it."

Suddenly about to recognize him, after how many years? I just listened, sick. "And you know what else?" he said. "I figure you've sold out to them. They got to you, too, didn't they. Sent you to buy me off, so I'll give up the hunt. But just to spoil any wrong impressions you might have about me . . ."

He straightened up and settled himself and a gun appeared in his hand, a flat little black pistol with a square shiny butt. "I'm not exactly helpless."

A patch of my scalp prickled and I turned my startled yip into a little cough and went on smiling, being a good audience. I had no alternatives. He'd locked the door again when we'd started up on Main; I had no way out.

"Whoa—that's pretty slick. How'd you do that, anyway?"

He showed me the bracket he'd fixed for the gun just under the edge of the seat, and made it appear and disappear a couple more times, smooth as silk.

"One thing I don't understand," I said. "First you say they're trying to kill me because I know something, and the next thing I'm on their side in some way. That doesn't track."

"You know how far we are from there?" Jordan said, and I knew he meant the Tenhagen house. "A little over two miles. Straight up."

"And that's where you want to go?"

"Read my mind."

Another string of ducks glided down the channel closest to us, always at the same pace, and otherwise so motionless they looked mechanical. Jordan looked at them and back at me. I returned his stare.

"You really think you can hypnotize me?" he said. "Better not try: you could damage your brain badly, and I'd hate to see you get hurt. You did a nice job on those ducks, though. You're planning to wait till they get to where the leader is just parallel with that white stick over there, and then the whole world will explode." The place on my scalp prickled again. "But you don't have to worry," he said. "I won't let it."

Fantásticos, Socorro had said, all kinds of wild ideas; but a good kid at heart. "You like to play games, don't you."

"You better hope I do. The truth is, I don't really need the gun—I have my kundalini powers, and nothing can prevail against them. But I don't want to use them unless I have to, because it could change the orbital paths and seriously derange the universe." Then he turned away, looking disgusted, and said, "It doesn't matter."

When he turned back to me his face was transformed by a big, relaxed grin. "Not bad, hey?" he said. A lone bicyclist had just come around the curve ahead, about half a mile away.

"Listen, I've really got to be getting back," I said. "You said something about a plan of yours?"

"Right. Being as you're in so thick with Deirdre. . . . Say you were out for a ride with her, in your car, of course—you'd have to have a pretty strong reason, it's quite a ways. There's a cabin I know about up in the mountains, off the Ortega Highway. Real isolated." He was waiting for me to react. I didn't.

"You want to get the truth as bad as me, don't you?" he said. "We'd have plenty of time to question her without any interruptions. No pain, nothing like that. Oh, maybe a little sensory deprivation. . . ." His eyes glittered behind his sunglasses and he had a naughty, gleeful smile.

"Oh, man—can't you be serious?"

"You want to see serious?" The gun had jumped into his hand again. The bicyclist was getting closer, and Jordan pointed it out the window, resting the muzzle on the door with his left arm lying over it to conceal it. "I'll show you serious."

The guy on the bike was really winded, red-faced and sweating under his blue-and-white baseball cap, in spite of the cool day—I was mortally certain Jordan wouldn't do anything, but still I hated him for jerking my strings. I wanted to yell something at him but I didn't say anything—how sure could you be? I didn't move.

Jordan raised his free hand and they both said "Hiya," and I made a sound, and the guy went on by.

"*Jeez*, you bother me," I said. "Come on, take me back now."

Jordan laughed and started the engine. The gun was already out of sight. "You don't care for my sense of humor." He pulled out and drove on ahead, instead of back the way we'd come. "Never retrace your footsteps, if you can help it," he said. "That's how terrorists get their victims, did you know that? They look for your routine, and use it against you."

As he turned onto Jamboree and into the afternoon traffic, the van hit a rough patch of street and bucked, and Jordan swore under his breath. "Maybe that's partly why," he said, talking to himself. "Because he figured I couldn't do all the things he could. And don't you ever try to scare my wife again with stuff like that 'danger' crap; you hear?"

"It got your attention, didn't it? Isn't that what games are for?"

We had a wild ride back, cutting in and out of traffic. I did try to convince him that threatening Deirdre or any of the Tenhagens would be the worst move possible. "That's never going to work. You do something like that, and the Tenhagens'll have their lawyers down on you so fast you'll never see daylight again. Then they'd have it all their own way. Not to mention how much worse off Lupe and the baby would be."

After that I just hung on to the handhold over my door and kept my mouth shut. Jordan glanced at me every now and then to see how I was taking it. I tried to remind myself that Jordan's problems were not mine, I had enough to do looking out for myself; but along with everything else, I wanted to get at the truth.

When Jordan let me out again in the T. Ambrose parking lot, he offered to find me a handgun so I'd have some protection, and I refused nicely. He shrugged. "It's your funeral. Well, I'll be in touch." He punched in a tape cassette, swinging onto the street with some heavy metal thing blaring, and I started back into the office. Now I had my wedge, my way into the castle. It was time to assault the Tenhagen citadel head-on.

 The office door was locked. I could see that Arlene's PC was turned on, but nobody was inside; and of course my keys were in my purse, in my office. She must've gone out for a taco, I thought, and I went over to wait for her in my car. I had plenty to think about—too much. My brain jumped with wild possibilities.

Jordan. Vera's original soft words, "Our first was stillborn." Had she meant dead to her, because she couldn't accept him? Say he was hers but not Arnie's . . . illegitimate, born before she married Arnie—then Jordan would have to be in his mid-thirties, and he didn't seem old enough. Of course, his sheltered life could explain that mixture of naïveté and calculation that made him seem so young. . . . Child of rape, or incest; and Vera's shaking fits, blackouts, times when she was suddenly reminded of what happened, and couldn't face it.

My shoulder ached from the rough ride, and the eggplant bruise was throbbing, each pulse beat a painful reminder . . . that was something else Vera didn't know about yet. I got out a tissue and started to wipe away the concealing makeup.

Arlene's Firebird bounced into the parking lot and she braked in front of the door with a screech, pranced up the steps, and unlocked the door one-handed, balancing a camera on her shoulder.

"Hey, you missed all the excitement," she said when I came in. She waved the office Nikon at me. "Crane tipped over on a big job in Orange, I mean a big one, and they needed pictures right now. What could I do? I couldn't find any of you guys— not that I know one end of a camera from the other, actually. Sure hope there was film in it. Seemed to be advancing okay, anyway."

"They're probably terrific," I said, crossing my fingers. The contractor would have a whopping performance bond, time was of the essence, and service to our clients was Leo's First Commandment. They'd better be.

I dropped off the roll of film at the lab on my way to the Tenhagens. Socorro had told me Vera would be home by six.

That fast white twilight you get on the coast had already dimmed down into night when I pulled into the Tenhagens' driveway. The ground lamps in the shrubbery made long split-leaf shadows sliding along the wall and sharpened the edges of those tropical plants that look like clusters of sword-blades.

Socorro opened the door, frowning. "She's not home yet. Comes anytime now. Listen; what you going to talk about with her?"

"You've been having a good time with me, haven't you. Letting me think Jordan was yours."

She grinned briefly and nodded. "Yah, pretty good. 'Ey, why not? We keep him alive, no?"

"So now I've got to talk to her direct. Something you should've done years ago, no matter what you promised Mr. Ten."

She shook her head. "Don't do it. It brings more trouble."

"Hey, I'm going to. After all this? What is it you're afraid of, anyway?"

"Is that you, Moz?" A familiar voice—Keith called up to me from the other end of the darkened hall, and my heart leapt in the old erotic surge, unwanted and at that moment worse, a distraction and a handicap. I could see him silhouetted against the window wall. "Come on down," he said. "Gee, this is a great surprise."

The living room was in darkness, and we stood side by side looking at the view. All the street lamps on the peninsula and the islands were jewels glowing through a thin fog that veiled the harbor in a tissue of light.

"Incredible," I said. Outside the lighted pool blazed blue, a huge crystal sunk into the ground.

"Isn't it terrific?" he said. "I never get tired of looking. Come on, let's go outside." He dimmed the pool lights and slid the door open, and helped me over the threshold, keeping hold of my hand.

"Watch your step here—" The gesture was paternal, a social courtesy that would've been Arnie's. Can all your senses lie? I still couldn't believe that Keith was capable of killing anybody. Whatever had happened between him and his father, Keith's personality, his whole world was saturated with Arnie's influence and always would be.

"Look, there's the ferry starting across." He pointed with his free hand. Then he turned toward me, holding both my hands cupped against his chest.

"I'm really glad to see you—probably you came for Mother, right?—because I've been wanting to apologize, and waiting for the right chance. I made sort of an ass of myself the other night. . . ."

"I agree." You could've called anytime, I thought. I could feel his heart beating strong and steady. Our pulses seemed synchronized. "Whenever you see something you want, you just go for it; right?"

"Oh, God, if I knew. What happened is I had too much, too much of everything, I guess. Anyway, I hope I'll get a chance to make it up. Show you that I have another side."

"We'll see." I pulled away. "Anyway, if—"

"What brings you up here? Any luck so far?"

"Mm—some stuff I've got to ask your mother about." He didn't pursue it, obviously because he didn't want to know any more. "Genes are fascinating, aren't they," I said. "You've got your mother's chin exactly, but then it completely skipped Deirdre. I'd know it anywhere."

He had such a resigned, wistful look—did Keith know about Jordan, had he for a long time? I could imagine him doing almost anything to conceal other people's secrets, to avoid the pain of getting involved. I pulled away and turned toward the ocean. I was doing it again; blocking out any thought of Keith as a liar, thief, murderer.

We heard the muffled sound of a powerful motor being gunned inside a closed garage, and he moved me back inside. "That'll be Mother," he said. "I've got some people waiting, I'll leave you two to your conversation. Catch up with you later, okay?" He started to whistle as he went back down the darkened hall. Whistling in the dark. Such a nice boy. . . . But Ted Bundy had been a nice boy too, and good-looking; lots of girls thought so. You can't go by looks, girls.

A minute later Vera strode by in her stocking feet with her boots under one arm. "Yes, Moz," she said. "We had some problems at the stables. Be with you in a few minutes, I just need to wash off some of this muck." She went on down the corridor, moving through the shifting light from outside, and opened a door at the end. That wing must be the master suite, hers and Arnie's.

I waited in the dim living room bathed in the quivering water reflections. It was like being underwater, or in an alcove alongside a huge aquarium. My head was pounding and I wanted to ask Socorro for an aspirin, but I didn't want to speak to her right now for fear Vera might find it suspicious.

Why would Vera possibly tell me anything? A family secret kept hidden all these years. . . . All she had to say was "None of your business, Moz," and "Get out," and that would be it. Because I was the most recent victim; and if Deirdre was anxious to keep it quiet, Vera would be even more so.

"Moz?" Vera called from an open door part way down the corridor. "Come on down."

She closed the door firmly behind me and then lowered the lights. "We ran into a little snag out at Twelvetrees this afternoon," she said. "The books didn't balance. Not a very large discrepancy, but I wanted to deal with it immediately."

The room was an uncurtained artist's studio with big north windows and fluorescent fixtures overhead, white walls with oil paintings stacked around and several of them framed and hung, all paintings of flowers. A bunch of larger-than-life-size daisies yellow and orange centered the inner wall, the flowers hard-edged and painstakingly ragged and monumental. Even the three fallen petals seemed to be of stone.

"My quote-unquote artistic phase," Vera said. "Therapy, really. I never spent enough time at it to get very good."

Vera was wearing a long cotton kimono with an abstract pattern, olive-green on white, and her hair was combed back wet. She motioned me to a wicker settee beside the window, looking out on the three-tiered fountain of terra cotta, its lifting spiral illuminated from underneath. She had already made tea, and now she filled our cups; but neither of us ever touched it.

"What's happened?" Vera said. "Must be something important, to bring you up here this time of day. . . . And you've hurt yourself." She said it almost reluctantly, the reaction so delayed that I figured Deirdre had already told her about it.

"Yes. I had a bad fall yesterday. I should've come to you right away."

"Me? What for?"

"I'll get to that. First of all, your first child wasn't actually stillborn, was he—"

Vera froze. "You're trying to pry into our family privacy, and I won't allow it. I don't intend to discuss anything."

"—And his name was Jordan. I'm afraid you'll have to—he's alive and well, practically. I saw him this afternoon."

"That's impossible." She snapped upright, frowning, but at the same time seeming to relish the challenge. It seemed an odd response, a little off-center.

"And that's why you're here?" she said. "You've been digging around, trying to get something on us— Oh, I can't believe this!" She threw her head back, hands over her face; then she crouched over her lap with her face still covered, shaking and making little whimpering noises that sounded almost like laughter. I was afraid she was going into one of the shaking fits Deirdre had described.

"Vera?" Finally she sat up and looked at me. Her eyes were wet but her face was calm, she was in control again. "I'm sorry," I said, "but you've got to deal with this. He's serious. He's convinced he belongs up here."

"Ridiculous. He's an impostor, and this is some kind of a scam. I guess you'll have to go ahead and tell me the rest of it."

I did, the phone calls and my meeting with Jordan, anyway, telescoping past any mention of Deirdre, let that be her responsibility; and finishing with his accusation of the other children.

"I'm shocked to think you'd be a party to something like this," Vera said. "Out-and-out blackmail, by the sound."

"Me? How? With what? Listen, I'm confused. I came to you with this direct—I could find out other ways, there must be records we can investigate. My God, I could even have gone to the newspapers, but I didn't; I wouldn't do that. I wanted to hear it from you."

"Oh, dear God. After all these years . . ." She leaned forward, hands clasped between her knees. "You wonder how such things can happen. We're decent people, we've always tried to do the right thing— All right; I'm going to tell you the truth of it, so you can see just how you're being used. This has got to be absolutely private. Do I have your word on that?"

I nodded and looked sincere, wanting to shake her to get her started. Yes, she said, their first child had been a boy, named Jordan—severely retarded, and institutionalized all his life.

"I didn't even know he existed till after Keith was born," she said. "Seven years. Can you believe that? The very first night I was home from the hospital. Arnie was pretty high, feeling no pain—he had two healthy, whole sons now, and he was on top of the world. So he finally told me his bloody little story. To relieve his conscience, of course.

"You have to understand how different the world was then," she said. They were in love, and it was 1951; her parents disapproved of Arnie, a nobody with no background, no family, and an uncertain future, to say the least. Arnie's pride was assaulted, terrible things were said all around, and Vera and her family disowned one another. "We've made it up long since, of course. Oh, we were so young and innocent—naive, really. None of my children has ever been that young."

They ran away to get married. Arnie got a government job he hated, working on the aqueduct, and they were living in a little desert town when she got pregnant. It was a perfectly normal pregnancy, the usual morning sickness but nothing else—she was to deliver in the local clinic. She went into labor on the Fourth of July weekend, when her regular doctor was out of town, and so she had to be tended by his alternate.

"The man was utterly incompetent. Drunk, to begin with; and he got drunker as the thing went on. Talking the way people do—you know, very careful, exaggerated. Arnie took an instant dislike to him, and utterly justified, as it turned out." It was a long labor, the baby was breech and the doctor couldn't get him turned. Arnie heard her screaming, and stormed into the delivery room threatening to sue the man, have him disqualified. The doctor had Arnie thrown out.

"I only heard about it afterward, of course—I was mostly out of it, they'd given me so much stuff, and the spinal made me cold and far away—that scared Arnie, too, he kept thinking, what if this drunken fool did it wrong and paralyzed me?"

She began to worry only after she woke up next morning, when she asked to see the baby and the nurse kept putting her off. When Arnie finally came in, she took one look at him and guessed the worst. He was haggard and red-eyed, haunted-looking. The baby hadn't lived, he told her. It was deformed, and even if it had survived, it would've been severely retarded.

"He was crying, we were crying together; we had nobody but ourselves and we had to comfort each other." Well, that was part of the story, but not all, Vera said . . . she seemed tired now and talked slowly, hesitating before she spoke. "He didn't get around to telling me the whole truth till seven years later."

Which was when Arnie confessed that the baby, Jordan, actually had survived. The doctor had told Arnie that his son was hydrocephalic, a vegetable, and couldn't survive more than a year or two at most. So Arnie arranged to have it sent away to an institution, afraid that if Vera knew the truth she would refuse to have any more children.

"Somehow he convinced me that this was a one-time thing, caused by this quack, and not hereditary; and so . . . you see? All those years he carried around that big lie. I was appalled. Stunned. Here I was with a houseful of babies—Keith had the worst colic, and Martin's asthma flared up, of course, reacting to the new baby—doing my damnedest to keep the family together.

"Oh, I know he was ashamed; he cried. And he was a good man, really—everybody saw him as so tough. You know, strong, independent; a doer. But when it came to the really tough personal decisions, he—just couldn't make them. Easier to let things slide, we'll see what develops—and that's essentially what he did in this case." She was weeping quietly now, remembering. I felt her pain, and my eyes filled with tears too.

"With Jordan," I said. It bothered me that she never called him by name. Because she couldn't stand to think of him as a person? She still hadn't come to grips with it. "Did you go to see him?"

"Never. Arnie didn't want me to; said he was this grotesque, pitiful little thing, that by rights should've died."

"I'm sorry," I said. "But Arnie lied about that, too. Vera, you've got to see him once, anyway. He's really quite competent, and he's the spitting image—he's absolutely a Tenhagen."

"Never," she said. "I have too much respect for Arnie's memory to ever do that. I know he never lied to me afterward, he knew I wouldn't've gone on living with him. Where the family was concerned, he relied on my judgment totally—if anything, our relationship was all the stronger for it. We had a good life together, as it happens, a wonderful marriage. No woman was ever happier. I trusted him completely, and I won't dishonor his memory with one minute's doubt."

The tears were sliding down Vera's cheeks, and she wiped her jaw along her shoulder. She'll never be able to admit he lied to her twice, I thought. I touched her hand and she took hold of mine, holding on tight, and we sat like that for a moment, not looking at one another. Then she got up and found a tissue and blew her nose.

"All right," she said. "Let's hear about this fall of yours yesterday. How did it happen?"

"I wish now I'd gone straight to the police." I described the thread of light—probably nylon fishing line, I'd decided—and my plunge down the concrete stairs. "I can only figure it was done because I know something—God, if I could figure out what!"

"Obviously it's some kind of blackmail business, and this is a way to bring pressure," Vera said.

"What? Where do you see that? Nobody's even made a move in that direction. And what good does falling on my head do? I'm not the one with the money."

"A gesture. A warning."

"Crazy. In any case, Jordan obviously couldn't've done it."

"Stop calling him Jordan! Of course they'd get someone crippled, and with some resemblance to us, to be the front person. You're being used, Moz, can't you understand that? And you can just go back and tell them to forget it; I'm not their— pigeon."

"That's ridiculous. If you seriously thought I was in on some blackmail thing, you'd be calling the police right now. Do you know why you haven't?"

"Because I can't handle any more public attention, I can't cope with it. What I am going to do is turn it over to our attorneys, first thing in the morning. Somebody very clever and unscrupulous found out about this—"

"Good. And they can straighten out this whole Jordan business. Maybe they'll convince you that you're in more danger now than ever."

"Stop this! There isn't any danger—can't you get that through your skull? It wasn't arson, it was an accident! An accident!" She sagged back in her chair with her hands over her face. "I think you'd better leave."

"Right." I went on out. What a mess. How could a supposedly capable adult refuse to look the truth in the eye? Vera certainly believed what she said—or else she was a wonderfully gifted liar.

When I was already at the end of the corridor, Vera called to me. "Moz?" She stood outside her door and the pool reflections crawled over the wall and ceiling and over her.

"I'm just too tired to think tonight, Moz. I'll call you in a day or two, when I've recovered a little more. Drive carefully." As if I were one of her kids. Being the good mommy.

As I passed by the darkened living room, the empty pool outside moved by itself, rocking, and Keith and I were swimming there, lifting our arms, stroking in unison. And the cool flesh afterward, relaxed drugged arms and legs smelling of chlorine. . . . Moz, you are a sick person.

A wonderful smell came from the kitchen, warm and spicy; a curry. Socorro looked up as I passed, she'd been watching for me. "How it goes?" she asked softly.

"Oh, she thinks he's a fake and we're . . . somebody's trying to blackmail her."

"What is this, blackmail?"

I started to explain, and Socorro understood all right. She snorted. "You see? I know she gonna say that."

"Well, you can certainly prove the truth of it, can't you? Listen, we need to get together and talk."

"I'm real tired of this place," Socorro said. "Too many rooms. Why one, two people need so many rooms for? I'm all fed up. Too hard on the legs."

"Socorro?" I jumped: Vera's voice was right in the room with us. Socorro laughed at me and pointed to the intercom speaker.

"Uh-huh—I think maybe about time to go somewheres else," Socorro said. She flipped the switch and answered. "Yah? Right here, Mrs. Ten."

I waved good-bye and let myself out. The Tenhagen palace was tainted. What else might Arnie have done to build his perfect little empire? The Rockefellers had their slave trade, the Roosevelts, opium. . . . How did you think millionaires got that way? I reminded myself. All Arnie did was hide away a damaged child; so, big deal. Theirs was just good business; this was a private matter. Personal. And Keith—had he maybe known about it all along? That might make one a bit cold-blooded.

 If not Jordan, then who? I'd swear Vera believed what she'd told me, and that Jordan did, too. Probably they were both lying somewhat, anyway, and what could I do? How can you psych out somebody who rearranges the world because he needs it to be that way? Hopeless. Tired, sick, I navigated home with a roaring in my ears that blocked out the evening traffic, and hauled myself whimpering up the narrow stairs.

If Vera pursued her blackmail nonsense, I'd be hearing from her lawyer soon enough, which Leo wouldn't care for at all. Deirdre looked to be right, Jordan was what he seemed to be, and I was back there at square one again.

Figure Keith killed the dog and set the snare for this rabbit. It didn't make any sense, but then dopers and drunks tend not to . . . . Get descriptions of what had been stolen from Tenhagen, and find out if anything had turned up. And if not Keith, who else?

Fran wasn't home yet, but otherwise everything seemed normal. The man next door was out in his garage hammering on something, Mrs. Chaney's green-monster yard light made everything look like a bad movie, and inside the main house, Toto yapped her little heart out.

At eight twenty-five, Deirdre called. "Just checking to see if you're still alive," she said. "What news?"

"I finally got to meet your brother in the flesh today: the secret one. Which you've no doubt heard about already."

"*What?* Where? What did he say? Why didn't you call me?"

"Why don't you ask your mother? She knows the whole story."

"Oh, my God—you didn't!"

"Ah, but I did. And she didn't crumble, or have any seizures—she's got quite a story to tell. Don't you girls ever communicate?"

"Where did you find him?"

"Under a toadstool, down in the dell—a little shop in downtown Santa Ana that sells tape cassettes, including secondhand. They're on the edge of bankruptcy, by the looks. Jordan's been right there all the time. Your mother can fill you in on the rest. She thinks I'm the front end of a sinister blackmail plot. I think she's been living in Newport Beach too long."

"What's the name of the place?"

"El Lobo Rojo. You go play detective for a while, and good luck. Speaking of which, describe to me exactly what was stolen from the *Spray*. Those 'antique nautical instruments.'"

"You're still going on with this. What are you, a glutton for punishment?"

"What are you, the one who pushed me? Or only related?" For a rare instant Deirdre was quiet, and I could feel her weighing and deciding. Be civil to Moz, she finds out things; versus, what if she finds some proof it was Keith?

"As I recall," Deirdre said, "there were three items taken. One was a dry card compass in a box maybe a foot square, with a sliding lid; that seemed odd, fairly bulky and harder to hide.

And there was a miniature double-frame sextant, and a Seth Thomas ship's clock with a bell that hung down from the bottom."

"Excellent. Worth how much, would you say? I mean individually."

"I don't recall. Generally we leave the price tag off our gifts . . . . Just tell me one thing more before I meet him. What, in your opinion, does Jordan want?"

"To be honest, I think he wants in. To be recognized as part of the family. Acknowledged. I'd imagine he has some rights to your father's estate."

"But we don't actually know that, nothing's been proved. The blackmail idea isn't too farfetched, is it. That may sound a bit hard; but remember, to me he's only a stranger, and a pain. How could I feel otherwise?"

"I think you better meet him yourself," I said. "Before you jump to any conclusions." Let her take a good look, and then see if she could believe Vera's claim that Jordan was an impostor. I told her how to find El Lobo Rojo.

"And you might want to stay out of his van," I said. "He can have his flaky moments."

Eleven P.M., and still no Fran. Something must have gone wrong at the hospital. I tried calling UCI Medical Center, but nobody could tell me anything. I could hardly bar the door tonight, leave her standing out in the cold. . . . I rigged up a pyramid of pans against the door, made up Fran's bed, and crawled gratefully into my own.

I dreamed that I'd fallen into an icy swift mountain stream and somehow dragged myself up onto a floating log and managed to straddle it. But the log kept twisting in the current as I tried not to get my legs smashed against the rocks. They were numb, I was slipping off and hanging on for dear life—I woke up and lay rigid, listening.

The pans went down with a crash. "Hey, what's this?" Fran said. I rolled over and looked at the clock: Three forty-nine.

"How come you're so late? How's Rick?" I hung on to my elbows, shaking so hard I could barely talk.

"It was like they thought, a blood clot. He got into surgery very late."

"And. . . ?" We looked at each other and Fran shrugged, exhausted and resigned.

"I waited till he came out of the recovery room," she said. "He wasn't conscious, of course. We may know more tomorrow. . . . Lord, but you look awful. Get back to bed, before you catch your death." We laughed ruefully at the irony of it and hugged one another.

Fran must've gone to sleep as soon as she turned out the lights—in a couple of minutes there was a light snore. She was still asleep next morning when I let myself out.

A pale sun had begun to percolate through the fog, melting the mist on the car windows into sudden braiding streamlets. Leo's car was parked outside T. Ambrose, and the smell of mildewed carpet was potent this morning. Arlene, deep in her periodic argument with Bob Fryer over his imaginative expense account, looked up with a strained little smile.

"Boss's been looking for you. Going to be here all morning?" I said yes, and they went back to their argument. Leo's door was closed.

There were two messages on my answering machine; one routine, and the other a man's voice, just a few words run together. A hesitation and then ". . . Hodges thinks you ought to know—" was what it sounded like, broken off in mid-sentence. The voice seemed vaguely familiar, but I couldn't place it, even after a quick trip through my files to see if any of the names there clicked. It didn't seem very important. This guy sounded too halfhearted and tentative to be a threat.

The top form in my "in" box had a note clipped to it, SEE ME, in Leo's vivid black felt-pen slash, and the form itself was popping with items circled in red. When I looked up, Leo was standing in his office door staring at me.

"Come on in, Moz, and close the door," he said, sitting down at his desk, and I got that old sinking feeling right away. Leo was in his shirtsleeves, with dark circles under his eyes— hung over, maybe? He was leaning his forearms on the desk and rolling a pen in his hands, looking at it.

"When you started here, Moz, I had high hopes. . . ." I knew then for sure that he was going to fire me. He exhaled and started again. "We have a certain level of service to maintain here. Provided we intend to stay in business, that is. Which I do. I've spent seventeen years of my life building this up—ah, hell." He hit his chest with the side of his fist. I knew the sign. I was giving him heartburn.

"To begin with, the Yeo case. Open and shut, no sweat; am I right? Well, evidently she couldn't stand the suspense, waiting for you to follow up, because now she's gotten herself a lawyer." There was plenty more; reports that were late, incomplete, just plain wrong.

"Not to mention these." He dumped out a sheaf of photographs on the desk, blurred almost beyond recognition, Arlene's lighthearted pictures of the crane accident. "What the hell good do you think these are? Do you have any idea the size claim we're talking about here?"

There was no point in arguing and I didn't, just stood there and felt the heat rising.

"What I think you want to do now," he said, "is get your act together. Clean up these cases, and then take a couple of weeks off to work on your private life. Once that's done, we can talk. You think?"

"Sounds fair." I didn't feel like discussing it. Everything was crumbling around me and blowing away. My future looked like the Dust Bowl and it was my own fault, I'd been kidding myself. The day I started at T. Ambrose I'd stood right here and nodded and smiled when Leo told me, "If you want to be treated like one of the boys, you've got to produce like one of the boys."

About as tough as buttermilk, Leo was, and underneath I

could hear him saying that maybe I could negotiate something later, if I got my act together in the meantime.

No tears, no pleading; I took it like a little man, like one of the boys, and Leo sagged back in relief. "Close the door behind you, Moz, okay? And good luck."

I felt like a balloon with the string cut. Arlene watched me come out of Leo's office and I knew she knew; her look was pure sugar crystallizing around the edges. Suddenly the gray-brown aerial map of Orange County in 1967, the reams of paper stacked like glossy green bricks, the whole office had the glaze of a scene remembered from the past. Instant nostalgia.

I sat down and flailed away at the paperwork for a while, ignoring that old out-of-a-job panic clutching my stomach. I had a few hundred put away, I could manage—about one month's rent and a car payment. Plenty of other things I could do. Earning a living was a damn nuisance anyway, interfered with the important stuff. Would I be eligible for unemployment?

This time it was Gage Pfeiffer on the phone. "You got a few minutes, we could meet somewhere? I've got some good news, and some bad news."

We met in a new little park just off the San Diego Freeway, a half-block of lawn with six saplings, some swings, and three picnic tables. When Gage turned to look at me, his pupils dilated in that universal *I want it* reaction that probably goes right down through the primates to the lemurs. I was vibrating like a bass guitar string, and surprised to be so vulnerable. Funny how having the right person interested can turn you on, just like that.

Gage had found out quite a lot about Jordan. Straight arrow, paid his bills, no criminal record. "The store was held up once, but they sure didn't get much. He's got a drinking buddy and a workout buddy; both relationships look to be normal. Works out at a gym several mornings a week. Other guy's a double amputee, stepped on a booby trap in Vietnam. They call themselves the Dynamic Duo."

None of it mattered now, and anyway, Gage could've told me over the phone; only then he wouldn't be here with me. "Was that the good news, or the bad?"

He looked at me. "Our witness is back in town, and I finally got to talk to him. Says it was foggy that morning, and all he ever saw was a guy in a black wet suit and blue fins climbing up onto the deck. Figured he was cleaning the hull. Never saw the face, too far away anyway."

My last lead, gurgling down the drain. "And that's it?"

"Hell, it's nothing to him. He just doesn't want to be bothered, I could see that. But what can you do?"

A flat-bed truck backed into the little parking area, and we both watched as the driver let down the back end and began to unload a riding mower. "Have you told any of the family about it?" I asked.

"Why? I did suggest to the guy that he go talk to the Newport Beach Police. But I know he won't. . . . That grass is too wet to cut," Gage said, as the mower's engine coughed and took hold.

"Tell him."

Gage grinned. "So, what else've you been up to. Anything?"

All the time I was describing my meeting with Jordan, and Vera's big story about Arnie hiding his deformed son, Gage sat leaning against a picnic table with his foot up on his knee, bouncing impatiently, and his scowl deepening.

"Which is it you don't approve of now?" I said. "The story, or me personally?"

"Not true. I think you're a very capable and intelligent woman, with all kinds of drive—too much, maybe. Because that's way out of line. Going into the woman's house and spying on her!"

"Oh, really. But if it's Jordan, that's okay, right? Because he doesn't have the big bucks."

"Come on—you can see the difference as easy as I can. Anyway; this pretty well locks it up, wouldn't you say? There's an excellent chance now that we'll never find out who did it."

I just waited. We were going to have a neat fight, and I was ready.

"You don't like that at all," he said, "but you won't say so. You don't trust me, so you're going to shut me out. Or is it men in general you feel that way about?"

I sneered. "I'm serious," Gage said. "You behave like a— female chauvinist. I believe that's your cute term for it."

"Whose cute term? Only one person here using it that I've heard. You must not have enough to do today." I was disgusted with myself for trying to play the laid-back young professional just so I'd fit into Gage's solid-citizen frame, which wasn't mine; no way.

"Leo fired me this morning," I said.

Gage got very quiet and I told him about it. "I can see his side," I said. "Tell you the truth, he was quite a bit in the right."

"So. What are your plans now?" Gage asked.

"Haven't made any yet. Clean up my open cases, and then we'll see. I'll manage."

We sat and watched the man bouncing along on his blatting mower, and then Gage looked at his watch. "Hell, I'm due in Dana Harbor." We got up and started toward our cars.

". . . Oh, I know you will. Manage," Gage said. He put his arm around my shoulders with a friendly squeeze that developed into an awkward smooch on the cheek.

"We can do better than that," he said, and kissed me square on the mouth. It was like discovering a new galaxy, the shape and feel of Gage mixed in with the snarling motor and the smell of cut grass, and I wanted not to stop.

We broke apart. "Huh."

"Yup," was all he said, grinning like a fool. He saw me to my car. "I'll call you later, okay?" He bent into the open window, kissed me on the cheek again and banged his head. I drove away not thinking about Gage, saving it for later, with a warm feeling under my ribs like soup on a cold day.

Ups and downs. I finished the day at the Newport Y, swimming laps to shut out the whole mess, ignoring the steady pulse of pain in my bruised head. The Y is situated at the head of Upper Newport Bay, and from the deck of the four-foot pool I could look down across dead plowed slopes to the water, now just after sunset a preposterous sheet of shell-pink foil spread between the dark bluffs, holding more light than all the sky.

When I dragged myself out, feeble and wrinkle-fingered, the lifeguard gave me a worried look. In the shower room I saw why: the makeup had all washed away and exposed the eggplant bruise.

Fran, just back from the hospital, said that while she was waiting to see Rick, he'd had a seizure. "That's good, believe it or not. Sign the brain is coming back to life."

Fran was fascinated by Vera and her story of Arnie's great deception. She listened without interrupting, her eyes narrowed. A contemptuous smile began to widen.

"What?" I asked.

"That's ridiculous," Fran said. "And you believed her? You can't live with someone for years and not be aware that something's bothering them. Unless you don't want to know."

"I don't agree."

"But then, you've never been married, have you," she said.

The truth was too complicated. "No," I said, "but I've lived with a man." Your son, for one. We exchanged the thought and left it unvoiced. "And I certainly didn't know what he thought, or even did, most of the time." Fran was shaking her head at my pigheadedness.

"Listen," I said. "I'm the one who was talking to Vera, and she told me the complete truth as she knows it. You'll just have to take my word for that." Fran looked away, embarrassed and still shaking her head.

"Nope," she said. "Vera preferred peace at any price. Sitting on top of the world. Up to her hips in clover, and didn't want to jeopardize it in any way."

"I can see that! What I think is, she's clinging to this because she's afraid to find out the truth. She's trying to protect her children."

"Nonsense. That woman has got you all tied up with a ribbon on it, hasn't she? When you've lived as long as I have . . ." I could have hit her. We were both totally exasperated and got up simultaneously, each of us reaching for a dish to take to the kitchen—any other time I might've laughed; but I was furious.

We kept quiet for a while, doing separate chores, and then Fran said in a small voice, "I've been quite stupid, and I hope you'll excuse me. You've gone way beyond anything called for here—"

"Come on, stop with that stuff. You're the one who's had it all on your back."

She sighed. "I think I'll make us some nice cocoa, would you like that? . . . You're quitting, aren't you? I don't blame you a bit."

"No," I said. "I couldn't if I wanted to. It's just that I'm fresh out of ideas. . . . Because he's still out there, you know?"

"In which case . . ." Fran picked up a chair and went over and wedged it under the doorknob, like the first night.

"If we could only draw him—or her—out," she said. "Scare them. Make them think we do know something."

"You mean, put out some bait. I thought I already did. Or was." Then, finally, the light came on.

"Something better," I said. "Gage Pfeiffer finally talked to the witness. And it's no good. He didn't see enough."

Fran sagged. "Well, that's a great help."

"Yes, it is. Because nobody knows that but us, so far. What if we tell them all the opposite?"

Below her gray-and-tan curls Fran's eyes gleamed, a wily old predator taking the scent. "Oh, I like it," she said. "Let's play around with that a little."

So obvious. Tell each of them that the witness could in fact identify the arsonist. Naturally the police don't want to reveal it yet, that would spoil their investigation. Why couldn't it work, if just for a little while? And I'd be off the hook, no longer the mysterious threat, but just a spectator again; watching to see who jumped, and which way.

16 I found out pretty young that to tell a lie really well you have to believe it, during the telling anyway. I delivered my news to Deirdre's answering machine with just the right tone of controlled excitement, winging in the little darts of disinformation as cool as any politician. By the time I got to El Lobo Rojo next morning, I was primed. Keep it low-key. "Right, exactly; a clear view. Said he'd know the guy anywhere."

But Jordan wasn't there; and Lupe was worried about it.

"He goes away very early this morning like always, to his gym. But then he didn't come back. Always he comes back for us so we can open up the shop. He never missed before, never. I had to call Chuy to bring us down so we could open up on time."

She looked at me with suspicion. "Last time you come in here, you talk about some danger. Now you tell me, please, what danger this is."

"Maybe you should talk to Socorro," I said.

"I already did. She doesn't know nothing, either." Two middle-aged women came into the store, and Lupe went to help them. I looked into the crowded little back room, where Miguel was pushing a milk carton around his playpen and making a spluttery motor sound. He sat back and gave me a Keithy-baby grin. No Jordan.

Lupe backed up to the doorway where she could keep an eye on both her customers and the baby—or me. I was trying to suppress the obvious horrible thought. What if Jordan had gone through with his dippy plan, and actually tried to kidnap Deirdre on his own?

"Maybe I'll call Socorro myself. Okay?" I said, pointing to the phone on the crowded desk, alongside a clutch of jars of baby food. Lupe nodded.

Socorro was worried, too. "I thought maybe you would know," she said. "Lupe say he talk to you, you give him some good ideas."

"Not me," I said. "He had plenty of his own."

". . . And that next time he goes for the real thing."

"What does that mean?"

"How do I know? Besides . . . you know yesterday Deirdre comes there to see him?"

"Whoa."

"Uh-huh. So now I think, what's going on? Anyway, I call Deirdre's, she not home. Could you maybe call her office, where she works?" She gave me the number.

Deirdre was out of the office, called away to a meeting. Her secretary was good at tones, too—sincere but reserved, and don't pursue it. I didn't envy her lot in life as Deirdre's sergeant.

I called Socorro back. "Are you thinking what I'm thinking? Socorro, if he's pulled some kind of dumb stunt—" I asked her to phone me at T. Ambrose if she heard anything.

"I have my afternoon off," Socorro said. "Tell Lupe I come see her later. First I got this appointment."

"What's happening?" Lupe asked, watching me closely.

"Nothing, that I know of." I gave her Socorro's message. "Listen, it's all going to work out, okay? I'm going to call you on the telephone in a little while. Probably Jordan will be here by then."

Crazy Jordan. I headed for my old and about-to-be-former office at T. Ambrose; because the more I thought about it, the surer I was that he had lured Deirdre away—taken her off somewhere for a little talk, a verbal duel, a double whammy of guilt, you name it.

Could he actually do what he'd threatened? Ingeniously rig some kind of a trap, maybe. . . . If he'd taken Deirdre off somewhere, he'd really have his hands full. And then he might even call on me—we were old phone pals, after all—to relay his demands, or help bail him out. He could hardly tell Lupe, 'Hey, babe, I'm going to be home a little late, I'm up here pulling my rich sister's fingernails out. Give Miguel a kiss for me."

Ridiculous. I just couldn't imagine Jordan being stupid enough actually to do Deirdre any physical harm. But he might have a great time terrorizing her. . . .

"You're here more when you're not working here than when you are," Arlene said. "If you know what I mean." I tucked myself in with my telephone machine, which had nothing more since the new mystery voice talking about Hodges, and decided to gamble the next several hours on my hunch about Jordan's big move.

Twice I called Lupe, who had heard nothing from Jordan and was getting more and more scared and hostile. Arlene went out for a Chinese lunch, and brought me back an order of mu shu pork. . . . On the other hand, if Jordan really was guilty, he might be doing something terrible right now. Should I be talking to the police about this, get them to start looking for Deirdre? An even wilder possibility: what if it was Deirdre who'd lured Jordan away?

The phone rang at three twenty-five, long after I'd given up any reasonable hope. It was Deirdre.

"Moz? Good, I need you. There's been rather a large misunderstanding—oh, have I had a day!" She sounded excited and in full charge of herself and the world.

"What happened? Where are you? Are you all right?"

"Of course I'm all right, considering I've spent the last six or however many hours with this mad Jordan person. Yes, you heard me right. Jordan."

"But that's a great—" relief, I was going to say.

"He dumped me," Deirdre said. "My doing, really. I dared him to, and he took me up on it." She was definitely pleased with herself. "I'm out here in Elsinore—do you know where that is?—and I need somebody to come get me, the bus arrangements are just unbelievable. Everybody else I can think of is too busy. Would you do it? Get some paper and I'll give you the directions."

"Did you tell him about the witness?"

"Yeah, he seemed really excited about that—why, have you talked to the guy already? What exactly does he know?"

"We can get to that later."

I'd been to Elsinore once, a little town in the back country tucked in behind the Santa Ana Mountains alongside Lake Elsinore, a big shallow lake with no outlet. During really wet winters it spreads out and floods all the lakefront places. Normally Elsinore would be about an hour away; but this was exactly the wrong time, the start of the great outflux through the Santa Ana River Canyon as thousands of Orange County workers headed for their "affordable" lodgings farther inland.

I could've said no, rent a car, or call somebody else; and, stuck in that sluggish stream of stinking vehicles, I almost wished I had. But not really. The Tenhagens might still have the answers we needed; and besides, I was wild to know what had happened between Jordan and Deirdre.

Once through the canyon, I got off the freeway and wound my way through groves of lemon and grapefruit trees and small towns, past stables and a hot-springs-and-spa advertising therapeutic mudbaths. Deirdre's directions were excellent, and I found her exactly as described, outside an Italian restaurant at the edge of Elsinore. She was sitting with her legs crossed on a folding chair to one side of the doorway, in front of a big clump of red geranium, and reading an issue of *Cosmo*; the perfect aristocrat, at home anywhere.

When I pulled into the parking lot she waved and got up, folded up the chair and carried it inside. She came out with the magazine between thumb and forefinger, took it over to a trash barrel at the gas station next door, and ostentatiously dropped it in. She looked especially elegant today in a beige knit Chanel-style suit with a string of pearls, and I could imagine Jordan taking her in, impressed.

"Well, you made pretty good time," she said as she climbed into the car. "Thanks. . . . Come on, what are you waiting for? Let's get going."

"I'm waiting to hear your story," I said, and pulled out onto the highway again.

"Ah. . . . He takes a little getting used to." She and Jordan had met at a coffee shop for breakfast, at her invitation; after which he suggested they go for a ride in his van. "We had plenty to talk about, as you may imagine."

"And what was the essence of it?"

"Family matters." They had wound up on the Ortega, the scenic two-lane highway that runs from San Juan Capistrano up over the crest of the mountains to Elsinore. "He said he wanted to show me the sights—they'd taken him up there when he was a kid to see a waterfall, carried him into it. And we got off on this back road, got stuck in the brush where he could barely turn around—I really think he was lost, but he wouldn't admit it."

She didn't say anything about a gun, and I didn't want to ask. By the time they got to Elsinore they were having a silly argument, she said. Up until then the conversation had been "pretty far-ranging and philosophical, really. But we got into this stupid little conflict and I was suddenly tired of the whole bit, just momentarily sick of the sound of his voice. So I told him, 'Stop and let me out.' And he did."

He came back around once. She waved him off, and he drove away and left her there. "He called my bluff," she said, pleased.

"A real Tenhagen," I said. "As arrogant as the rest of the family." She smiled, agreeing. "As if the looks weren't enough," I said. "What do you think? Now maybe you can help with your mother. She's convinced he's an impostor."

Deirdre didn't answer. If Jordan's resemblance to Vera had shocked her, she wasn't about to let me know. And she obviously hadn't talked to Vera about him yet—why? Because she was afraid to find out the truth of it?

"You haven't talked to Socorro yet either, have you," I said.

"No . . . Soky's good at keeping secrets."

"Like the rest of you."

"It's actually none of your business," Deirdre said.

I veered onto the shoulder and stomped on my brakes. Pulling a Jordan, I thought, and, whatever works. We sat there without talking.

Finally Deirdre looked at me. "We've got quite a long way yet," she said. "'Miles to go before I sleep.' Isn't that Robert Frost?"

"I want to know what Jordan told you today."

". . . Jordan didn't have anything to do with the boat accident, if that's what you mean. He wanted to see Daddy alive more than anybody. We just generally got acquainted, and explored each others' viewpoint. . . ." She gestured for me to drive on, and I gave up and pulled out again.

"It was quite a high-level conversation," Deirdre said. "Tactical. We got some stuff ironed out, and I think he understands how vulnerable Mother is right now. We'll resolve everything, but it takes time. He's able to see that now, I'd say. We have to be patient."

"So you did agree on some things."

"I'm sure he understands that he'll be dealt with in a fair and reasonable way."

She's bought him off, I thought; promised him a cut of some kind if he'll stay out of sight. "A modest monthly allowance, for starters."

Her chin lifted. "That's between the two of us," she said, and I knew I was right, at least in substance. We drove through Corona and back onto the freeway in silence.

"He seems reasonably intelligent, wouldn't you say?" Deirdre said. "For somebody who's been in a . . . a pretty weird situation. Naive, of course, which is to be expected, given his limited background. He has a totally unrealistic idea of the way we live—like something out of "Dallas." Do you know he's never been out of Orange County? I couldn't believe that. I trust you a whole lot, don't I. You're really on the inside of this."

"Why not? What am I getting out of it all? Nothing but a long, slow ride." I realized then why I was the one Deirdre had thought of calling first—so nobody else would know about today. Nobody who mattered.

"He may tell himself it's the money," I began.

". . . Wanting to get as much as he can out of the situation. It's understandable." Of course, I thought. That's how she, any of them would react in his place.

"He's actually quite creative," she said. "Imaginative. Although I think his . . . isolated circumstances have maybe distorted his perceptions in some situations."

"Did he try that hypnosis routine on you, too?" I grinned at her and she capitulated, grinning back.

"Well, you can't take him quite at face value," she said. "But then, you can't disregard him, either."

She leaned back against the seat and closed her eyes, smiling a little to herself. Resting after her labors. She'd lassoed the problem and tied it up, and her world was back under control. I wondered how long she'd try to put off talking to Vera about Jordan. Maybe indefinitely.

"Oh, God," she said, coming upright. "What day is it? Thursday, isn't it. I've got to call Mother; stop at the next place you see. We always eat together on Thursday night, it's Socorro's afternoon off and we throw together little messes, or else I stop at the deli. She'll be wondering why I haven't called yet."

I pulled off at the Coco's at the head of Santa Ana Canyon and sat squinting into the late sun, barely able to see the trailer park and tree-shaded golf course below. The trailers were nosed up together under the knoll like a flock of alien sheep. Then I saw Deirdre coming back from the phone booth at a dead run, her fists clenched and her mouth twisted shut.

She yanked open the door. "Quick! Something terrible has happened." She scrambled in. "Hurry up, we've got to get back there!"

I was already in gear and backing around. "What's wrong?"

"You want me to drive? It'll be quicker—" She was twisted around in her seat, looking back too, helping. "Mother's had a burglary, she caught him in the act—right there in the house, can you imagine? He had a gun."

She was still panting, her breath squeaking in her throat. "Joyce Landis answered the phone; I knew as soon as I heard her voice that something was wrong. . . ." She pushed her hand against her chest, trying to catch her breath. "Oh, my God—"

"Was she hurt?"

"Oh, no, thank God. She managed to get it away from him. She shot him."

"What?"

A miracle Vera hadn't been hurt or even killed, she said. The police were all over the house; trying to be civil, but it was a madhouse, Joyce Landis, the family friend, had told her. Joyce had called the doctor to come and see Vera; she'd absolutely insisted, even though Vera said no. And that was really all Deirdre knew about it.

"But how terrible for her," I said.

"Yes," Deirdre said, staring straight ahead and nodding. "Yes."

I drove as fast as I reasonably could, cutting in and out of traffic—luckily, most of it was on the other side of the freeway, still going up the canyon toward Riverside. If we'd been stuck in that, Deirdre would've had a stroke.

"Who was it?" I asked, even though I was sure she would've said so already, if she knew. I had a terrible apprehension that it was Jordan's doing, that maybe he'd set it up with somebody and then decoyed Deirdre out of the way. Socorro's afternoon off? A natural. "Who was he? How could he get in there, anyway?"

"I told you, I don't know!"

"Then he got away."

"Oh, no. He's dead."

She was staring, bent forward and gripping the dashboard with both hands as if to make us go faster. "You mean your mother killed him?" I couldn't take it in.

"That's right! Now you know exactly as much as I do; so why don't you just—keep quiet and drive."

I believed her—she didn't know any more and she didn't want to know. Soon enough she'd be into the whole mess. I kept seeing Vera in all kinds of situations, struggling with a burglar, fighting him off—had he tried to attack her? I didn't want to suggest that to Deirdre.

"What a horrible thing to happen," I said. "After everything else she's had . . . it just isn't fair. Like the woman's under some sort of curse."

The traffic was thickening up on our side now, too. And it got worse after the Newport Freeway split off in Orange. Deirdre kept tuning the radio back and forth looking for news bulletins, but all she got were descriptions of traffic tie-ups. "Vehicle over the side . . . stalled car in the fast lane on the Santa Monica at Western . . ." From the I-5 to the Corona del Mar Freeway, the whole way was a nightmare, stop and go and stinking fumes under a sky like soap scum.

"Oh, just shut up," Deirdre kept muttering, rocking back and forth. "Shut up, can't you?" We didn't hear anything about the shooting.

The Tenhagen driveway was full of cars: a county van, two

police cars, and several others. Deirdre was out before we'd stopped. There was a patrolman at the front door; she shouted an explanation at him and I hustled to keep up as she ran past. A black-and-yellow plastic tape was stretched across the hall, blocking it off.

"They're over in the sunroom," the policeman said, pointing through the kitchen.

It was a glassed-in room, the outside blinds lowered now and the glass reflecting a big television sitting diagonally in the middle of the floor. "Mommy!" Vera, haggard, her eyes sunken and her hair wild, stood up when she saw Deirdre and they hugged, rocking back and forth, Deirdre patting her back and crooning, "There, now. It's going to be alll right. . . ."

Vera buried her face in Deirdre's neck, whimpering. Keith was there, too, hovering with his hands up, glancing back and forth from the television to his mother; and a woman of about sixty in a red three-piece knit suit who would be Joyce Landis.

"I've been trying to get her out of here," Joyce Landis said to Deirdre. "She'd be much better off over at my place—there's no need for her to stay here, they already said she could go. You talk to her."

"No!" Vera cried, raising her head. "This is my home, my place, and nobody's going to force me out of it! I'm going to fight, I'll fight anybody for it—I made it all, this is my life. Don't let them pull me out of it—Deirdre? Keith?" They patted her, trying to calm her. Vera's eyes fell on me.

"What are you doing here? Go away, can't you? Oh, somebody, Keith, can't you get them all out of here?"

"I'll take care of this," Joyce Landis said. "Now, miss." And she gave me a little push to turn me around. We moved out of the room and into the kitchen.

"What a terrible thing," and "I'm so sorry," I murmured automatically. "Who was he, do you know?"

"I can't see that this is any of your business at all," she said, and turned her back on me.

"Then you do know."

"You heard her. You don't belong here." She rapped away across the big kitchen and I followed the hair dyed walnut-brown, the knobby spine under the red knit suit.

"Just give me his name. It's bound to be public information—"

"Vera's said what a pest you've been." Her eyes sparkled with excitement, the thrill of being the protector in this great emergency. She opened the front door, and the cop outside turned to watch us. "Now, out!"

**17** "Could you spell that last name?" I said. My brain was in a stall, trying to absorb what Tom Forster from the NBPD was telling me. I stared at what I'd written. Edward Mowatt. Eddie from the boatyard? "Oh, yeah. Thanks a million, Tom. I really appreciate this." A gritty wind blew across Pacific Coast Highway, cold around the ankles, and outside the phone booth the home-going traffic crawled along as always. . . . Eddie, the beached Viking, had got himself shot trying to rob Vera? I was astounded. This was incredibly wrong; it just didn't compute.

Come on, brain, crank. Eddie obviously craved the rich life, didn't he? But holding up somebody you know has got to be suicide. He'd never have gotten away with it. Unless he'd been planning to kill her after? That would make it self-defense. Which it had to be in any case. Oh, the lady had guts. She must've had a gun of her own on hand. An honest-to-God shoot-out up on Sea Hawk Ridge.

Another disaster in the life of Vera Tenhagen. A real soap, that's what Fran will call it. And won't she be excited? I was trying to be cool and adult, but my brain kept playing the same picture. Cornered, I squeezed the trigger and felt the gun kick, saw Eddie hit and falling away, his startled dying look—it made my stomach turn. It all felt wrong, wrong.

I nosed my Toyota back into the sluggish stream of traffic. There was no news of the shooting on the car radio yet, just the endless roll call of freeway snarls. . . . If Eddie could do something that crazy, what else might he have done? Blow up the *Spray*, maybe? What a great idea—why didn't I love it? If Eddie was the killer, that would solve everything.

Hold on here. Eddie could have wanted to kill Arnie because Arnie knew he'd stolen his antique compass and the rest from the boat—maybe he even caught Eddie at it. And then, say Eddie thought that Vera suspected him. Or maybe he just lusted after more of the Tenhagen goodies, couldn't get them off his mind. Obviously crazy even to try such a thing. Too bad about poor Vera, really awful. Or was it? Maybe it hadn't been that way. Maybe Eddie knew Keith had done it and was trying to blackmail Vera, and she set him up.

I didn't like that idea at all. Imagine Eddie actually dead, and in such a dumb-ass way. I'd only met the guy once but he seemed okay, and after all, he was a human being.

But for once I was going to play it smart and keep my opinions to myself till I knew a whole lot more. No shooting from the hip; I'd been wrong too often lately. Watch and wait. Wonder how Fran will take this? If she figures the same way, that Eddie was responsible for the boat, too, she'll dance on his grave.

Talk to Socorro in a day or so, when things cool down—ah; today was her afternoon off, she hadn't been there. Maybe Eddie knew that, too.

Fran was sitting up close to the television, holding a wooden cooking spoon in her lap, smearing her apron. "Guess what's happened!" she cried, and punched the buttons to change channels. "Vera Tenhagen shot somebody! I heard it on the radio in the kitchen, they gave her name. 'Preliminary report, wife of prominent Newport yachtsman—'"

"That's right. Wait'll you hear who it was."

"A burglar, they said. Who?"

"Eddie Mowatt. One of the guys who rebuilt Arnie Tenhagen's boat."

"Oh, boy! Is this a fine mess!" I'd been right. Fran was fascinated. Especially by my description of haggard Vera, and of getting thrown out of the Tenhagen house.

A bright-eyed, solemn Japanese commentator, female, materialized against a plain blue wall. "A woman homeowner in an exclusive Newport Beach neighborhood shot and killed a burglar in her home this afternoon," she said. "Stay tuned for film at eight."

"There's more to this than meets the eye," Fran said.

We settled down in front of the TV, switching from channel to channel in search of news, running out to the kitchen during the commercials to fill our plates with Fran's eggplant spaghetti and salad.

"A daring daylight robbery attempt this afternoon in Newport Beach's exclusive Sea Hawk Ridge section failed, thanks to the courage and quick thinking of the intended victim. Mrs. Vera Tenhagen was alone in her home when she was allegedly confronted by a man who demanded that she give him all of her jewels. The man reportedly had been employed by her husband some months ago to do some work on his yacht."

View into the Tenhagen driveway from the front gate, where two paramedics in bright orange rolled a stretcher loaded with a bulky body-sized yellow plastic bundle up to the rear of an ambulance and slid it in, folding the stretcher legs back. The next shot was taken from across the street, the camera panning along the Tenhagen's white stucco wall with red-tiled roofs above and then back to the crowd: neighbors, probably; a couple of teenagers and six or seven middle-aged men and women in casual clothes.

As the ambulance pulled out, someone cheered, and there

was a spattering of applause from the watchers on this side of the street. The camera drew back and panned them. They were all in sunglasses and most of them turned their heads away, but one man leaned forward grinning and shouted something, making a thumbs-up sign.

"Their place is a mansion," Fran said. "I don't think you really told me. There's well-off, and then there's *rich*."

Fran was insatiable, milking me for every detail of my meeting with Eddie at Dickerson's boatyard and speculating nonstop about his behavior. "You know," she said, "he could've been the one that blew up the boat, too."

"You think so?"

"You already thought of it! Why didn't you say so? I bet it was your telling everybody about the witness that smoked him out."

"Only I didn't tell him. I wonder if somebody else did. . . ."

"And making you fall downstairs," she said. "That fits in, too."

"How do you figure that?"

"Because you were on his trail and getting closer, you must've been. You knew something about him, and he was scared."

"Then why didn't he kill me outright?" She turned away without saying any more, but I could see the wheels turning.

Fran took charge, tuning back and forth among the channels looking for more news. "Shot him dead," Fran said. "Now I ask you, does that sound like a frail little female that falls down with hissy-fits? Oh, she's had them all buffaloed for years." She came back to the news broadcast just as the sports section was finishing up.

"We have an update on that Newport Beach shooting," said Unflappable Sam. "It appears that Mrs. Vera Tenhagen, who was alone in the house at the time, actually shot the robber with his own gun; that somehow she managed to get it away from him and pull the trigger. Stay tuned for late-breaking developments in this and other top stories."

"Whoo-ee!" Fran squealed like a steam whistle. "Are you ready for that?" She looked carnivorous, transformed.

I didn't say anything. "You hardly seem surprised," Fran said.

"Me? I'm still stunned by it all." I shook my head. "I can't believe any of it." I knew I was keeping a poker face to hide my real reaction. I felt a sick fear in my stomach, like a little kid abandoned on a street corner. Like betrayal.

"Took it away from him?" Fran said. And she was off. "Vera and Eddie. Well, well."

"Now that idea is ridiculous."

"Oh? Because your rich lady friend, butter wouldn't melt in her mouth, is too nice for that; play around with a hunk of muscles. Is that it?"

"You'd have to know her to understand," I said. Fran gave me a long, speculative look and went back to her channel-hopping.

When the phone rang, we both jumped. It was Deirdre.

"Hello, Moz? I hated to call you, but I had to; we've got things to discuss." Her voice sounded almost normal, only weary and hard, resigned to taking care of business but still resenting it. She asked me to corroborate her story to the police about how she'd spent her day. "Everything's in order, it's all exactly the same," she said, "only I left out any mention of Jordan. I had a missed connection. I got stranded in Elsinore and you came out to get me, and that's it. Okay?"

"That seems to be fairly reasonable," I said, being vague. I was in no hurry to perjure myself just because it suited Deirdre's purposes. "How's your mother doing?"

"She's sleeping now, thank God. We couldn't even persuade her to take any kind of a sedative. We had to trick her, put it in her glass. Frankly, we just figure it's a miracle she's alive. That's one tough lady."

"Listen, about this afternoon; is there some problem? I mean, are we talking here about suspicious circumstances?"

"Absolutely not!" Deirdre paused; she read me well

enough—my cooperation should certainly be worth some inside details. "Listen. I'll tell you exactly what happened, all right? Only, see to it you keep this to yourself."

"Be serious," I said.

I'd guessed right. Eddie had talked his way in by persuading Vera he had to discuss the damaged boat with her. But once in the house, he told Vera that Arnie owed him $850 for some side job he'd done on the *Spray.*

"Naturally enough, Mother asked him for some proof," Deirdre said. "He didn't have any, not a shred, he was even vague about the dates. So of course she refused. Which is when he went berserk and started ransacking the house for things to sell. Smaller stuff; binoculars, cameras, Daddy's pocket chronometer—can you believe it? This heap of stuff, piled up on the desk. The police took pictures."

They wound up in Vera's bedroom, with Eddie stuffing her jewelry in his pockets. "My grandmother's pearls—the diamond-and-emerald necklace my father gave her two years ago, and the earrings to match— She was terrified, shaking so badly she was afraid her legs wouldn't hold her up—she just kept piling things in his hands, anything loose. That's when he put the gun down, and she grabbed it. He tried to get it back. They fought for it. It went off."

"Wow. What an experience."

"And that was it," Deirdre said. "Now you know the whole story."

"Incredible," I said. "She was incredibly lucky."

"You are so right."

"Would you tell her for me how thankful I am—"

"Certainly," said Deirdre. "In the morning."

I gave Fran a verbatim repeat of Deirdre's half of the conversation. She listened with her mouth pursed, but all she said was, "We'll see what develops."

By ten o'clock the shooting had become the major story of the evening. "Tragedy strikes a millionaire Newport Beach household for the second time in little more than a week," with a still shot of Arnie and Vera at the opening of the new Performing Arts Center. ". . . Tragic death of Vera Tenhagen's husband Arnold in the explosion of the family yacht." The *Spray* riding at anchor trailed wisps of smoke under the lights in the debris-littered water.

"The rather amazing story of how this unarmed woman managed to defend herself and her home by tricking her assailant out of his loaded gun and turning it on him. Recently widowed, Mrs. Tenhagen reportedly . . ."

Fran snarled deep in her throat. "Oh, yes. Look at that. They're already making her into a heroine. The brave pioneer woman standing in the cabin door, holding off the savages single-handed."

"Who knows? Maybe she is."

"And maybe they were 'getting it on,' like the kids say. And she got him to kill her husband, and then they fell out, someway. Murderers do."

"You're still not satisfied; you want more misery, is that it? A deep dark conspiracy, something big enough to balance off all the pain and blood and broken bodies. . . . Not enough to have it be a simple dumb coke-head maybe, doing any crazy thing to feed his addiction. You keep wanting more, more—you're insatiable!"

Her thoughtful glint warned me. I could see her wonder if I was siding with Eddie because of the alcoholism. In any case, my judgment was hopelessly skewed and there was no point in arguing. I jumped up, ready to leave, just to get out of there, but I knew that would be as bad: I'd have to come back sooner or later and she'd be waiting up for me, or awake, anyway, worried that maybe I'd gone out and started drinking again. So instead I slammed into the shower feeling absolutely murderous myself.

When I came out, Fran was still at it, which turned out to be a piece of luck. They were rehashing the shooting, same shot of the ambulance driving out and the crowd applauding. The alleged robber had been identified as Edward Mowatt, thirty-nine, of Newport Beach.

"Now we're going live to the Orange County Coroner's Office, where Mowatt's body was taken earlier today and some sort of disturbance seems to be in progress." Night shot, glare of TV spotlights and a police car with its red spot turning, lighting up a scattered crowd of ten or twelve people watching a couple of policemen in dark blue arguing with a tall young woman, curly-haired and smeary with mascara. Another girl and a man hung on to her arms and talked to her, trying to calm her down as the camera jostled in close. She pulled away from them and a hand stuck a mike up to her mouth as she hollered,

"No, you're not! You're not going to get away with this, and neither is she!" There was something familiar about her, even with her nose fat and red and her eyes swollen. She'd been crying, but she wasn't now; she was raving. "Think you can just shoot somebody down like a dog, in cold blood—"

A murmur away from the mike, somebody apparently was asking her, "Who?"

"Vera Tenhagen, that's who. Mrs. Rich-Bitch, thinks she can get away with this—she's a murderer, that's who!" She made a sudden lunge toward us, shouting, "What's your problem, frog eyes?" and stuck her face right into the camera. Abruptly the scene cut to a thin blond reporter in green, holding the mike to her own mouth.

"That was Catherine Malena, a friend of the dead man, who's just come out from identifying the body and is obviously distraught. This is Trina Paradis, live from the Orange County Coroner's Office for Channel Five News."

"I know that girl," I said. "Anyway, I've seen her before." At the Crow's Nest, the day after the explosion; she was the long tall Sally stumbling around as if she were loaded. "Only I didn't know she was Eddie's girlfriend." Cat Malena; Eddie's kitty-cat.

Next morning Fran and I were both subdued and civilized. While I was still drinking my first cup of coffee, Fran went out and bought all the papers, and we went over them together. Eddie had been shot twice in the chest at close range. They rehashed the whole *Spray* explosion, but there wasn't much else that was new.

"Twice?" Fran raised one eyebrow, and shut her mouth.

"She's got everything on her side," I said. "If it happened otherwise, somebody'll have to prove it."

Ben Dickerson's Boatyard was cooler and grayer than the first time, with the ghost of Eddie strong in the place. The asphalt was freshly swept and the tools all put away, everything ready for company. Ben leaned against a boat, sitting on a high wooden stool with his heels hooked over a rung; just sitting there, hands on his knees. He had on a new black-and-white shirt of houndstooth check, polyester jersey, with the fold marks sharp across the chest; and he looked badly hung over, sorry-eyed and sallow, his nose a spongy pink.

"I knew he had some money problems," Ben said, "but I had no idea they were that serious. If he'd only just talked to me. What a dumb-ass thing to do." They'd called Ben as well to identify the body, and afterward he'd gone out and got drunk, and planned to go again tonight. The story of Arnie owing Eddie any money was "pure poppycock. I knew every inch of that boat and exactly what was done to it. There is no way he could've worked on it and me not know."

"Somebody suggested to me that he might've been, you know, interested in Vera."

"I wouldn't've thought so," he said. "They weren't exactly each other's types. But you never know, do you." He looked faintly interested, like I'd started him on a new train of thought.

"The truth of the matter is," Ben said, "I think it was that shitty damn car of his. He had a real severe case of Zooportitis. You know, run with the big boys. That old Jag never ran right from the first day he got it, he was always in hock for repairs. And the way he's been the last couple months, slipping around—jumpy. I was afraid he was dealing." He rubbed his belly, and then pulled out a roll of chalk tablets and tossed two into his mouth.

"But why?" Ben said. "For what?" His voice peaked, plaintive. "You imagine his being so stupid, trying to rob her in broad daylight? Figure he'd have to shoot her after that, being as she knows him. Nope; she did the smart thing, I don't fault her there. She's lucky to be alive."

I had to agree. "You mentioned going down last night to identify Eddie's body," I said. "Were you there at the same time as Cat Malena?"

"More or less," Ben said, suddenly expressionless.

"She made quite a splash on television. Accused Vera Tenhagen of murder."

"Poor old Cat," he said. "She never has learned to control her drinking, or her mouth. Not that she didn't have pretty strong reasons to be upset at the time."

"You know where I can get in touch with her?"

"Nope. I expect Cat'll be unavailable for a while. By now, Mrs. Tenhagen's attorneys have probably gotten word to her that they consider such statements as hers in the nature of libel. I understand the television station's already sent Mrs. Tenhagen a letter of formal apology. No . . . old Cat's probably holed up somewhere, sobering up and getting a grip on herself."

"I know a little bit about that stuff," I said. "I'd like to help her out, if I could."

"Frankly, I'd advise against it. You see, Cat's got a little sort of a record; couple of dumb things, related to her drinking and so on—"

"She might be safer if she went public," I said. "Instead of hiding herself away. Where she could easily become the victim of some kind of accident."

Ben looked at me, not asking what I was getting at. Which was just as well; I didn't have anything solid to point to. "She'll never do that," he said. "The police are looking to question her; but she figures they want to arrest her for breaking probation, and she'll have to go to jail."

Vera's attorneys, hey? Ben must've had some recent dealings with them himself, I figured. Us ordinary people just call them lawyers.

". . . You know the one I really blame." I didn't hear him at first, because I was remembering my little mystery message,

"Hodges wants you to know." Could it have been Eddie? I'd have to go by the office and listen to the tape again. Ben was waiting, looking at me from under those shaggy eyebrows with an unhappy frown.

"Who's that?"

"The originator of this whole mess, with his precious god-damn boat." He pointed a knuckle across the yard at the *Spray*, up on chocks. "I'm not afraid to say it; the jinx boat. Rich man's ego trip. The money he sank into it . . . That sideways eight, the infinity sign? It's a hex mark. Go anywhere, do anything—power dreams. Dreams of power."

We talked a little about Eddie, his likes and dislikes, and Ben told some stories about Eddie's practical jokes, both of us trying to keep his memory green a little longer. It was getting warmer, the sun broke through, and the rank smell of Ben sweating out last night's booze in that new polyester was overpowering. I had an idea that Ben's liver wasn't in great shape, and maybe he wouldn't be around too much longer, either.

"If you should see Cat," I said, "just tell her I'd like to help her. Would you do that?"

"Why, I surely will," he said, meaning he surely wouldn't. I left Ben sitting on his stool, rubbing his palms on his knees and sucking in his cheeks as if his mouth was dry.

18 If Ben could accept Eddie's shooting, why couldn't I?

Give it up, Moz—that's what Gage or any other sensible person would say. What you can't change, accept. Quit fighting the real world. What kind of dummy are you? But I couldn't. The trail was full of tiger traps I'd never suspected, and I needed to learn the signs.

None of the Orange County telephone books listed any Malenas, C. or otherwise. I went around to the Crow's Nest and found it locked up tight, dark and dead inside, with that OPEN sign still hanging crooked in the door.

The afternoon sunlight weakened as I started along the dock toward the *Vagabunda*, John and Sandra Healy's floating retreat, and a faint haze spread over the harbor, graying the sky and the water, which seemed just right. Through *Vagabunda*'s open porthole came the sobbing voice of a tenor in the drawn-out falsetto refrain of "Malagueña Salerosa." I rapped on the hull. The music stopped, and in a moment Sandra Healy's head popped up in the stairwell—tan, teeth and fringe of curly bangs brilliant in the subdued day.

"Well! What brings you back here?" She motioned me aboard.

"I just . . . I want to know why."

"You haven't exactly covered yourself with glory, have you."

"You haven't exactly helped, have you." She slid onto the bench behind the table, and I sat down opposite. "But you're right," I said. "I haven't accomplished very much at all. You have any further thoughts on the situation?"

"A tragedy, of a sort—for poor Eddie, certainly," she said. "Whatever he had going, I don't think he deserved to end up like that."

"My feelings exactly. I'm trying to make some sense of it. What did he have going; does anybody know?"

"Oh, God . . . Eddie's been part of the harbor scene since I can remember. His only real claim to fame was that ill-conceived trip he tried to make around Baja in an old wreck, a piece of junk, I mean really. Jim Farnsworth and Botty Means found him on the beach somewhere north of Loreto in simply wretched condition, ragged and covered with sores from malnutrition, and took pity on him. Brought him back here."

"Arnie Tenhagen wasn't involved."

"No." Sandra looked at me, speculating. "Eddie wasn't a planner, and he certainly wasn't malicious," she said. "He might have been crafty in his own little way; but it was the sort of thing anybody'd pick up on about fifteen seconds after he'd thought of it."

"Okay. Still, he went up there for something."

"Oh, I know exactly what they'll say. That there was some of the old belly-bumping going on between him and Vera. Patent nonsense."

"I quite agree."

"Do you." She sneered and turned away. My being there was a distasteful intrusion.

"What galls me is that she's getting away with it," I said. "I just want to know why. But you'd prefer not to be disturbed, I gather."

"Indeed. And what makes you think you're the slightest bit equipped to understand? Breezing through here in your utter ignorance— You never even knew the man."

"Ignorant; okay. But I'm still trying."

"He was leaving her."

"Arnie?" I was ready to hoot, and caught myself.

"He was suffocating. Oh, I'll admit that as a couple they weren't entirely ill-suited," she said. "In his own masculine, guilt-ridden way, Arnie understood Vera and, I'd have to say, to some degree even approved. He said to me once that he accepted Vera's motherhood rights as supreme; seeing as she had so little else. That household is her entire life, she has no other."

"But . . . nobody else has even hinted at such a thing."

"John and I spent a month cruising with Arnie in the South Pacific last winter," Sandra said. "A bare-bones charter—we flew to New Zealand. Bay of Islands and then Fiji—summer there, of course. It was idyllic, a wonderful . . . interlude." She took a deep breath. "He'd been going about it very gently, to spare the family the slightest public suggestion of a rupture."

"I guess. Are you sure you're not—"

"Disengaging from his business," she said. "First this cruise, and then there would have been others, longer, so that his absences would gradually become the norm. Last spring he arranged a big life-insurance policy for her. That's just one example."

"But I hardly think she needed the money—"

"Is that what you think I've been talking about? You've missed the point completely, haven't you."

I laughed. "So. You're saying that, to preserve her marriage, she had her husband killed."

"We'll never know now, will we." She stood up. "If you'll excuse me. I have to go out shortly." And then, in one of her lightning changes of mood, Sandra Healy escorted me off the boat and partway up the dock, growing more cordial as our parting neared. "I hope I've helped," she said, patting me on the shoulder. "Do come back anytime."

Not bloody likely. The woman sat in there weaving fantasies for herself; or if not, she was perfectly able to accept the murder of her dear, dear friend without lifting a finger to retaliate . . . . Think about it. If Arnie really had been planning to leave . . .

Nobody was in the T. Ambrose office but Arlene. "You see the story about your buddy in this morning's *Tribune*?" Arlene asked. She handed me the paper, folded back with Vera's photo uppermost. "Hey; she's loaded, isn't she. Kind of risky. You never know who's watching you, thinking of taking a crack at it. No wonder those rich guys are so security-conscious. I would be myself."

I shut myself into my office and listened to the tape with the mysterious little message about Hodges. "Hodges wants you to know—" Only now I could hear plain as day, "I just want you to know." Sounding exactly like Eddie. Could I swear to it? Yes.

What was it you wanted me to know, Eddie? If you'd told me a little more, you might still be around to discuss it. Too late now, too late, too late . . . "A day late and a dollar short," Ada would say. "That's our Moz."

The story and pictures of Eddie's shooting filled up half the *Tribune*'s front page. There was just one mention of Cat Malena.

> After viewing Mowatt's body, a friend of the dead man, Catherine Malena, questioned the circumstances of his death. "I'm not letting her get away with it!" Miss Malena said, distraught. Friends sought to console her, and she was led away weeping.

The story had been written by Tessa Kocher, who by now must be the *Tribune*'s Tenhagen expert. I picked up the phone.

After the third transfer, I finally heard Tessa Kocher's voice.

"This is Moz Brant. My friends Rick Tyler and Judy Christensen were injured when the Tenhagen boat blew up. You called me about them, remember?"

"Oh, yes. The girl died, didn't she. That's a shame. How's he doing?"

"His left side has been paralyzed. But they did surgery yesterday and removed a blood clot—we'll know more in a couple of days. Listen; I saw your latest story. Do you have anything more from Cat Malena? I know she's claimed Eddie's shooting was out-and-out murder."

"Not yet, but I'm trying. I just haven't been able to locate her."

"I've got the same problem. But I do have a lead I'm working on. I'll let you know what I turn up."

"Great."

"Any new developments?"

She hesitated. "Yes, as a matter of fact. We just got something from the Newport Beach PD. . . . The gun Mrs. T. shot him with, that Mowatt used for the holdup? It was registered to Arnold Tenhagen. Her dead husband."

"*What?*"

"Yup. She said her husband always kept it on the boat. But when they started looking through the wreckage for it after the explosion, they were never able to find it. Pretty interesting little connection."

"That's right. I remember Vera telling me about it." Oh, you bitch. "What you mean is that Eddie must've taken it when he blew up the boat."

"Well, of course right now that's just speculation," Tessa Kocher said quickly. "We'll wait for the police report." She sounded happy.

"You find any other connection between the two of them yet? Vera and Eddie, I mean."

"Why . . . is there one?"

"I don't have any personal knowledge, but I've heard some rumors."

"We can't print rumors. From what I understand, she'd sue my ass. But I'd love to have any leads you get, and I'll follow them up myself."

"Right." Right. I hung up the receiver, and then I straightened the phone, aligning it with my desk blotter. Tessa Kocher wouldn't get any leads, no incriminating pictures would turn up, no motel registrations in a telltale hand. Nobody would ever be able to prove she'd made it all happen; because Vera was too smart for that.

My middle desk drawer was open and I started separating the paper clips from the pushpins and rubber bands. I was putting off going home, because I'd have to tell Fran that Eddie had been Vera's murder weapon, only nobody would ever believe it, because Vera was even smart enough to get him to self-destruct.

But I finally went. Fran was watching the news, of course, sitting in the middle of the couch and crocheting away at her blue placemat. She jumped when I came in.

"That housekeeper, Socorro, called, and wants you to call her back," Fran said. "She said you've got their number."

"Well, yes and no. Never mind. Are they talking about the gun yet? They will be."

When I told her about the gun registration, Fran whooped and yelled. "We got it!" She was jumping around like a kid. "She must've had the gun all the time," Fran said. "She planned the whole thing and this proves it. This is it!"

"This is nothing! Don't you see? This is going to justify her completely. Without realizing it, she managed to kill her husband's murderer. They'll all say it's an act of God."

"No!"

"Don't take my word for it. Just watch."

We spread dishtowels over our laps and ate our chicken tacos while watching the news. Another Sea Hawk Ridge resident was being interviewed, a blond woman around fifty, curvy and straight-backed, probably a former sorority girl who'd always been a good sport and a lot of fun. She twinkled up at the camera, shading her eyes.

"Absolutely; I'm proud to have Vera Tenhagen for a neighbor. I only wish more people had her intestinal fortitude. If you can't be safe in your own home nowadays, where can you be? After all, this is what America's all about, isn't it?"

"Sheep," Fran muttered. "Cow."

"Just wait. I haven't asked yet. How's Rick today?"

"Well, it'll sound worse; but he's definitely better, Dr. Towner says. He's had a couple more seizures. Unfortunately they have to keep him tied down now. For his own good." She sighed. "Sort of awful to see. He's too big for that, they have a hard time with him."

It came on the eight o'clock news program from Los Angeles; the late-breaking news about the weapon that killed Edward Mowatt.

The announcer was one I particularly disliked, a tall man with crinkly close-cut black hair and a handsome skull, and a serene, untroubled manner, as if nothing that he read ever penetrated to his brain. He shifted his head to the most becoming three-quarter angle, certainly rehearsed in his mirror, and gave us a look at once friendly, confiding, reassuring, and solemn.

"Something akin to Divine retribution would seem to be at work in yesterday's robbery-related shooting in a fashionable Newport Beach area," he said. Fran put down her taco. I went out and cleaned up the kitchen. I didn't want to watch.

"There must not be a shadow of a doubt," I said. "By the sound, the police consider the case all wrapped up." Fran just sat there without moving. I should've thought of something kind to say, but a black bitter current was eating out my insides and I couldn't stand to be around Fran for another minute. I put on my jacket.

"I've got to go out for a while, see one of our clients," I said. "Don't worry if it turns out to run pretty late."

Damp cold tonight, with a sheet of moisture condensed over everything. I had to run my windshield wipers before I could see to pull out. I just drove, staying with the traffic and not thinking. The chill went clear to the bone, and I recognized the old bellyache from drinking too much coffee. What I needed was something soothing to calm me down.

Sherry, that would've been, once upon a time—"A spot of sherry?" Ada used to say. "Settle your stomach." Not that I ever needed an invitation from her, I'd already found the way for myself. I could taste it now, feel it sliding down hot and smooth right to where you need it, the warmth percolating into your blood.

I'd graduated from sherry soon enough, and developed my own reasons and excuses. Just that bit to calm the nerves—very sensitive, they are. Hereditary, you know. Delicate nervous systems run in our family. Now I was passing all kinds of grocery stores and liquor stores—even the little corner quicky-markets would have a few brands. In the velvet dark the neon shone yellow, red, green—beautiful; emblems and signs of human warmth, the civilized comforts.

There's a nice little place; looks clean and quiet, nobody in the parking lot. Then I was sitting nosed up to the front window and looking in through the open door, so close I could taste it.

Jesus, I thought. Have you forgotten already how much harder it is not to? So easy to let the current take you, go with it warm and swift and secure, and why not? It made sense. . . . I dug around in the glove compartment and got out my AA directory.

The Alano Club on the west side of Costa Mesa in the midst of an industrial area was easy enough to find, but the parking lot in back was a mess, all gleaming mud with pools of water still shining in the ruts from the last rain. The meeting had already started and the table was full; a long narrow room with fluorescent ceiling tubes and plain painted walls, a chipped brown enameled table with about twenty-five people around it. They moved over and made room for me, and unfolded another chair. Jeans, leather jackets, sweaters; this was a young group, in their twenties and thirties, and maybe a quarter of them girls.

The first step: one more time, one more time, one more time. The affirmation: yes, I'm limited. I admit that I'm powerless to help myself, and I entrust myself to a higher power. Whatever that may be.

Another man took over the readings. He was older, gray, a decent haircut, dressed well enough and freshly shaven, with a face like six miles of bad road, as Ada would say. Will I still need to come here, too, when I'm fifty? Oh, yes.

When they started around the table taking turns introducing themselves, the voices answering together vibrated through the wood and through my chest. My nose stung and I wanted to cry. "My name's Kevin, and I'm a drug addict and alcoholic." All of us answered in unison, "Hi, Kevin."

It was my turn. "My name is Moz, and I'm an alcoholic." "Hi, Moz."

After the meeting I had a cup of coffee with a nice-enough guy named Hank who asked me if I wanted to shoot a game of pool. But I was too jumpy—when Hank moved, his black leather jacket gleamed like the wet mud under the lights—and I went out alone and got back in my car and started driving. Eventually I wandered onto the freeway and headed south. I wasn't going to go out and poison myself again: no way. I was going to do my damnedest to poison her.

Easy enough to see now that Vera'd been using me all along. That was obviously why she'd been so nice: to keep in touch with me—and hadn't I lapped it up?—so she'd know just how I was doing, what I'd found out, and then going right back to Eddie with it.

Or, turn it around. Everything is exactly the way Vera tells it. Crazy Eddie did it on his own entirely, and Vera is just the victim of a fabulous set of circumstances. You don't have any proof otherwise.

Then I'll find some.

Hey, Moz. Isn't it interesting how hot you are about this now? Not because of Rick and Judy; and certainly not for poor dumb Eddie, who must've been the perfect tool—oh, no. It's because your pride is wounded. You got kicked right in your big fat ego, and it hurts, doesn't it.

Yes, yes! My head was filled with bloody images. Vera run down by a car, smashed and bloody and screaming. Vera taking poison; the agony, Vera clutching at her throat, and then one awful look of understanding before she collapsed. . . . No good. I wanted her to suffer, and I wanted her eliminated from the world. But only after they'd all seen what she was. I wanted revenge.

When I thought to look at my gas gauge, it was dead on E. I moved into the outside lane, looking for an off-ramp with a lighted gas-station sign and dreading that sickening moment when you stomp on the accelerator and the car dies under you. Finally I spotted a big yellow GAS sign and pulled off.

"Where am I?"

The kid in the bulletproof self-service booth answered, "Del Mar," looking interested. "You know, the racetrack. Happens to be closed right now"—with a grin, being cute. "You lost?"

"What? . . . No; thanks." Del Mar. More than halfway to San Diego, heading toward Mexico. Was that where my subconscious was wanting to run? Waking up now, I made myself get out again and check the oil and water, too.

. . . Here I'd been trying so hard to do the right thing, whatever that was—like a fool, because who could ever figure it out?—and what had it gotten me? Fired, for one thing. Nothing but misery.

I looked around for my keys and finally discovered them in my left hand, and realized how tired I was. Then I dug up my seat belt and fastened it, thinking about some turkey coming toward me in the dark, driving down the wrong side of the freeway with no lights; and headed back up the coast.

Well, no more nice-guy crap. From here on I'd smile and cheat and lie with the best of them. Good-bye Dr. Jekyll; hello, Mrs. Hyde. I was going to be Bad.

19 I woke up to a stripe of sunlight swaying across the wall with the moving curtain, and the smell of fresh coffee. Once again Fran had brought back all the morning papers she could find. The *Tribune*, maybe scenting a shift at the core of Vera's drama, had the Tenhagens' floor plan drawn by computer, with the dashed path of Eddie's rampage through the house and a fat X like a Greek cross where he'd finally come to rest.

"In her bedroom," Fran said. "Now, I ask you."

I shrugged. "What can we do?"

"Exactly. You're supposed to know all the legal angles."

"But what's the woman done? Defend herself, is all. Hey, how's this? You could maybe sue her for infringing on Rick's civil rights." I could see Fran taking that seriously, and I was ashamed.

"Or for medical expenses, anyway," she said. "And the therapy, that could go on for years. Do you know what his first bill from Coast Community was, just the partial? . . . Never mind."

"Say we just accept it was all Eddie's doing, and let it go at that. At least you'd have peace of mind. And he's certainly suffered the ultimate punishment. Which I guess is fair, in a way."

"Not good enough," Fran said, scowling.

"Why not?"

"I don't know why! Yes, I do. Because there's got to be some justice. Because it stinks to high heaven! I want to be sure. Nothing's sure. . . . I don't really know why. Some days I think maybe I'm losing my mind."

"Yeah. I know what you mean."

Ting-a-ling— Gage on the telephone, sounding as if he were on the bottom of an empty swimming pool.

"I'm over here on Catalina, been here since yesterday," he said. "Drunk in a brand-new thirty-two-foot Wellcraft; clipped three boats coming into the harbor. Can you believe it? Now I find out I've got to fly up to Frisco tonight and appraise this eighty-foot yacht some Arabian sheikh just bought his son. You available for lunch before I go?"

"Sure; why not?" We agreed to meet at La Rancheria at twelve thirty.

Fran reminded me again of Socorro's message, so I phoned her, not wanting to.

"This is Moz. I understand you called me yesterday."

"Yah. You know this shooting?" Socorro sounded tired, her voice hoarse.

"Everybody in the county 'knows' it."

"Listen; now she's gonna leave here. She got real estate people to come and talk about sell the house. She says maybe Arizona? This Scottsdale? Ah, or maybe Santa Fe."

"It figures. You going with her?"

"Don't kidding. No way. I got another job ready now. Nice lady, she waits till I can come. Little place down on Lido, all one floor, no too many rooms—so listen, we got not plenty time. I want to see you somewheres."

"What for? It's a little late now, isn't it? She's getting away with everything. You know it, and so do I. But all you ever cared about was your dumb secret and your feet hurting. If you'd spoken up, maybe a lot of things would be different."

Socorro was quiet a minute. "—Yah, she comes now."

"That's your problem. You know where the front door is. I'll talk to you later." And I hung up.

The maze of UCI Medical Center isn't so bad if you have a good map, like the one Fran had made for me. Rick was tied hand and foot in a bed with barred metal sides like a big crib, curled toward a fetal position, except for the hand that was dragged back and the feet splayed.

I walked around to where I could see his face. The movement caught his attention, and he scowled at me, trying to focus. He moved his head slowly from side to side and began to stretch out his hand, everything in slow motion, like a derelict I saw once in downtown L.A., an old guy too far gone to reach anymore.

Being tied, Rick's hand couldn't move very far. I stood there and talked to him, friendly reassurances in the tone of voice you use for babies and strange dogs. His eyebrows were starting to grow together—huh. Old Rick the natural man must've been shaving a path between them at the top of his nose.

He kept trying to reach out in that slow, tentative way, and then he started making a sound. "Nah. Nah," the same sound over and over, turning his head but not fixing on anything. After a few minutes a nurse came in, looking surprised to see me.

"Oh no, you can't be in here," she said. "You'll have to leave now."

I stopped in the doorway to take it in, the wreck that used to be my friend Rick; burning it into my mind, the sight of him and the sound. I knew what I was doing—using Rick to whip up my hatred, like some poor creep jerking off with a dirty magazine—and I was ashamed. But I needed it. All the way down the hall I heard Rick's voice, "Nah! Nah, nah, nah!" and the bars of his bed jingling like chains as the nurse struggled with him.

I armed myself with a boysenberry pie from Marie Callender's and drove over to El Lobo Rojo. Jordan was hitched up close to a bin sorting tapes, with a yellow plastic dishpan full of cassettes in his lap, his face hidden by a big straw cowboy hat with a curvy brim turned up on both sides. He had the shop halfway pulled apart, rearranging the stock and giving Lupe all kinds of directions in a mixture of English and Spanish.

"Hello!" he said. "What's happening?" I asked if he'd heard about the shooting, which seemed to be the standard opening that morning.

He looked surprised at the question. "Hell, yes, we heard. A lot of guts there. That lady is pur-ty strong. Strong. Take his gun away from him like that? Woo! Deedee says they're going to do an autopsy, find out if maybe he was full of dope." Deedee. Already he considered himself one of the family.

Jordan swung his wheelchair around and banged into the counter behind.

"Damn! This place is too small. Well, it's only temporary." He was calm, even complacent, and I could see that his day in the country with Deirdre had gone well from his point of view, too.

We headed for the little back room to have our pie. Lupe produced real plates and forks, and cut up the pie and served it; but she didn't take any herself. "I have mine later," she said, giving me a look that was frankly mistrustful. "I need to stay out here and tend the store."

"Strong is right," I said to Jordan. "It's a real shame, the kind of rumors they're spreading around about her."

"What rumors?"

"Vera and Eddie? Well, guess. You're a big boy now. I mean; they were in her bedroom. Fairly nasty stuff." I looked disgusted and shrugged it off. This web-weaving might be fun. "I'm glad to see the business between you and Deirdre getting smoothed out," I said. "You met the rest of the family yet?"

"These things take time," Jordan said.

"You mean, things like wills; or anything else having to do with money. Oh, for sure. I just hope she hasn't promised something she can't deliver."

"Meaning?"

"Frankly, I wonder how much real control Deedee has over the Tenhagen assets. If any. You know she still hasn't talked to her mother about you?"

Jordan was feeding Miguel bits of pie with a spoon between his own bites, and appeared to be indifferent; but I figured it was a pose.

"Just as well," I said. "Otherwise I'd begin to worry about Miguel. The woman's death on race-mixing. I mean rabid." Jordan looked over at me, his expression a mixture of boredom and contempt, and I knew I had him going.

"Strong, and tough as ice," I said. "A wall of ice." I kept thinking about Jordan making his little gun appear and disappear. What I wanted him to do was go up there and challenge Vera, confront her. I didn't dare suggest it directly, but I tried to send him the idea; I could feel it vibrating in the air between us. The gun. Get the gun. Do it.

He maybe wasn't picking up anything, but Lupe was. She watched me from across the shop, beside the cash register, with a look of fear and loathing. Take the gun along. Do it, do it!

"You're so full of it," Jordan said.

"Right. What it is, you've sold out. Haven't you?"

"What?"

"That's what I said—they bought you out. And with what? A bigger shop, maybe? Some little bone, a couple of promises. Keep quiet, don't make trouble, and you'll get yours. Someday."

He started to roar, he was furious. "What the hell business is it of yours? You don't know jack shit about this situation. So who asked you to butt your nose in?"

"You forgot already? You did. And it just so happens I got fired for it. Neglecting my work, my boss called it. Now I'm out looking for another job. So thanks a lot."

Then he calmed down, and even halfway apologized.

"You get yourself a lawyer yet?" I asked.

"Yeah, I've been thinking about that. Chuy's in real estate; he'll know somebody." We fell into a neutral silence and I could hear Lupe waiting on a couple of girls, the murmuring exchange in Spanish.

". . . I just can't figure where Vera's coming from," I said. "I guess it's true about rich people, they never have enough. Or maybe she's afraid her others won't have as much, if you get your rightful share. Holy Christ, that woman is supposed to be your mother? I mean, we're talking millions here."

"Bag it."

"No. We're also talking murder here. Woman that gets her lover to kill her husband? Shoot the poor guy and then stuff his pockets full of her jewelry—they were in her bedroom, doesn't that strike you as a little strange? Did she have to screw him right there to set him up?"

Jordan gave me a big lopsided sneer to convey his utter and complete contempt. "Just how stupid do you really think I—" Then he turned and slammed his plate against the back door. Miguel jumped and started to howl; Lupe cried out and came running. The plate stuck for a long moment and then slid, leaving a rosy purple smear down the white-painted door. Jordan already had Miguel against his shoulder, joggling and patting him.

"*Nada, nada,*" Jordan said to Lupe. "It's okay; *no importa.*"

I got up to leave. "I hope you're right and I'm wrong, and it all works out eventually," I said. "If I hear anything more you ought to know, I'll be in touch." I went away feeling tough and only a little nauseated, thinking about the power of the poisoned word.

At La Rancheria, Gage was waiting at the same table under the pepper tree in the patio, quite at home among the big pots of fuchsias, tilted back with his legs out straight and his ankles crossed, drinking a bottle of beer.

"Don't have to go to Frisco today, after all," he said. "Put it off till next week. Aahh . . . this is the life, isn't it? . . . You look a little peaked. What's on your mind?"

"Vera Tenhagen. Our high-society killer."

"Oh, that." Reluctantly he came upright. "Pretty exciting, huh."

"What's your view? As clear-cut as it looks to me—that Eddie set the explosion, and Vera put him up to it?"

"I did have some passing thoughts—we'll probably never know for sure. You know, it's awful, isn't it? Someone you've lived with like that, slept in the same bed—that you could actually do that? Side by side. She really would have to've hated him."

"Unbelievable."

"It's also possible somebody was just trying for the boat, and blew up Arnie Tenhagen by mistake. Stranger things have happened."

"But what if she gets away with it!"

"Then might be she will. No way on God's green earth to catch her, not if she was halfway careful. And. . . ?" He was watching me.

"It isn't fair!"

"Who said anything about fair? Life's not fair, it just is. What're you going to do about it, anyway; shoot her?"

"That'd be the simplest."

Gage grinned and frowned and shook his head all at once. "You do hang on to things, don't you?" he asked. "I've been hoping you'd pretty much be over this obsession of yours by now." And pay some proper attention to me, is what he meant. "But not yet, I see."

"That's right," I said. "Not yet."

And from there on, things went downhill. I wasn't hungry. Gage tried to talk music—he had a lot of country records, everything from Chet Atkins to funky old Bob Wills, who wrote "Faded Loves" and his precious "San Antonio Rose"—and he seemed to be interested in my blues collection; Bessie Smith and Pinetop and the Jimmy Yancey slow boogies, strongly hinting for an invitation to hear them.

"I'd invite you over," I said, "except for two things. One is Fran, Fran, everlasting Fran; and two—obviously I'm not very good company. You're right: it is an obsession. I think she planned it all, right from the beginning."

"Moz, Moz . . . and after you've yelled and sworn about how rotten it is, then what? It's not up to you to take care of this, it's the police. Frankly, what happens to Vera is not your problem."

"And I should just let it go. Forget it. Let her get away with playing Lady Wonderful. People should see what kind of a person she really is!"

"It's not a matter of money, or therapy, or any of that crap, is it," he said. "This has gotten to be some kind of vendetta for you."

"You got that right."

"Not for Rick at all," Gage said. "For your own self. Because you can't stand to get beat. She faked you out; she made you think you're incompetent. Hell, that's—"

I stood up, knocking my chair over. "I'm certainly sorry that your lunch is being spoiled by a, an—incompetent, power-mad female. Obviously you're a man who prefers the peace of total solitude." I stomped out of La Rancheria, furious. Nothing could make me quit now; even though—especially because I understood perfectly why I was so mad at Gage. Because he was right.

I couldn't quite believe it at first—the door of the Crow's Nest was finally open, and there were lights on inside. The cook, all in white with a little boxy cap, was bent double leaning on the counter talking to two happy fishermen having hamburgers. I could tell they'd been successful because their clothes were stiff and stinking with saltwater stains, scales, and what must be fish blood and bait slime, their hands stained and fingernails dark-rimmed, and they both had stubble beards and the dazed, windburned look of men who'd spent the last sixteen or so hours on the water.

"'Ey, George," one of them said; jerking a thumb toward me. "You got a customer. Wait on her, quick, before she figures out she's in the wrong place."

"I'll just have some coffee."

George, smiling behind his wire-rim specs, was maybe seventy, brisk and squeaky-clean, his scalp pink under the close-trimmed white side hair. "How about a liddle piece pie?" He had a strong accent. "Doughnut?"

"Okay, a doughnut, then. That chocolate one. . . . You weren't born in Newport either," I said.

George smiled happily. "Oh, no. I come from Greece, forty years ago now. More. Liddle island—you wouldn't know the name if I told you. Always sunny. Not like here."

When the fishermen had finished and left, George told me about how they used to shoot the little birds with slingshots, about the flocks of birds that got so fat from eating the figs. "We used to wrap the birds up in grape leaves, you know? Pack mud around, build a fire and put them right in it to cook them." He smacked his lips and kissed his fingers. "Mm! Wonderful!" He eyed me slyly. "Right about now, Americans, they go 'What? With the feathers and everything? Ugh.'"

"The feathers come off with the mud," I said.

"That's right! You got it! You priddy smart little girl."

"I wish I were a little smarter. To tell you the truth, I'm here because I've got a problem."

He straightened up and waited, still smiling, his expression a perfect blend of interest, skepticism, and friendliness.

"I need to talk to Cat Malena." His face didn't change. "Did you know her boyfriend, Eddie?"

"Yah. He was priddy nice guy, really. Can't imagine what went wrong there."

"I can. He was set up. Cat was absolutely right, what she

said, because Vera Tenhagen's nothing but an out-and-out killer. I've got to see Cat. Is she here?"

"Right now? No. But she be back. To get her money." He nodded toward a little cork bulletin board hanging above the refrigerator, shaggy with pinned-up papers, where I could see a paycheck stuck among the coupons and utility bills. "Cat's always short of money," George said, smiling. "What's the matter, you don't believe me? Take a look, see for yourself."

"Why, thank you. I'd love to." I was up and around the end of the counter before he could change his mind. The tiny kitchen, grimy but orderly, was empty. The screened vent above the grill was coated thick with dusty grease, a real hazard, a fire waiting to happen. There was nobody in the little storeroom either, or the tiny dark toilet, its washbowl with a twenty-year drip stain shaped like a skull.

"Thank you," I said. "I appreciate that. Can you tell me where Cat lives?"

"Costa Mesa, over on west side. Freedom Homes. You know where that is? Bonch of dummies she's got over there. I don't know any street nomber."

"What about her telephone number?"

"She took it out last year. The dummies, they ran up this great big bill. What you going to do? It was in her name, she had to pay." He shook his head. "Mostly she stayed with Eddie by his place."

Of course. "And he must be in the phone book."

George handed the telephone book to me. "Oh, yah. But he don't live there anymore." He smiled at his own joke.

Eddie's place, 721 Sandpiper, was a weathered frame house not six blocks from Dickerson's Boatyard, around the corner from the Stuft T-Shirt and in among the boat showrooms and engine mechanics and bikini shops and sailmakers. The police had been there and left the door sealed with yellow and black tape and a DO NOT ENTER warning. To one side, over the doorbell button, a faded bumper sticker said PARTY HEARTY. And that was that.

"Need any help?" The call came from the other side of the street; an older man shading his eyes was watching me. He had the biggest belly I'd ever seen on a human. He wasn't that fat overall, certainly not obese, but under the blinding white T-shirt his belly pushed out like a separate organism, as if maybe he'd swallowed a pig whole, like a boa. He had to lean back like a pregnant woman to balance it. Maybe it's a tumor, I thought, or some kind of elephantiasis.

"I'm looking for Cat Malena."

"Is that right. Guess you don't know what's been happening around here," he said happily. He hooked both thumbs in his belt, balancing the belly on his fists, and lumbered across the empty street, ready to tell me the whole story. From the beginning.

Twenty minutes later I had a bona fide address for C. Malena out of last year's phone book, which my friendly stranger located around the corner at the ice house, where Tim the manager never threw anything like that away; which demonstrates the value of behaving nicely, even when you don't feel like it.

And fifteen minutes after that, I was knocking at the door of 4144 Republic. It was a forty-year-old stucco house on a corner lot, its open carport stuffed with decaying furniture, a green plastic recliner, a brown plaid sofa on end. Roof-rat heaven. Clumps of pink oleanders thirty feet high towered above the house and pressed close on either side, walling it off from the side street.

The grass was short and dead, with two vehicles parked on the front lawn, a red Toyota truck and a white Chrysler Imperial, about a '74 and the left rear fender scrunched beyond recognition. I wondered which, if either, was Cat's.

"Hello?" Although the current of warm air flowing out the opened door was rank with old burrito wrappers, mildew, and maybe a backed-up sink, the young man who stood in the doorway, blinking a little in the light, was presentable enough in a clean shirt and jeans. Somewhere around twenty-two, with wisps of pale hair floating.

He ran a hand through his silky blond hair. "Hello," he said, and with a wonderfully serene smile he began stroking his left forearm. Then he said, very slowly, "Can I help you?" He was definitely not on Pacific Standard Time.

"I need to talk to Cat Malena. It's really important. About her boyfriend, Eddie Mowatt?"

A frown appeared between his eyebrows. "Oh, I don't think that's possible," he said.

"Why's that?"

"Because I don't think she's here right now." He considered that a while. "Wait a minute, and I'll go check." He went away, leaving the door open. The coffee table was piled high with taco wrappers, and a cache of beer cans almost hid a pizza box on the floor at the end of the couch. He came back and closed the door.

I waited five minutes, figuring he'd probably floated on down the river of time and forgotten about me. I knocked, and decided to wait some more—what the heck? I'd given Jordan longer than this.

Angel child opened the door again, smiled, said, "You're still here, I see," and nodded at me, serially. I waited.

"I really do need to see Cat," I said. "I think she's about to get a raw deal here, and I don't want to let that happen." I spoke rather loudly and distinctly, figuring Cat herself might be standing just out of sight behind the door.

"I'm really awfully sorry," he said, and stopped to look sorry. "But I'm afraid that's not possible."

"Why not?"

"Because Cat isn't available."

Somewhere in the neighborhood a car was warming up, I could hear the motor of an old crock being gunned . . . certainly a four-cylinder missing on at least one, and with a blown muffler besides. I had plenty of time to listen.

"Then can you tell me when she will be available?" I asked.

"I wish I could do that."

From around the corner with a blatting roar came a yellow

VW with a clay-colored left front fender stripped and primed, and a cloud of smoke pouring out. The girl at the wheel—yes, it was Cat—swerved into the curb and yelled, "Suck-er!" and raised one hand through the open sunroof in the immortal middle-finger salute. Then she rattled on down the street.

"The thing is," he said, "she's not at home right now." And his shoulders shook in a soundless chuckle.

I ran for my car thinking never mind—with a noise like that, I can track her anywhere. And I could, more or less. I heard that blown muffler racketing through the neighborhood, first from one side and then the other as I bounced in and around those T-cross streets and cul de sacs and sudden street bumps to slow through traffic. The sound of Cat's bug got farther away, and then it was gone.

Figuring maybe she'd stopped and parked somewhere, I spent the next half hour working the network of streets with my Thomas Bros. map book. But I knew I'd lost her. For the moment.

Look at it this way, I thought. Of all the things she could've called you, 'sucker' is certainly the most polite. That must mean something.

 This time George was alone in the Crow's Nest, standing in the doorway to the kitchen with a mug of coffee.

"Hello, there!" he said. He put his mug down beside the pie case, shaking his head with the corners of his mouth pulled down. "She didn't . . ." He saw me glance toward the board where Cat's check had been. It was gone.

"You just missed her," he said. "She been here and left already. That's too bad." There was a plate with a half-eaten hamburger and a heap of french fries on the counter, at the place nearest the end. George sat down on the stool, picked up the hamburger and took a bite. "Oh," he said, chewing. "How about it? You want some food?"

"Yeah," I said. "That smells good. I'll have a burger, myself." George, I thought, you'd make a rotten spy. Food in one place, coffee in another—he was eating Cat's dinner.

212

He went out in the kitchen and threw a patty of ground meat on the griddle. "You ever find that place where she lives?" he asked. He had his back to me, scraping the griddle.

"Oh, yeah. We almost connected, in fact. But she ran away. I guess she doesn't understand yet that I'm on her side." I figured Cat was in the little toilet, probably sitting on the closed seat with her legs crossed and the door open, listening. George just shrugged.

"I'd hate to see her ruin her life because of a misunderstanding," I said. "If she just hangs back and lets Vera Rich-Bitch run the show . . . Cat isn't guilty of anything. In fact, it's the other way around. Jeez, you'd think she'd be interested in some justice for Eddie, the poor guy. His memory, anyway. I really admired her when I saw her speaking out on the TV."

"I don't know anything about that," George said. "It don't concern me."

And he didn't have anything more to say, no matter what tack I tried. "I imagine Eddie ate many a meal, sitting right here at this counter. Breakfasts?" George lifted one shoulder, agreeing. Eddie stowing away his pan san and sausages would've been about three hundred yards from *Spray* and the Tenhagens. And a couple of light-years.

I wiped the grease and mayo off my face and hands with some paper napkins and paid. "If you do see Cat, let her know I'm still looking for her," I said. "I'm known as the best damn tracker in my company; and I've only just begun to hunt."

I went outside and stood a minute, trying to decide where to look first. The home-going traffic on Pacific Coast Highway was beginning to lessen somewhat. The Crow's Nest was almost in front of the signal for the cross street that dead-ended into PCH. The stores in the left-hand block opposite, on the inside of the highway, were all rustic wood and mostly dark now, except for the big marine hardware. The right-hand block was more stores and a Mexican restaurant, Pepito's, closed for remodeling now.

I was parked in one of the big lots behind the stores, and

maybe Cat was, too. I sauntered across PCH with the signal, hoping Cat was peeking out watching me.

It only took me a few minutes to find Cat's yellow VW, parked up close behind the restaurant and completely hidden from the cross street by a big blue metal trash bin. The car's sunroof was not only open but gone, and the evening damp was already condensing on the car, inside and out.

I found a spot in the parking lot across the side street and behind the hardware store, where I could look one way and see the door of the café between the buildings, and also keep the approach to Cat's car in view, and moved my dusty maroon Toyota to it. Then I settled down to wait.

The lights were on in the Crow's Nest now, and I could clearly see old George moving around, waiting on the few customers who appeared as the evening wore on. Hardly enough to pay the rent, I thought. Maybe he owned the building. And no sign of Cat Malena. You planning to spend the night here? I thought about that.

The parking-lot lights came on, bathing everything in a bronze light which fell across my thighs. I was sitting close to one of the lights, so that my head and upper body were in darkness, but I figured that anyone really looking this way might be able to see my silhouette.

It was beginning to get cold. When I first started at T. Ambrose, I'd stowed a pair of black sweats in the trunk, secretly thinking of them as my commando clothes, for night surveillance. Now I dug them out and wriggled into them gratefully, pulling them on over my daytime shirt and slacks.

Maybe she left when you weren't watching, I thought. She's not a very patient kind of person. Probably she's wise to you and already left by the back way, is long gone. By nine-thirty I was totally lame and already beginning to worry about staying awake. I put on a talk radio show, low, for a while.

At ten of eleven the lights in the café went off and George came out the front door. Twelve-hour day? The old man must be made of iron, I thought. He paused with the door almost closed and turned to say something—aha! Then he slammed the door and tried the knob a couple of times to be sure it had locked, and walked away up the sidewalk, his hands in his pockets. Anyway, now I knew Cat was still in there.

Doing what—sleeping on the counter? There was only a night-light left on in the kitchen, and around eleven I thought I saw a flicker, as if somebody had moved through the doorway to the customer side. But I was so tired I could've imagined it.

When I looked again the café door was open, a foot-wide slab of black under the streetlight. It was eleven-ten. Then slowly, slowly, a curly head came out, and Cat looked up the street, down the street, across the highway. She stepped outside and slammed the door so hard I could hear it clear over there. She was wearing jeans and sandals with heels, and an athletic jacket, blue and white.

Cat walked over to the traffic signal and pushed the button to change it, tapped one foot a couple of times and then started across without waiting for the green light. In the middle of the street she held her arm out at full length, palm out, evidently signaling a car some distance away to stop. My key was already in the ignition. I stretched my legs to limber them and fastened my seat belt, getting ready for whatever. Cat looked drunk to me.

Moving up the cross street, alongside the building opposite the parking lot, she began stepping with elaborate care, and stopped once suspiciously to look all around. I froze, and then I thought, so what if she sees me? I didn't have anything like a concrete plan for cornering Cat and getting her to talk; I was strictly improvising.

She disappeared behind the trash bin, and I heard the cough and rattle of the VW's engine turning over. It took her about five minutes to warm up, and the racket was horrendous. The highway runs along the foot of the bluff there, and I halfway expected somebody in one of the houses up on Cliff Drive to call the police about the ungodly noise she was making down there.

Finally Cat started to pull out—whang! She backed into the trash bin. Of course. She pulled away again, bumper rattling, and onto the street, without her car lights on. At the corner she slowed down momentarily and then pulled out onto the highway, heading up the coast.

I was only a few car lengths behind her, blinking my headlights on and off, trying to get her to turn hers on. Cat stayed in the outside lane, moving at a sedate speed in wide slow arcs, correcting as she drifted over the line into the next lane, the dead giveaway of a drunk driver. She must've had something stashed in the café; or else she'd brought it with her. Finally I saw her car lights go on.

About six blocks along she stopped beside a liquor store and got out, leaving her motor running and her lights on now. I watched her talking to the clerk, a dark-haired man with thick eyebrows and a hawk nose, both of them laughing and waving their arms. She cashed her paycheck—he pointed, asking her to endorse it—and she came out with a six-pack of beer.

Before Cat started up again she popped the top on a can of beer, tipped it up and took several long swallows. Then she lowered the can and her head drooped, her whole body sagged, like a parched man on the desert who'd finally reached water. Is Cat what I used to be? I wondered. She finished the beer, bent the can double and flipped it up through the sunroof in an arc onto the highway, where it landed with a clank. Then she started up again, in no hurry; so how could I be? Eventually she'd have to alight; and I'd be right there, waiting.

Cat rumbled under the Newport Boulevard overpass and then gunned her motor and swung right, looping up and over the highway and onto the Balboa Peninsula. I couldn't believe the luck. There were only two roads off the peninsula. Now I had her for sure.

She blatted on down the peninsula in the light late-evening traffic, slowing just past the Newport Beach City Hall as if she were going to turn left toward Eddie's place. Instead, she speeded up again. I stayed the same distance behind her all the way along divided Balboa Boulevard, past Newport Pier and down the length of the peninsula toward the little town of Balboa.

I couldn't figure out where Cat was going. The peninsula broadens at its tip, ending a mile beyond the town in a quietly expensive residential neighborhood. There was no other way out but the water. The gray-shingled cupola of the Balboa Pavilion came in view ahead of us and on the left, outlined in white lights against the overcast night sky. The divided street became one again, and Cat suddenly veered left down the side street, toward the bay. I had to wait for an oncoming car, so by the time I could follow, she was out of sight.

I turned left after her, rolling my window down to follow the sound, and then turned right, and saw her taillights ahead of me. She slowed down, and so did I. We were just about two blocks apart now, in a residential neighborhood parked solid, and the only cars moving on the street. Cat found a parking spot, and swerved into it. I cut my lights and motor and coasted to a stop, half across somebody's driveway.

Cat got out, hitching up her little white shoulder bag with its skinny strap, and stood a minute leaning against the car. Half-screened by some shrubbery, I slid across and got out on the passenger side, keeping my eyes on her. But my car door bumped the bush. Cat saw the movement, stared my way a moment and was off like a startled deer.

She had the advantage of a stride twice as long as mine, and a head start. Cat cut down a side street to the right and back toward Balboa Boulevard and was temporarily out of sight. As I rounded the corner I saw her again, galloping across Balboa, and tires screeched as a car braked to avoid hitting her. Cat was heading straight toward the beach, only a block beyond. What's she got in mind? I wondered; drowning herself?

From the other side Cat looked across, saw me, and raced on. All she had to do, I knew, was cut down the alley that runs parallel to Balboa Boulevard and behind the ocean-front houses, and then step into some doorway, and I'd lose her. But instead she plunged straight ahead, up the three concrete steps at the street end, and onto the wide misty beach.

She had slower going in the soft sand, and I gained on her temporarily. I was close enough now to hear her noisy breathing as she ran.

"Cat, wait!" I yelled. "Just to talk . . ." It was hopeless. With those long legs she had, I'd have to run her to a standstill to catch her. Beyond the band of pale sand the ocean stretched dark and indistinct, unseeable after the bright lights, and I could hear the surf now, the *crack-crack-crack* as an invisible wave started to break echoing all down its length. Ahead of me Cat spread her arms, jumped, and dropped out of sight.

"Cat! Don't!"

The beach dropped away toward the water at a sharp angle cut by the last high tide. Crouching, I slid partway down the slope, blinking my eyes to adjust to the faint light and trying to catch a glimpse of Cat, or the sound of her splashing. Then I saw her to my left, racing along the hard wet sand, heading toward the Balboa Pier.

I started after her again along the slanted beach, staying close to the water's edge. Cat seemed to be slowing down, and I had some notion that if she made a desperation move into the water I might be able to cut her off before she got out too far. Then she screamed and went down, sprawled out flat. I froze in a crouch, trying to make myself invisible.

"Oh, shit!" Cat sat up, yanked off her sandal and threw it as far as she could. "Damn things!" Then she yanked off the other one and threw it. I had my mouth open to call out something friendly and reassuring, when suddenly a spent wave hit me and knocked me into the icy water, drenching me.

Cat was up and running again, and I struggled to my feet and thrashed after her, holding up my soaking sweatpants with both hands. She was winded now, I could hear her gasping—but so was I. Near the big parking lot alongside Balboa Pier she cut up away from the water and fell at the top of the sandy incline and lay there a minute, panting.

"Hey there," I yelled, toiling along after her like a squirrel too fat in the haunches. "Wait up. Ain't we a pair?"

She pulled herself to her knees and then stood up. "Aren't you ever going to quit?" she hollered back, and loped on across the parking lot.

"No!" I shouted back, exhausted. "Make up—your mind-toit!" Cat jogged past the Studio Café, that jazz spot at the foot of the pier where I'd met Keith, and on down the Boardwalk, widening the distance between us now. I stopped and leaned on the wall, trying to summon up some energy. Inside they were partying, as always. The music pounded through the air and through the stucco against my back.

Oh, you idiot, I thought, and dropped the sodden sweatpants and stepped out of them. I jogged on, my feet squishing in the sneakers at every step. Cat was nowhere in sight.

I cut back to Balboa Boulevard just in time to get a glimpse of Cat crossing about three blocks ahead of me, and after that it was only a matter of time. I finally ran her down sitting on the sand in the shadows at a street-end between two tall houses, facing the dark waters of the bay with their liquid reflections of the lights from Balboa Island across the way, smoking a cigarette.

Cat turned her head. "Don't come any closer," she said. "Or I'll go straight out in the water and you'll never see me again. I'm bigger than you are; I've got to be stronger and faster."

"Right," I said, and sat down cross-legged on the sand where I was, grateful for a little rest.

She took another drag on her cigarette, and then examined the glowing tip. "Eddie wasn't actually that nice of a guy, sometimes," she said, her head turned my way. "Sometimes I didn't even like him that much, you know? Only, I just can't stand it without him." She began whimpering. "I feel like I'm going to die." Then she started to bawl out loud.

"Hssh!" I said, coming closer. "You'll wake the neighbors, and they'll call the police."

She quieted down, threw her cigarette in the water and went on snuffling.

"Well. Before you do," I said, "would you just tell me about Eddie and Vera? Or maybe you don't know anything after all, and I've been chasing you for nothing."

"I wish he had of killed her," Cat said.

"So do I."

Cat looked at me. "Bitch." I decided she meant Vera. "I don't think they ever really, you know, did anything together," Cat said. "But he sure had plans. Did you know, he started making me hide, wouldn't let anybody see us together, or let me stay over at his place anymore. For fear it might get back to her. Making out how crazy he was about her."

I inched closer, not wanting to miss anything. The little breeze coming from the water was agony, freezing my bones, and I hugged my knees. "She was just using him," Cat said. "Anybody could see it. Except him. They were using each other." She laughed. "See, he was convinced she was hot for his body. Like, she'd sort of accidentally brush by him, he said, real subtle, so nobody else would notice. 'This woman's going to be my ticket out of here,' he'd say. 'Even though she doesn't know it yet.'"

"How?" I said. "What did she want him to do? What did she say to him?"

"I can't remember exactly," Cat said, suddenly mulish. "Why?"

"Well, you know, she's the guilty party." My teeth were chattering and I braced my jaw against my knee to control the shaking.

Cat rolled her eyes toward me, getting nervous. "He was real vague about it. Anyway, he'd had a couple of drinks."

"Yeah. I know how that goes."

She leaned back on her elbows. "We used to fight about it a lot, and you know what he said to me once? He says to me, 'She smells like money, and you smell like hamburgers. And that's it.' Asshole."

"So why did she want her husband dead? She could just as well have divorced him. . . ."

"Oh yeah, right. Perfect example. She told him it was just the boat he was supposed to do. And then he finds out her old man's inside at the time? He was scared shitless. . . . You're wasting your time, I hope you know. If they ask me, I deny everything." Cat tilted around to smile at me with malice, momentarily enjoying herself. Then she lay back in the sand with her arms folded under her head and stretched out.

"I used to think if I slept with smart guys it would make me smarter, you know? Boy, was I wrong." She rolled onto her side, curled up with her cheek on her hand. She was going to sleep.

"Listen," I said. "You can't stay here all night."

"Right."

"You could stay at my place for tonight. That way you won't be hassled, at least."

". . . told me they had orders to take me in. And they're supposed to shoot to kill if you're resisting arrest. You believe that?"

"Actually, no." I knew there was no chance I could get Cat up on her feet and all the way back to my car. I'd have to go back and bring it here, and pray she wouldn't be gone.

"Listen," I said. "I'll get the car, be right back. Okay?"

"Okay," Cat said. "Right."

**21** Jogging back down Balboa Boulevard started to warm me up. The Balboa Theater was just letting out—Gerard Depardieu in *Jean de Florette*. What a hunk. Remembering him in *The Return of Martin Guerre* helped raised the temperature, too. But the sand and water inside my sockless sneakers started to rub blisters, and I had to slow down to a walk the last half-mile or so. Then I saw two Newport Beach police cars with their blue rooflights turning pulled up alongside Cat's yellow VW, and I started jogging again, bloody feet or no. Cat was right, then; they were looking for her.

But when I passed them with a smile and a nod, I saw the reason why. Cat had parked smack up against a fire hydrant.

When I finally got back with my car, Cat was still there at the darkened street-end, stretched out sound asleep on the sand. It took me a while to wake her up. "Come on, Cat, it's starting to get light! The neighbors are liable to call the cops when they see you out here. Let's go home."

She got up in stages, complaining. I knocked some of the sand off her, and she limped over to the car. She slid onto the back seat, groaning, and stretched out, and I saw a fresh gash in the sole of her foot, with sand, blood, and guck crusted in it. I folded the long, dirty feet inside and closed the door, feeling as if I'd captured a twentieth-century unicorn.

On the way home I started to wonder how I'd get Cat up those stairs if she turned unwilling. But she solved that for me. Halfway there she sat up in the car and said, "I need a restroom," her eyes dark and worried in the rearview mirror.

"It's right up here, just a few more blocks. Can you make it?"

"Certainly," she said, insulted, and lay back down again.

So I worked her up my stairs, one step at a time. Fran heard us and stuck her head out. "What's this?" she said. I scowled and waved her back inside.

Once I had Cat safely in and with the door closed and bolted, I said to Cat, "That's Fran, the woman who lives here. Don't mind her. She doesn't hear very well." And to Fran, loudly, "Fran, this is Cat, a friend of mine. She's going to stay here tonight. Stay, okay? You got it?"

Fran nodded vigorously and said, "Mm. Hm."

"Do you mind if I use your restroom?" Cat asked, blinking in the light.

As soon as the bathroom door had closed behind her, I ran to get the little tape recorder in my dresser drawer, and then showed Fran how to work it. "You'll have to hide it someway— stay as close as you can," I whispered, shucking off my wet clothes. "Eddie told her all about everything. He said it was Vera's idea." Fran lit up like a torch, opened her mouth and then closed it. "And see to it you get every word," I said. "No matter what you have to do."

The bathroom door opened, and Cat limped out. "What's the matter?" Fran asked, pointing at Cat's foot. When she saw the gash, she shook her head and clucked, "Tsk, tsk, tsk"—

overacting a bit, I thought, but then Cat wouldn't know—and went to fill the dishpan with warm water.

We settled Cat on the edge of Fran's opened-out bed with a blanket around her and her foot soaking in the dishpan. Fran fixed us all mugs of hot cocoa. Cat said, "Thank you very much," and sat looking glumly at hers. I figured she'd rather have had something like brandy; and if I'd had any around, she would've gotten it. Cat was sobering up, and getting more sullen and withdrawn by the minute.

"You hungry?" I asked her.

"No, thank you." She wouldn't look at me steadily, just glanced and then away. How to get her talking again?

"What I don't get," I said, "is Eddie claiming it was all Vera's idea. Isn't that just what he would say? Frankly, I find it hard to believe."

"Well, I don't give a . . . burp if you believe it or not," Cat said. "That's exactly the thing of it. She's too smart. Like crying around all upset about how Arnie was getting brainsick or something, wanting to play like Marlon Brando on the beach in Tahiti. See, she didn't ever *say* anything bad herself, right out. Just hint around and work it around till she got Eddie to say it. Oh, she's a smart old . . . bat, all right." Fran's presence, whether or not she could hear, seemed to be inhibiting Cat. She was being a good little girl.

Fran sat on a straight chair pulled up behind the couch, with her knitting bag on her lap (and the tape recorder underneath, I figured), crocheting away at one of her eternal blue place mats.

"Poor Eddie," I said.

"Oh, Eddie knew what was happening. But he had it all figured. He was going to come out of it a *big man*."

"So then, this line across my stairs. That was Vera's idea too, right?"

She took a swallow of cocoa and made a face. "Huh-uh; his. To scare you off. When you came around and left your card and all, he figured you were on to something. Why couldn't you mind your own damn business!" she yelled.

"Good question," I said.

"If you'd kept your nose out of it, nothing more would've happened! He'd still be alive, anyway." She whimpered a couple of times and gave it up.

"You think so? You think Vera'd want to leave a witness hanging around?"

"You got it." Cat yawned suddenly. "And then she has the gall to say it's all his fault, he did it all, it was just some terrible mistake. . . ." She was falling asleep again.

"Nah," I said, shaking my head. "Where did they even get a chance to see each other?"

"At the boatyard, when Eddie knew Ben would be gone. See, Arnie being in it was so much more serious that he started to figure Vera'd try to nail him for it."

"So he decided to go up there and talk to her about it."

"'I've got to get this straightened out,' he said. He didn't say how, or when. Jesus, but he was scared. . . . She's so rich," Cat wailed. "Nobody's ever going to touch her." She lifted her foot out of the water and looked at the cut, and Fran leaned over the back of the couch, looking, too. The gash was about an inch long, and not deep enough to need stitches, I decided. The sole of her foot was white and wrinkled.

I handed Cat the towel and she dried her foot, yawning till her jaws cracked. "Woo! I'm beat."

"You can sleep in my bed tonight," I said. "This one is Fran's."

"That'll be okay. Listen, I appreciate this, don't get me wrong. But just don't figure any of it, what I told you, is going to go any farther; because it isn't. I'll deny everything, I'll look them straight in the eye and say, 'Eddie who?' I want nothing more to do with the cops. Nothing." She shrugged. "Sorry. That's just the way it is."

"Right," I said. "I got it."

I took Cat into my bedroom and left her to get into my bed, which luckily is a queen-size—where else would I sleep?—and came back out to shower. Fran was fizzing with excitement.

"What do you think?" she hissed. We went into the bathroom and rewound the tape partway and hit the "play" button. Cat's voice said, ". . . Eddie could tell what was happening." Fran whooped soundlessly. I turned it off.

"Will this do it?" she whispered. "Have we got enough?"

"Well, we've got something. I'm too tired to say right now. Let's talk about it in the morning."

I lay in the dark on my side of the bed listening to Cat's peaceful breathing, trying to get myself unwound. When I was sitting on that little beach in the dark shaking with the cold, it had all been so simple—I was on top of the world. And now I'd come down; because I knew we'd won and lost, both.

True, we'd been right about Vera. But even if by some freak of luck I could persuade Cat to testify to what she'd told us, it would never stand up in court. Cat would be a rotten witness, utterly unreliable; anybody could wind her around and trip her up with no trouble. To start out, they'd demonstrate that she's an alcoholic. In addition, everything she'd told me was hearsay. But I can't give up now, I thought, I've come too far. There's got to be a way to prove it. . . . I was too tired; I slid away into sleep.

Terrible dreams woke me, gushes of blood flowering in the dark, a severed leg, crying mutilated babies, and a chainsaw biting into live flesh. Vera did it, she'd made it all happen. Play the tape for Jordan; make him see. Edit it, even—the best stuff from the bay beach wasn't on there, but it was still true. Get him to go up there—Socorro could sneak him in the back way.

Say I got it set up with Socorro ahead of time, and the intercom was open. He could listen in Socorro's room while I talked to Vera. Push her, get her going—insult her with Eddie, work on her till she cracks and finally admits it, contemptuous; I'm nobody, anyway. And then Jordan would come charging in; the confrontation, argument; he'd pull out his little hidden gun and shoot her dead.

Better yet—someway I'd get her kids up there, Keith and Deirdre both, so they could see it all. Behind my eyelids the whole beautiful thing unfolded, Jordan tearing her apart with terrible cutting phrases, and then the gun in his hand and the crack as he fired, *pam! pam!*—Vera's look of surprise and horror, the bullet holes in her chest and the blood spreading. . . .

I opened my eyes and stared into the darkness. The dim light from around the blinds gave the room solidity and contour. I was afraid to close my eyes again and see the bullets hit and the blood spurt, and I stared at each familiar thing in turn, around to the chest of drawers with the clean clothes Fran had folded piled neatly on top and the little Rembrandt drawing of the lion hanging above it. I was as crazy as Vera, as vengeful and vicious, and just as willing to use anybody to get what I wanted. Ruin Jordan's life—what did I care? I wanted to write JUSTICE up in the night sky in huge glittering fireworks. Right on, Gage. I wanted to play God.

Sometime later Cat groaned, turned over and then sat up and looked around. She held out her T-shirt and sniffed down her front. "I stink," she said. "I can't stand myself. I need a shower."

"Go ahead," I said. The night was shot anyway.

By the time Cat came back and got settled again, the clock said three forty-seven. I arranged myself for a little rest, at least, and just let it all slide away, I abandoned the whole struggle. In the sycamore outside the birds had begun to twitter, which was crazy: this was late October, not spring. . . . If you can't have everything, then what? Choose the one most important thing, and go for it. Which is? The solution came over me all together, as sweet and wonderful as rain falling on the desert. I curled up and fell asleep.

Next morning Cat hunched scowling over her cup of coffee and refused Fran's wonderful offers to fix her breakfast. "Omelet?" Fran asked. "Pancakes? Grapenuts? Shredded-wheat biscuits?" Fran dashed around the kitchen demonstrating each, and then her own all-time favorite, toasted Health Nut muffins spread with low-calorie cottage cheese. Overdoing it a little, I

227

thought. Anybody sharper than Cat would be more than skeptical.

"I just hope my car's still there all right," Cat said, sticking out her lower lip. "I just hope it hasn't been stolen. How'm I supposed to get back down there to it, anyway? I don't even know what buses you've got out here."

"Fran can drive you down okay. I'll give her the directions." I figured Cat was in a hurry to get away from here because she needed a drink.

When I managed to get Fran aside, I explained about Cat's parking her car beside a fireplug. "I'll bet you it's been towed," I said. "But don't you tell her; let her figure it out for herself." I took out three twenty-dollar bills. "You can give her this toward the impound. I guess I owe her that much."

Cat went slapping down the cement stairs barefoot without looking back. "Take it easy," I said.

"Oh, right. Sure I will."

Just as I'd expected, at 9 A.M. Gage was in his office, cranking away. "What's this?" he asked, startled but pleased, and then he looked worried. "What's happened?"

"It's not an emergency, you can relax. I just wanted to talk to you. Ask your advice about something. After I apologize for losing my cool yesterday."

"Oh, hey," he said. "I was—I could've kept my mouth shut, to say the least."

I had to laugh, it was so typical. Gage still believed he was right, and couldn't bring himself to pretend otherwise. "This is true," I said. Gage pulled a chair around for me, and closed his office door.

"It's about this Vera thing," I said. "I had a chance to talk to Cat Malena, and sure enough, Vera got Eddie to do it. But I can see now we'll never get her convicted, even though she's guilty as sin. So I got to thinking: what about that great big life-insurance policy Arnie just bought? Wouldn't the company at least investigate, if they thought they'd been taken? I mean, if the designee is involved in some very suspicious circumstances . . ."

"Why, hell yes, they would," Gage said. He was tickled to death at my return to sweet reasonableness, and falling all over himself. "They're going to go at it six different ways if there's even a hint of attempt to defraud. Arnie had a policy on himself, with his wife as beneficiary? What kind of money we talking?"

"We must be talking seven figures here . . . I don't think Sandra Healy said how much exactly."

"Course they may wind up eventually paying anyway, if they can't definitively prove intent to defraud. But she'd get herself listed as a shady lady, on the wrong side risk-wise. They couldn't let her flat-out get away with it, as a matter of principle. And it might drag on for months. Those big companies have resources. They're deep."

"What might drag on?"

"The investigation."

"Too long," I said. "I can't wait."

22 "We need to get together," I said. "Say, your place? Six o'clock?"

"Not a chance," said Deirdre. "Give me one good reason why."

"Because I've talked to Cat Malena, and I taped the whole conversation. She makes some pretty radical accusations." Silence. I knew Deirdre couldn't resist. Besides being vitally concerned, coping with problems was her specialty. She loved the sense of power it gave her.

All or nothing. Keith opened the door of Deirdre's apartment and smiled at me, and I was back inside the living peach. I held the little tape recorder against my shirt, mostly hidden by my arm. "Deedee's on the phone," he said. "Can I get you something? Perrier?" With a shy grin, to show that he remembered.

"No, thanks."

Deirdre stood in the kitchen door talking on a peach-colored phone with a long cord. "Be right with you." She gave me a samurai sort of glare, ready for combat.

There was a glass of whiskey on the white marble coffee table, but Keith passed it by and we went out onto the little balcony overlooking the ravine. The chaparral was still mostly a dusty brown, waiting for the winter rains, and the wedge of bay we could see to our left was gray and still.

"How are you holding up?" I asked.

"Oh, okay. Not really. Everything is totally bizarre. Seeing my mother sitting there in the morning reading the newspapers—I can't believe it, I mean the whole thing is incomprehensible." He blinked; there were tears in his eyes. He hasn't the foggiest idea why I'm here, I thought. Doesn't Deirdre ever tell him anything?

"She's completely stripped the room where it happened; says she'll never sleep in there again. Had some guys come this morning and cut out part of the carpet, the . . . you know . . . stained section. They wrapped it up in a sheet and carried it out like a body. Agh! Listen, that was my parents' bedroom, I've lived in that house all my life! I used to bring the Sunday papers in there and we'd all pile on, read the comics together. . . ."

"Moz, you want something?" Deirdre called. "I've got this— no, I already told you, he has to be back in Washington on the twenty-sixth."

"I don't think she likes you talking to me," I said to Keith.

"I don't think I like any of it," he said. ". . . That's what I wish I was right now." He pointed at a lone sea gull gliding toward the bay.

"Finally," Deirdre said, exasperated. "Come on in here, and let's get on with it."

I put the tape recorder down on the amber-veined marble of the coffee table, and we sat down around it. Keith picked up the glass and took a swallow of his whiskey.

"First of all, I'd like you to understand my position in this,"

I said. "I'm frankly not the least interested in who was responsible for what, where, and how, and I've got no intention of involving the police." Deirdre snorted at that, such an absurdity. "All I care about is an adequate settlement for my friend Rick and his family. I'm going to make sure he's properly taken care of."

"Ah; a settlement." Deirdre sat back with a disagreeable smile. Now she was on familiar ground. "Maybe you'd better tell us the circumstances where this great revelation occurred," she said.

"About one o'clock this morning, at my apartment, after a long, hard night," I said.

"—And with Cat Malena, it would be that," Deirdre said. "She's one of our more prominent local drunks, I guess you know."

"Let's just get it over with," Keith said, looking bored and unhappy. I started the tape.

At Cat's first rambling words, Deirdre let her shoulders drop, visibly relaxed. When they heard ". . . brainsick or something, wanting to play Marlon Brando on the beach in Tahiti," she and Keith exchanged an involuntary glance.

"I don't want to hear any more of this garbage," Keith said, and leaned toward the tape recorder. Deirdre stopped him.

"Wait. Let's call her bluff. None of this has a shred of validity. It's absolute schlock." Hearing my own voice pushing Cat, leading her, and Cat's ramblings, "Jesus, but he was scared," and "She's so rich!" I knew Deirdre was probably right.

"I want to see how far out on her limb Miss Cobra's willing to go," Deirdre said.

"Elemen-tree," I said. "All the way."

The tape finished and Deirdre said, feigning wonder, "And that's it? All this fuss over that trivial bit of—twaddle?"

"You know what?" Keith said. "Why don't we just erase it and be done with it?" Deirdre opened her eyes wide and then closed them, which was enough to convey her instant conclusion that Keith was possibly loaded, for sure hopelessly naive, and that, besides, now she had to manage him, too, push his little buttons along with everything else. But I saw that Keith was sincere, even knowing it was useless; he was bone-weary and wanting to be out of it. He hadn't even been surprised. It was as if he'd been anticipating the worst. Sitting there watching the tidal wave roll in.

"I don't think your father's life-insurance carrier will find it so completely trivial," I said to Deirdre.

"Oh," said Keith.

"Yes; oh," said Deirdre.

"Fine," I said, getting up. "Then I see my attorney, and we contact the insurance people. Or maybe it's something your mother ought to hear first."

"Don't you go near her," Keith said. "Haven't you brought her enough misery already?"

"Me?"

"Why not?" said Deirdre. "Yes, let's. She's obviously bluffing, she knows this can't go anywhere. It's a load of bullshit, speaking frankly. Which is exactly what Mother will say. So we can put an end to this stupid nonsense, once and for all."

"But I don't think that . . ." I hung back, trailing the bait, still not believing she'd take it.

"Come on," Deirdre said. "Let's get it over with. Let's go."

"Hey, not so fast," Keith said. "Some of this is pretty ripe stuff. I think we're talking libel here."

"Exactly!" said Deirdre. "Not to mention harassment. You think we can't handle this?"

And she even insisted in riding up in my car with me, as if I might have second thoughts and try to escape. "You can bring me back after," she said to Keith.

When we were stopped at the gate, Deirdre leaned over to say, "It's all right, Chuck. She's with me." Chuck, every blond hair sprayed in place and his uniform shirt creased in thirds like a policeman's, gave me the fish-eye and Deirdre a toothy grin, and raised the barrier.

Deirdre leaned forward, eager for the challenge. This was

real, the outcome could profoundly affect their lives; and she loved the contest. Had Arnie been like that? I wondered. At first, anyway.

Going up the hill I began to realize that I had absolutely no strategy for dealing with this situation. I'd been running so hard that I never stopped to consider what I'd do when I got there. Worse: I was probably walking into some kind of a trap, or why had Deirdre acquiesced so readily? Three against one. I'd be lucky to get out with a whole skin. I began the mental thrash, trying to churn up a plan. Then I realized it was impossible, and let it go.

Vera's black BMW was sitting in the middle of the Tenhagen driveway. When Keith got out of his little white Porsche convertible he looked haggard, his skin pasty, and I saw that he was sick with fear.

Socorro had served Vera her dinner at a small table set up in the sunroom, overlooking the view of the harbor and the open ocean. In the last of the light, the waters of the harbor and the ocean moved pale and alive, but points of light had begun to appear in the dark, indistinct land mass framing the water.

Vera turned to take us in without getting up. "This is a surprise." I sensed that she was annoyed at seeing the three of us come there together. She gave me a long, knowing look, and for a mad moment I believed she already knew everything I'd been doing and what I intended, and that she was completely in control.

"Do you want your coffee now?" Socorro asked. Vera looked at me, paused, and said,

"No. I'll take it a little later," making clear that she intended not to offer me anything. Socorro, stolid as a deaf-mute and meeting no one's eyes, cleared Vera's place, her hands dark against the white gold-edged china, the crystal water goblet and wineglass etched with stalks of wheat. Deirdre pulled a chair up and sat down. When I moved up to the table, Vera glanced over to be sure Socorro was out of earshot and then said to me,

"I'm really quite stunned to see you in my house. My first impulse is to call someone and have you removed."

"Good," I said. "Do it. Then maybe we can get this all out in the open and cleared up."

"If this is supposed to imply . . ." Vera began imperiously, looking from Keith to Deirdre.

Keith began to stammer something, and Deirdre said, "It implies nothing, Mother. We've come up against an . . . interesting situation, you might say, and we're going to deal with it. Among ourselves." She nodded toward the tape recorder as I laid it on the pale blue linen tablecloth.

"You've been through a simply awful business, and we really want to get the pressure off," Deirdre said. "But first we have to decide how to deal with this bit of unpleasantness. What we've got here is a tape recording of very dubious origins—"

"—Which you don't have to listen to more of than a little," Keith said. "So you'll see where we're coming from. Actually, you don't have to hear it at all if you don't want to." That clinched it, I thought. Keith was wonderful at promoting other people's aims.

"Crashing in without understanding a thing," Vera said to me. "Doing just irreversible damage. You ought to know," she said, looking from Keith to Deirdre, "that your father hasn't always been well over the years. Even though you never saw him as anything but completely competent and in charge of the world, I have to tell you that he suffered from a . . . a kind of monomania now and then. When Jordan was born—first of all, he couldn't stand anything not in perfect working order; you know that."

"Mother," Deirdre said, "this isn't about Jordan."

"Then what is it about?"

"I'm here because I've been talking to Cat Malena, Eddie's girlfriend," I said. "He said some things to her about the boat, before and afterward."

"Moz managed to lead the girl into making some pretty farfetched and absurd charges," Deirdre said.

"Really." Vera smiled.

"Moz seems to have the illusion that the insurance carriers will be interested," Deirdre added.

"What I do think is that Rick's going to get what he needs."

"I think she's dreaming dollar signs, myself," said Deirdre.

"As in settlement?" I said. "You're right."

"It does begin to smell a bit blackmailish," Vera said. She talked only to them, as if by ignoring me completely she could will me out of existence. Wonderful self-control; even then I had to admire her.

"I know how nasty this will sound, what with Eddie's being dead," Vera went on. "But it just goes to show. All the signs were there, long before— No; let's just hear what this girl has to say."

I pushed the "start" button, and Cat said sullenly, "Thank you very much." Vera listened with an expression of deepening disgust and contempt until "work it around till she got Eddie to say it." Then her arm lashed out and she tried to knock the tape recorder off the table; but I got my hand there first and kept it clamped down. The buckle of Vera's watch raised a welt across my arm.

I pushed the "stop" button. "I beg your pardon," Vera said, and drew a ragged breath. "Lies; a parade of them. A whole life's work of lies! If you could've seen him that day, Keith. I wasn't going to tell either of you, I wasn't going to tell a living soul about it ever. Pushing me around, rubbing himself, getting all excited. . . . 'I know what you've been wanting,' he said. I saw the way he looked at me even before then, but I always figured he had more sense. And then when he told me, actually bragged about what he'd done—I couldn't believe it! I couldn't go on living in the same world with him after that, could I?"

Vera bent over weeping into her hands and they both went to her, stroking her hair, rubbing her shoulders, "It's all right, Mom," and "Come on, Mom, it's okay now."

"Just a terrible accident," Vera said. "I adored your father, you know that. It was only the boat I hated." Keith and Deirdre exchanged a look above her bent head and I turned away.

"Yah," Socorro said. She stood in the doorway, her hands folded together making a knobby lump under her apron. "What about the gun?" Socorro asked, looking at me. She was scared, she kept her eyes fixed on mine. "You hear what I'm telling? She had it before, all the time. I see it in the drawer, in the back underneath her clotheses."

"You're crazy," Vera said, straightening up.

"You saw a gun?" Keith returned, sarcastic. "Where? When was this? Do you remember the date?"

"What kind of a gun was this?" Deirdre demanded. "Can you identify it? What do you know about guns, anyway?"

"Yah," Socorro said. "I know what I say, you don't change me. And don't worry to fire me," she told Vera. "I quit. Right now."

"This I will not tolerate," Vera said. "Keith, call the police. Now."

Nobody moved.

"Keith . . ." Vera began, and stopped.

"Mommy, we can't do that," Deirdre said.

"Mom? It doesn't matter," Keith said. "We love you."

"We'll always love you," Deirdre said.

"Yes," Vera said. "I know what I see." She looked from one to the other, shaking her head. "To think that I'd—but everything was for you; everything. You never wanted for a thing, did you? I always saw to it you had it. I! Me! You've been my whole life." Vera pushed back her chair and stood up. Deirdre reached toward her but Vera dodged the hand—"No!"—and ran out of the room. Socorro stepped back to let her pass.

The front door slammed. Nobody said anything.

Deirdre looked at me. "Bitch. Why couldn't you mind your own damn business?" Just what Cat had said. We heard a car starting and Deirdre, leaning against the table as if too exhausted to move, stirred herself. "Come on, Keith. We better go after her."

Socorro and I walked out onto the entryway and watched the white Porsche back out the gate. I was so tired I was staggering, like I'd been climbing a long way, or maybe holding my breath for a week.

"I tried to told you," Socorro said. "About the gun. I called you up."

"That's right. You did." She offered me a cup of coffee, but I didn't think I could drink it, my stomach was too jumpy. Then we heard a dull *whump!* from somewhere down the hill, and a glow lit up the evening sky.

"My God," I said, and ran for my car.

Even before I came around the last turn and onto the long grade to the entrance gate I could hear Deirdre screaming. I took it all in at once: Vera's black BMW still blazing, the roar and crackle sending up a column of oily black smoke. She'd hit the corner of the stone gatehouse dead-on and then rolled over at least once—the top of the car was crunched, and the front end had been driven so far in by the impact that there was no front seat left.

Chuck, held off by the heat, hopelessly pumped a dead fire extinguisher; the spurts of white powder on the ground had never reached the car. There was a terrible stink of burning fuel and roasted flesh; Deirdre was thrashing and trying to tear herself away from two women, Keith leaning on his car and holding his arms in front of him, but they looked weird—they were charred. The awful stench. Then I was on my knees in the gutter, vomiting.

They said there was an overflow crowd at Pacific View Cemetery for Vera's memorial service. I'd even thought about going myself, till I saw the look on Fran's face. She went instead, and told me all about it.

"Everybody kept saying, 'What a terrible accident, such a tragedy,'" Fran said. "Poor woman, just shattered by the death of her husband, just couldn't go on. Like they thought she did the right thing."

Socorro and Lupe came in with Jordan, all three of them totally in black and wearing wraparound shades, and somebody behind Fran said, "Whoa—is that Hollywood?" and someone answered, "Mexican Mafia." They went right on up to the front. Lupe wore high heels and had her hair pinned up, looking quite the determined young lady. Getting ready to take on anybody.

I went to visit Socorro at the house she and Benita were buying in a quiet barrio in Santa Ana about half a mile west of the Orange County Courthouse. It has a fence of big black wrought-iron fans all around, iron grilles over the windows, and twenty different kinds of roses pruned back with new growth coming, sprays of little red leaves.

"You have a lovely place," I said.

"Yah. She don't take it away now."

"You mean Vera?—Because of the money?" Socorro nodded, her mouth tight. So she'd been afraid all these years that Vera might try to get it back, the money they'd earned for Jordan's keep. Chains of gold.

"How are Jordan and Lupe doing?"

"Good," she said. "Except for Deedee all the time hanging around. Mikey need this clotheses, bring Mikey that—a real little car to ride on, red, goes by itself. Too much!"

"Trying to take over. Does that sound familiar?"

"Yah," said Socorro. "She wants him, all right."

Of course; the only Tenhagen grandchild. "Is Lupe tough enough?" The electronic chimes in the church across the street started, a wall of sound that blocked everything. I lip-read Socorro's answer: "Got to."

We moved around to the side of the house away from the chimes, talking mouth to ear. Auntie Deirdre was also arranging for some plastic surgery for Jordan, to repair the forceps damage.

I was hypocritically praising Socorro's six-foot bird of paradise, one of California's uglier specialties, when the chimes stopped. "So okay, Socorro. Can we talk about Arnie's big secret now?"

She let go of the flower stalk. I could see that she still didn't feel right about telling it. ". . . He let me to think he did this to Jordan. Cripple him, hurt his back so he never walk. The nurse in the hospital say the baby's okay when he first come out, kicking and everything. But then next morning, something happen. Yelling in the room. She see the baby's on the floor and Mrs. Ten yells at the mister, 'It's all your fault!' Like he drop the baby, or maybe even throw him down. Because he's ugly, you know, his face spoiled?"

She stood with her fingers pressed over her lips. Then she said, "But now I think it's not Mr. Ten at all, it's her. I just don't know. I don't know."

I told Gage all about it that night while we were having oysters on the half-shell down at The Crab Cooker, opposite Newport Pier. Cold, slimy things—well, you've got to eat something, and I still couldn't stand even the smell of meat.

"One thing I'd be willing to bet," Gage said. "They never scattered Vera's ashes at sea." He grinned and so did I, but still he was keeping a sharp eye on me. I slopped some more sauce on my oysters.

The best thing that had happened so far was seeing Rick the day before. He was sitting up in bed big as life, eating scrambled eggs with his hands out of a square plastic foam dish and patiently picking every bit out of the corners. He stopped with a clump of egg halfway to his mouth, thinking, and then he said, "Ha," and grinned.

I talked to him for a while, told him how great he looked and how happy I was. When the last crumb was gone, he licked his fingers and leaned back against the pillows to rest. And when I told him good-bye, he stopped and frowned. "Wheh Dudy?" he asked. I didn't answer.

"Good to have you back," Gage said.

"Good to be back." He slid his shoe alongside mine under the table. Yes, that was a definite nudge. I didn't nudge back yet, but I didn't move away, either. Gage took his own sweet time, but he knew where he was going.

He'd heard through the grapevine that Arnie's antique compass turned up in San Francisco, and Deirdre quietly got it back. "Funny thing," he said. "Arnie died by fire, and so did she." Everything so chancy, I thought—even the distance from home to the gatehouse: time enough for Vera to work herself into a frenzy, but not far enough for her to think up an alternative.

I pushed the rest of my oysters across to him. "Here, you finish these. I've had all I'm going to." The waitress came right over, and I ordered some more rice and salad.

"What do you think about the service?" Gage asked, teasing me. While I got myself situated again with Leo, clearing up my cases, I'd taken a part-time job waitressing at an ice-cream parlor.

"Adequate," I said. "It's respectable work. . . . Actually, I think Arnie was as much to blame as Vera. Maybe more."

"Now, wait a minute."

"It's true. After all, he made the whole mess possible. Went along with Vera because he couldn't stand unpleasantness. Babied her, took the blame on himself all those years—let her go on living in la-la land, thinking life should always be wonderful."

"Well then, he paid the price, didn't he." Gage's hand lay next to mine, and he rubbed his thumb across the back of my hand. "Nice color," he said. "Doesn't come off."

"That's for sure." Now what?

"You know, seems like damn near half of Oklahoma's part Indian nowadays," he said. "It's right in style. I'm one-eighth Cherokee myself; but I'd never tell anybody. Jump on the bandwagon like that?"

"Sure you are." He was poised like a kid in some mischief,

waiting to see if it would work. I just had to laugh, and so did he.

"Anyway," Gage said, "you handled the whole thing pretty damn well, by the sound."

I should've told him how wrong he was. But why dim the glow? "No," I said. "I just got lucky."